HALO of BRIMSTONE

HALO OF BRIMSTONE

KINGDOM WARS SERIES

BOOK THREE

JACK CAVANAUGH

Halo of Brimstone: Book 3 of the Kingdom Wars series
Copyright © 2019 by Jack Cavanaugh

Published by Enclave Publishing, an imprint of Third Day Books, LLC

Phoenix, Arizona, USA.
www.enclavepublishing.com

ISBN: 978-1-62184-075-6 (printed softcover)
ISBN: 978-1-68370-206-1 (ebook)

Cover design by Kirk DouPonce, www.DogEaredDesign.com
Interior typesetting by Jamie Foley

Printed in the United States of America.

19 20 21 22 23 24 25 / 5 4 3 2 1

An increasing number of corporations with larger boats and modern equipment were mercilessly cutting into his profits. Then a month ago, the Department of Fisheries had enacted new conservation fishing bans that would limit the number of months he could work. But the worst blow came last week when the *DAVID's* engine gave up the ghost and had to be towed to port. He didn't have the money to repair it and he was down to one ship. And now he was going to have to replace *BATHSHEBA's* weather radar. How was he going to do that and pay the crew?

Already he'd lost four seasoned crew members to the corporations. "Sorry, Yagil," the departing crew members said, "but the bigger boats are offering more money *and benefits,* and a man's got to take care of his family, no?"

Which left him with what? Zalel, his wife's good-for-nothing younger brother. The man never did an honest day's work in his life and was most recently fired from a government job. A government job! A corpse could hold a government job, but not Zalel. The man couldn't keep his mouth shut.

A self-professed expert on everything, all Zalel ever did was stand with his arms folded and tell people how they should do whatever it was they were doing. As a boy, he told women how to cook, mothers how to breastfeed, children how to play, and old men how to die; as an adult, he told his coworkers how to do their jobs, his employers how to run their businesses, his supervisors how to treat their workers, and political leaders how to run the country. It was his advice to a visiting female dignitary on how to get rid of unsightly facial hair that got him fired.

"But he's family," Yagil's wife insisted.

This was Zalel's first voyage aboard a fishing trawler and already there were murmurs about throwing him overboard. Crew members were taking bets on how long he'd be in the water before he started telling the fish how they should be swimming.

Off the Coast of Israel

THE STORM POUNCED WITHOUT WARNING. ONE MINUTE THE fishing trawler was scudding along under clear night skies; and the next, pummeled by fierce winds and high seas beneath churning black clouds.

In the wheelhouse, Captain Yagil Dahan gripped the padded armrests of his skipper's chair. He stared at the panel of instruments—navigation, communications, fish detection, and trawl sensors. While he'd come to check the trawling sensor, it was the weather radar that occupied his attention. The instrument showed no indication of clouds or wind, let alone a storm.

Dahan rubbed his bearded chin that showed a disturbing amount of gray. "I'm getting too old for this," he said.

Yagil Dahan had inherited the twin trawlers *DAVID* and *BATHSHEBA* from his father when he was thirty-nine years old, and for nearly three decades had managed to put food on the table for his wife and son and two daughters. But these last three years the family fishing business had struggled to stay afloat.

To Luke, Lily, and Calvin.
Can't wait until you're old enough to read Kingdom Wars.

The starboard side of the trawler heaved, and once again Yagil checked the weather radar screen.

Clear skies. Light wind. Calm seas.

Yagil cursed.

"Papa! Papa! Come on deck!"

There was an urgency in his son's voice. Chaviv was the same age Yagil was when he took over the family fishing business.

Yagil grabbed his tattered captain's hat. Then, spurred by a sense of foreboding intuition, he opened a drawer, retrieved his handgun, and tucked it into his waistband.

Emerging on deck, a gust of wind and salty spray knocked him back a step. The trawler's mechanical winch clanked loudly as it pulled the night's catch onboard.

"Papa, you have to see this!" Chaviv shouted over the wind.

He was pointing at the net.

There, nestled among the grouper, cod, and yellow mouth barracuda was something smooth and round and definitely man-made. The winch ground to a halt. Under normal conditions the crew would be cutting the bottom of the net and spilling the catch into the hold. To the man, they watched the captain's progress as he made his way along the port side under the eerie glow of ship's lights.

"Look, Papa," Chaviv pointed at the net. "There. There. And there. Three of them."

The burnt-orange bulge of clay jars, ancient from the look of them, stood out among the restless mass of gray fish scales.

"Treasure, Papa!" Chaviv said.

Years of life experience—hammered and shaped by disappointment—kept Yagil's emotions in check. Still, he couldn't help but wonder. Could it be that his luck was about to change, that on this God-forsaken night good fortune would favor him?

But treasure? He knew better. Israel was lousy with historical artifacts. You couldn't plant a vegetable garden without digging up a thousand-year-old bone. Most often clay vessels such as these contained grain or wine residue, sometimes scrolls. And then there was always the Israel Antiquities Authority. They were legendary for their strict punishments and severe fines for illegally excavated objects.

Yagil knew fully well he was at a crossroad. His next decision could alter the course of his life, the future of his family, his business, his son. His responsible side told him to leave the jars untouched and hand them over to the authorities. His adventurous side, the side that counted the cost yet took risks, urged him to open the jars so that he knew what he was dealing with.

"Let's see what we've got," he said. "Cut them out of there."

Chaviv grabbed his knife and sliced open the bottom of the net, a small opening to control the flow of fish as they spilled into the hold. As if floating down a silvery river, the jars slid toward the opening. Chaviv grabbed the first one with careful hands and passed it to a waiting crew member. He repeated the process until all three were on deck, each one steadied by a member of the crew.

Yagil knelt to inspect the jars. They were sealed, and it appeared each seal was intact. The crew gathered around, eager to hear what their captain would say next.

"Open one of them," he ordered.

Chaviv didn't have to be told twice. He dropped to his knees, cradled the jar, and examined the sealed lid. He tested it with an exploratory cut and found the seal waxy.

"Actually," Zalel said, stepping forward, "instead of a knife, you should use a torch to melt the wax."

Yagil rolled his eyes with exasperation.

"By melting the wax, you avoid scratching the—"

"Shut up, Zalel," Yagil snapped.

Chaviv continued working his way around the rim

methodically. When he had completely cut the circumference, he set the jar upright and leaned back. Opening it was the captain's privilege.

Yagil kneeled opposite his son.

"I need some light," he said.

Several of the crew members were recording the event with their cell phones as best they could, given the tempestuous pitch and yaw of the deck. One of them swiped his screen and punched the flashlight icon. A bright light illuminated the top of the jar. Yagil positioned the man's arm to shine the light where he wanted it.

He looked at his son who was all smiles, then back at the jar. Wrapping an arm around the container, he gripped the lid and twisted. The wax seal, old from age, crumbled as the lid rotated.

Yagil knew he'd broken the law the moment his son's knife cut the artifact. Had he stopped then, he could have explained it away as an impulsive error and probably gotten no more than a stern lecture from the authorities. But once he opened the jar, he was without excuse. He could only hope that the contents of the jar would prove to be so valuable—monetarily, historically; it didn't matter—that the authorities would overlook his indiscretion.

He set his jaw and removed the lid.

Leaning forward, he peered inside.

The escaping presence hit him with such force it slammed his body against the ship's gunwales, knocking the breath from his lungs.

Free from the jar that imprisoned him, the demon Ashmedai found himself occupying a living container, and felt the body he was possessing fight instinctively for air. He let it. The man's hands, shocked by the realization that something was inside him, tore at his clothing, clutched his face, his head. The struggle was of no concern to the demon.

"Papa! Papa, are you all right?"

Through the man's eyes, Ashmedai saw a young male, his chin and cheeks heavy with black stubble, peering at him with frantic concern.

"Chav—" the man tried to say.

Ashmedai clutched the vocal chords, cutting off any further sound.

While the man's son, and others with him, hovered over their captain, Ashmedai fed off the life streaming through the body—the beating heart, the pumping blood, the stretch of muscles—and the sensation soothed him like the pleasurable scratch of a long persistent itch. The torment of being without a body melted away in luxurious satisfaction.

The man's struggle to regain control of the body was proving to be an annoyance, so with the practiced control that came from centuries of possessing humans, Ashmedai engaged in the struggle, ripping the man's spirit with talon-like strokes, piercing his heart with razor thrusts. The blows were exquisitely painful to the man, the demon saw to that. The battle was brief. The man, though robust in body, was feeble in spirit and soon his will was broken.

In total control of the body, Ashmedai sat up and opened his eyes.

"Papa! What is wrong?"

Ashmedai stood and looked around. He was aboard some kind of ship. Men encircled him. As they should. The sight of two more clay jars on the deck pleased him.

"Open them," he commanded.

The man's son hesitated, still concerned for his father.

"Open them!" Ashmedai shouted.

As he had done before, but this time with trembling hands, Chaviv cut the seal on the second jar and removed the lid.

The man who was standing next to him recoiled as though hit by an invisible bludgeon, tugging violently at his clothes. The other crew members stepped back, alarmed.

"The third jar. Open it!"

His eyes wide with fright, Chaviv glanced imploringly at his father. "Papa, please. . . ."

"Do as I say," Ashmedai commanded.

The third jar was opened. This time it was Chaviv who flew backward and writhed on the deck as the crew watched in horror. After a time, the writhing stopped. Chaviv and the other crew member stood before their captain.

Ashmedai greeted them. "Ornasis. Lilith."

The two demon-possessed men took in their surroundings with wide eyes, particularly fascinated by the overhead torches affixed to the pilot house that gave light without flame.

The spirit of the captain made a valiant effort to control his arm, reaching for a stiff object that was stuffed in his waistband. Yagil managed to grip the object. Curious, Ashmedai allowed him to pull it from the waistband, then seized control of the hand to see what had so emboldened his host. The object was hard, like a block of iron, but not sharp like a blade. The man wanted to press it against his temple. To what end?

Show me, Ashmedai thought.

The man resisted. Ashmedai squeezed the man's heart. With his free hand, the man clutched at the pain in his chest.

Once subdued, the man did as he was instructed. His index finger curled around a metal appendage and pulled.

A loud *CRACK!* caused the crew members to jump, as a plank on the deck erupted with splinters.

"It appears to spit some sort of dart," Ornasis said from within Chaviv's body.

"Do it again," Lilith said. She scanned the crew, her gaze falling on one of them. "At him."

Zalel recoiled at being singled out.

Ashmedai leveled the blunt dagger that spit darts at the stammering crew member, curled his index finger around the metal appendage, and pulled.

Zalel's chest exploded with blood. He dropped to the deck as the other crew members scrambled for cover, some of them jumping overboard.

Ashmedai grinned with wicked satisfaction as he sought out crew member after crew member, spitting darts at them until the quiver was empty. Ornasis and Lilith followed him with the expressions of children playing with a new toy. At one point, Ornasis attempted to grab the weapon from Ashmedai, who backhanded him and ordered him to remember his place.

With the weapon no longer able to provide them with amusement, Ashmedai got down to the business at hand. As he questioned his host, two voices came from Yagil's mouth.

"Is Solomon still king?" Ashmedai asked.

The question perplexed his host. Ashmedai tried a different approach.

"Who is your king?"

"We have no king," Yagil replied.

Not liking his answer, Ashmedai squeezed his heart until the captain pleaded with him to stop.

"I will ask you again, who is your king?"

"We. . . we have not had a king for centuries. We have a prime minister now."

Another squeeze of the heart.

"Please . . . I'm telling you the truth! The prime minister is like a king."

Placated by the answer, Ashmedai's grip on the heart eased.

"And what is your country?"

"Israel."

Ashmedai exchanged glances with his cohorts. "This boat is an Israelite boat?

"It is registered with the State of Israel," the captain said.

"State of Israel." Ashmedai repeated the unfamiliar designation.

A sense of fear welled up inside the captain's body. Ashmedai gave it free rein, fear being a demon's most useful tool.

"Take us there," he said to the captain.

The man's fear escalated to alarm.

"Show me how to sail this boat."

The captain's instincts took a stand.

"You might as well kill me," Yagil said, "because I will never surrender my boat to you." He braced for the pain he knew would follow.

It didn't come.

"I believe you," Ashmedai said. "A captain and his ship, such a noble sentiment. But your misguided heroism leaves me with a dilemma. Do I kill you and persuade another? I think not. A captain should be at the helm of a ship when it enters port. So, where does that leave us?"

Ashmedai turned the captain's head toward his son. He spoke to the demon possessing him.

"Ornasis, if you will."

Chaviv's face contorted with pain. He dropped to the deck, writhing, tearing at his flesh, his eyes. Chaviv's screams ripped at what was left of his father's aching heart.

"All right! I'll do it!" the captain cried.

"Ornasis, it appears our negotiations were successful," Ashmedai said.

Chaviv fell limp, wounded but still alive. At the sight of his bloodied son, Yagil wept.

"Get control of yourself, captain," Ashmedai said. To Ornasis and Lilith, he said, "Indulge yourselves."

Lilith was especially pleased with the order.

"This body is disgusting," she said, her arms wide to illustrate her point. Her sultry voice came from a hairy body with a belly extending far over the belt.

"You never looked lovelier, my dear," Ashmedai said.

With the captain at the helm, the bow of the *BATHSHEBA* swung eastward toward the lights of Haifa to the screams of what remained of its crew.

CHAPTER
1

"I HATE YOU. YOU KNOW THAT, DON'T YOU?" JANA SAID.

I grinned as the waiter set an impressive bowl in front of me, a heaping helping of the restaurant's signature dish, The Devil's Own Decedent Mac And Cheese. It was a culinary carb-load of smoky bacon, wild mushrooms, cheddar, fontina, pepper jack, and mozzarella cheeses, a generous pile of caramelized onions for sweetness, and spicy roasted tomatoes for tang, topped with seasoned panko breadcrumbs and truffle oil.

In front of Jana the waiter placed a small garden salad with a wedge of lemon, no dressing.

Shrugging apologetically, I said, "Two things I've missed most on the East Coast. Sunsets on the beach and this bowl of mac and cheese."

"I'll try not to take that personally." Jana took up her fork.

"Things," I emphasized, "things I missed. Not people."

Having speared a single piece of lettuce, Jana's fork hovered between plate and mouth as she watched me shovel a mouthful of noodles, cheese dripping off both sides.

"You weighed a hundred and fifty pounds in high school," she observed. "And now what? A hundred and sixty?"

"A hundred and sixty-five. I've been putting on weight."

She leaned forward and spoke in a conspiratorial whisper. "Is it a Nephilim thing?"

"Could be. Now that you mention it, I've never seen any fat angels."

Jana chewed her leaf of lettuce, decided the salad needed something, and squeezed juice from the fresh lemon wedge on it. She'd always watched her weight religiously. In person, she appeared slightly gaunt, especially in the cheeks; on camera, she looked perfect.

Our booth was situated beside a window overlooking the downtown San Diego intersection of Broadway and 4th Avenue with the U.S. Grant Hotel on one corner and Horton Plaza on another.

We fell to eating; me relishing every bite of cheesy goodness, she staring absentmindedly out the window. The focus of her attention was turned inward.

"What did you do to Sue?" she said.

"I didn't do anything to her!" I tried not to sound defensive.

"She's rarely at home," Jana said, "and when she is, she barely speaks to me. She's withdrawn, sullen, and goes about her business like a zombie."

I put my fork down. There was no avoiding Sue's absence any longer; the plan had been for the three of us to celebrate my return to the city.

"Where is she now?" I asked.

"At the college."

When I'd called to give Sue my flight arrival information, she said something had come up and I'd need to make other arrangements. Not a problem. I could take an Uber. But then Jana called and offered to pick me up, and now it was time to settle up.

"So, what did you do?" she asked again.

"What makes you think I did anything?"

Jana gave me a look.

We had a history, one I'm not proud of. To say I'd been an immature jerk would be an understatement. But that was a different time, a different place, and a different girl. I'd been nothing but patient with Sue.

"I guess I committed the unpardonable sin," I said.

"Grant! Not Christina?"

"No, not that! You're asking the wrong question. It's not what I did—it's who I'm not."

Jana leaned back. Her expression indicated she understood.

"The professor," she said.

Sue and the professor—a man I loved like a father—had an intimate history. For years she had been a life partner to him in every way except the marriage bed.

"I thought after he died, in time, she'd get over him. But it's been two years, Jana. And if anything, it's gotten worse."

I didn't have to recount the entire two years to her. How Sue had fled to Chapel Hill, North Carolina, following the professor's murder by my rebel angel nemesis Semyaza. How, after battling Semyaza and Belial—the Laughing Jesus—in Sheol, I followed her to Chapel Hill. Sue completed her PhD in physics. I wrote a book. Things seemed to be going well for us. We almost had a normal life together. For a time. Then a headhunter recruited Sue for a firm that was developing quantum computers, the next big evolutionary leap for the industry.

"Sue never adjusted to the high-level stress and politics at Q-Wave Labs," I said. "She missed the academic life she had with the professor. Jana, she never even told me she'd approached

Heritage College for a position, not until the day she boarded a flight to come out here."

Jana shoved lettuce around on her plate. She didn't look up when she said, "They gave her the professor's old office."

This was news to me. I slumped sullenly, my cheesy, gooey bowl of goodness having lost its allure. "I can't compete with a saint," I grumbled. "Tell me, what else can I do?"

Before Jana could answer, a flash of light momentarily blinded me. My heart jumped into overdrive—my usual response to bright stimuli, given my death-defying encounters with angels.

Jana reacted to my reaction. "Grant? What's wrong? Do you see something?"

There was another flash.

I traced its source down the street to a high rise with a crane on the roof. Workers were lowering a large pane of glass over the side of the building. It was reflecting the early afternoon sun.

"It's coming from your building," I said. "They're putting in a new window."

Jana looked over her shoulder. KTSD broadcast the nightly news from the ground floor. She smiled a knowing smile. Apparently the repair had a story behind it.

"The 20th floor," she said. "Offices of the law firm of Hirsch and Zdrowski. Scuttlebutt is they're being audited by the IRS. Zdrowski took exception to one of their rulings and threw a chair, cracking the window."

There was another flash as the yet-to-be-installed window swung at the end of its tether. It concerned me not only because it was in my eyes, but because the blinding light was sweeping across downtown traffic.

"Grant, it takes time."

It took me a moment to catch up with her. At first I thought she was talking about the window, but she'd circled back to Sue.

"She's fine living with me for now," Jana continued. "I have plenty of space. Eventually she'll find a place of her own."

We both knew Sue moving in with me when I found a place was not an option for either of us.

"I just wish I could get into that head of hers," I said. "To know what she's thinking."

"No, you don't. Trust me, Grant. No man could survive five minutes inside a woman's head."

"What about you?" I said, picking up my fork, eager to change the subject. "Any prospects?"

"I've had the random date. All disappointing."

"That's understandable."

"Grant Austin! What do you mean by that?"

I shrugged as though it was obvious. "I'm a hard act to follow."

I got the laugh I was fishing for. Jana had a smile that could turn the head of a male statue.

"It's true," she said. "You are the standard by which I measure all other men. If any of my dates do anything that reminds me of you, I dump them on the spot."

I laughed in spite of myself. I loved this woman. We could never be a couple—we both knew that. But she was intelligent, witty, cool as ice under fire, and loyal to her friends. That loyalty went both ways. There wasn't anything I wouldn't do for her.

"How are things at the station?" I asked.

"Quiet . . . too quiet. I've fallen out of favor. You know how actors become associated with a particular role?"

"Yeah. Christopher Reeves will always be Superman to me. Mark Harmon is a NCIS Special Agent named Gibbs. Jim Parsons will always be a nerdy physicist named Sheldon."

"Exactly. Well, in the news industry, I'm the angel lady. So," she leaned forward and whispered conspiratorially, "can you help a girl out? What are the angels up to lately?"

"Sorry," I said. "All is quiet on that front."

"No presidential assassinations? No adventures in Sheol?"

"I'm adept at seeing swords now," I said. "Yours is looking good, by the way. And I pass the occasional angel on the street, both faith and rebel persuasion, some visible to the human eye, some invisible. But if they recognize me, they don't show it."

"Does that bother you?"

"Are you asking if I'm bothered that Lucifer's minions aren't stalking me? Plotting against me? Ripping my molecules apart and pulling me through membrane portals? I've had my fifteen minutes of fame, thank you very much."

"Walk through any walls lately?"

I stopped mid-chew. "Why would you ask me that?"

"You have!" she laughed. "You've been practicing walking through walls!"

It frightened me sometimes how well Jana could read me.

"I'm getting pretty good at it," I said sheepishly.

Another flash of light.

This was getting annoying. I looked out the window to check the progress of the installation. This time, next to the crane atop the high rise, I did see an angel. An angel with a black sword.

"How are your book sales?" Jana asked.

The sky over the intersection was growing dark as rebel angels began to assemble, dozens of them, then hundreds, until the firmament resembled a stadium with the intersection of Broadway and 4th Avenue the playing field. I was familiar with the venue. The angels call it a Spectacle.

"Grant?"

"Huh?"

"Your book. How's it selling?"

"Um . . . mediocre sales. The publisher is losing faith in it."

"Are you working on another project?"

Angels began appearing on the ground, strategically placed. On the sidewalks. Two in the middle of the street; one on Broadway, the other on 4th. Every one of them had black swords.

This wasn't good. This wasn't good at all.

CHAPTER

2

My blood pressure rising, I scanned the intersection that was center stage for an angelic Spectacle, the entertainment of choice for Lucifer's armies.

Four faithful angels made an appearance. One appearing on each corner. The good guys. But if they were alarmed by the developing Spectacle, they weren't showing it. They stood expressionless, serene, if not bored.

They didn't bother the rebel angels, the rebel angels didn't bother them.

But surely, I thought, once the action started, once human lives were in danger—human lives were always in danger at Spectacles, that's what provided the entertainment—the faithful angels would step up and rescue them, wouldn't they? After all, they were the good guys.

Two memories clambered to refute that proposition, both of them involving the professor. The first was the traffic accident that killed his wife and two daughters. That was a Spectacle and the faithful angels on the scene did nothing to prevent their deaths. The second was the professor's torture and death. I was there. Powerless to do anything to stop it. But so were Abdiel and his boys. The faithful. They observed, but didn't interfere.

"We are pleased to serve the Father." That was Abdiel's stock reply whenever I questioned his actions. Or lack of them.

"You know, I've been thinking," Jana said, unaware of what was happening on the other side of the restaurant window. "What if you wrote a novel?"

A sudden realization hit me like a bolt of lightning. I could have gotten the same sensation by sticking a key into an electrical socket. Was I the featured human sacrifice in this Spectacle? Was Jana?

"Grant! You're not listening to me. I've done some research on Amazon.com and found about a dozen supernatural suspense books on the bestseller lists, not to mention movies and television shows."

"Huh?"

"What if you took your experiences and fictionalized them, turned them into a novel or a screenplay? Isn't that what Harper Lee did with *To Kill a Mockingbird?* And Mark Twain with *Huckleberry Finn?*"

I glanced around the restaurant, looking for angels. Didn't see any. But that didn't necessarily mean anything. They could appear at any moment and overpower either one of us.

Instinctively my spirit was reaching for my sword.

"So, what do you think? It's a good idea, isn't it?" Jana said, casually taking another bite of her salad.

"What is?"

"Turning your experiences into a novel." She put her fork down. "Really, Grant. What has you so distracted?"

The only movement up and down our aisle of booths was a slender Asian mother gathering her things to leave. She slid out of the booth, checked her infant in a stroller, slung her purse over one of the stroller's arms, and began making her way to the front entrance.

"Um . . . won't work," I said to Jana. "At least my agent didn't think so."

"Why not?"

"Too far-fetched. Americans are no longer interested in anything related to the Bible. He said it might work if, instead of angels, I had invaders from a distant galaxy, a race of beings that have been taken over by artificial intelligence and controlled by a master computer with plans to take over the universe."

"Well that's just ridiculous," Jana huffed.

The woman with the baby had reached the entrance where a rebel angel appeared and was waiting for her. She couldn't see him, of course.

There was another flash of reflected light from the dangling window pane and things began to happen on the street.

A half block from the intersection, an angel appeared in the middle of Broadway directly in front of a brown UPS truck. It looked like the truck was going to plow into him, when the angel brandished his sword and thrust it into the truck's engine. The vehicle jolted to a sudden stop and traffic behind it backed up.

On 4th Avenue, a Yoohoo chocolate drink delivery truck sat at the intersection waiting for the signal light to turn green. The driver pulled out a cell phone and with his free hand reached for a cup of coffee. A rebel angel appeared in the cab beside him.

In front of the restaurant, the rebel angel that had met the woman and baby was escorting her toward the intersection.

Inside the restaurant, diners chatted and ate; on the street, pedestrians went about their business—all of them oblivious to the Spectacle unfolding around them.

Reflected sunlight swept back and forth across Broadway, flashing across the windshield of the UPS truck. Swatting at the blinding light with one hand, the driver raced the engine, unable to comprehend why the truck wasn't moving forward.

The four faithful angels looked on. Did nothing.

"Not on my watch," I said.

"What are you talking about?" Jana said.

I reached across the table.

"Can I borrow these?" I grabbed three cherry tomatoes from her salad.

There wasn't time for explanations. Ignoring Jana's startled expression, I slipped out of the booth and ran down the aisle and through the entrance doors.

"Hey! Come back here!"

It was the restaurant hostess. She thought I was skipping out on the bill.

"Security!" she shouted.

I bolted left, toward the intersection where the WALK signal to cross Broadway turned green. A cluster of pedestrians started to cross. The flow bottled up when three of them—rebel angels appearing as teenagers, complete with hoodies and dangling earbud wires—began jostling one another, good old-fashioned horsing around, or so it seemed. Because at that same moment, as the driver of the Yoohoo truck looked up and saw that the signal light had changed, the angel beside him knocked his hand, the one with coffee in it, spilling it all over the man's cellphone and shirt and lap. His curses could be heard above the horns of the cars queued up behind him.

I took it all in. Like a Rube Goldberg machine—the kind popularized by the board game Mouse Trap—all the pieces were in place and being set into motion just as I reached the corner.

The angel escorting the woman and child gave a signal. The three teens stopped horsing around and cleared the way for the woman to cross. She pushed the stroller into the crosswalk.

The angel beside the Yoohoo driver nudged him in his side, taking his attention off the spilled coffee. "Yeah, yeah," he shouted at the horns behind him. Ramming his truck into gear, he entered the intersection.

The drivers behind the UPS truck were equally loud, both with voice and horn. The driver was beside himself, staring at his instrument panel and pounding on the steering wheel. That's when the angel blocking him extracted his sword. The engine was whining at a high pitch as the transmission engaged and the truck lurched forward.

At that exact moment, the reflected light from the swinging pane of glass settled on the face of the UPS driver, blinding him—

To the red signal light.

To the Yoohoo truck halfway in the intersection.

To the woman and her baby in the crosswalk.

That's when I threw the tomatoes.

Whap!

Whap!

Whap!

In quick succession the cherry tomatoes splattered on the windshield of the UPS truck. Startled, the driver hit the brakes.

The screech of tires brought all manner of human attention to the intersection, which had been the plan all along, only not for the reasons intended.

The pane of glass atop the news building was shoved into place by workers on scaffolds and no longer reflecting the sun's rays on Broadway.

The UPS driver, seeing tomato juice trickling down his windshield when it could have been blood, tilted his head heavenward in thanksgiving for avoiding what might have been.

The Yoohoo truck continued on its way, oblivious to what

nearly happened, but probably still muttering curses over spilled coffee.

The woman with the stroller had stopped in the middle of the crosswalk, startled by the screeching tires, her face registering shock and fear at how close she and her child had come to being hit by a truck. With one hand pressed against her chest, she hurried to the sidewalk.

With nothing more to see, the four faithful angels disappeared, as did the rebel angels on the street, with one exception. He was on the sidewalk across from the restaurant, leaning against a building. And he was staring at me.

As I returned to the restaurant, I ran smack headlong into a young man barreling around the corner. He was wearing a t-shirt with the name of the restaurant on his chest, and by the way his shirt's short sleeves were straining against his arm muscles, you didn't have to be Sherlock Holmes to deduce he was security.

The fact that I was heading back to the restaurant surprised him.

"Um . . . excuse me, sir, but—"

"Sorry about the sudden departure," I said. "Thought I saw an old high school buddy, but it wasn't him. Turns out it was some guys from the company he works for, though."

As we passed the hostess, she smiled sweetly at Mr. Security for apprehending the bad guy. Her sugary smile and the way patrons were glaring at me was more than my male ego could stomach.

I circled back to the hostess.

Speaking loud enough to be heard by all those who were glaring at me, I said to the hostess, "I don't appreciate you sending security after me. It was uncalled for. Obviously, I was coming back."

Her smug smile vanished. "I thought you . . ." she stammered, her mind grasping for words. "How was I to know—"

"My date is still here," I said. "If I didn't pay the bill, she would."

The hostess glanced down the aisle and saw Jana.

"Oh, sir, I'm so sorry! I didn't know. I didn't—"

I walked away. I'd made my point and patrons were no longer glaring at me.

For several moments after I slid back into the booth, Jana said nothing. Then—

"What did UPS do to tick you off, Grant?"

"You saw that, did you?"

I glanced out the window. The skies were clear; not an angel in sight. Except the one across the street. He was still there. Still staring at me.

"A Spectacle," I said.

Jana's expression went from being amused to fear in the blink of an eye. She was fully aware of what a Spectacle was, having witnessed one in Jerusalem and having nearly been killed in one on the Bay Bridge.

"You see angels, Grant?"

"It's over," I assured her, at the same time checking on the angel across the street.

He was still there.

"Rebel angels?" she asked.

"Swords as black as sin. We should probably get out of here."

I looked over my shoulder to see if there was a back way out.

At that moment our waiter appeared. He placed a silver bowl of ice cream all decked out with rivers of fudge and piled high with whipped cream.

"Compliments of the manager," he said. "And he extends his apologies for that little misunderstanding."

Jana was already out of her seat. She pulled some bills from her purse, more than enough to cover the check and a generous tip. She handed it to the waiter and, when he took it, she placed a hand on his arm and flashed one of her award-winning smiles.

"My friend and I would like to leave rather discreetly," she said. "Do you think you could help us out?"

He was putty in her hands.

"I recognized you immediately, Miss Torres," he said, no longer a waiter, but an adoring fan.

"Do you think you could help us?" Jana pressed.

The waiter looked to the front of the restaurant and when he didn't see anything or anybody to stop him, he said, "I can take you out the back."

We followed the waiter into the kitchen and out a back door.

"Thank you so much," she said, again touching the waiter's arm and this time giving it a little squeeze.

We stepped into an alley and made our way to the street.

When we reached C Street, we turned a corner and there was the angel, the one who'd been staring at me. He didn't block our path. He stood there as casually as he'd done on Broadway.

Without saying anything to Jana and without acknowledging that I could see him, we walked several blocks before circling back to the KTSD building. Only then did I look over my shoulder to see if he was following us.

The angel was nowhere in sight.

CHAPTER
3

Jerusalem, Israel

THE NARROW STREET OF MA'ALOT E-KHANKA WAS ITS USUAL press of bodies, shoppers and tourists mostly, as Ashmedai, Lilith, and Ornasis worked their way through the crowd, sporting freshly possessed bodies. Ashmedai was in his body of choice, a trim, muscular Israeli soldier, in uniform, the kind of man who spent a great deal of attention on his physical appearance, not so much on spiritual strength. Lilith preferred to possess modest and chaste young women. She took perverse delight in their shame when she forced them to play the role of a harlot. Ornasis liked variety. Since landing in Haifa, he'd possessed a pompous money-lender, short in stature; a shapely female academic who could speak twelve languages; and a baker, for no other reason than he loved the way the man's clothes smelled after a night of baking, a tangy mixture of sweat and flour. He was currently wearing a religious student who wore all black, an ankle-length coat, and a round broad-brimmed hat, with long curls dangling down his temples.

As they were passing a restaurant that boasted the best hummus in Jerusalem, Ashmedai raised a hand, signaling he was stopping. The other two followed his gaze past the patrons huddled around small street-side metal tables into the establishment, past the ordering and delivery counter, to a box mounted on the back wall.

What caught Ashmedai's attention was the way the demons inside the box pressed their faces against the transparent front of the box and spewed a flurry of words without taking a breath. He thought the female demon inside the box was a seer, for she knew everything they'd done since landing in Haifa.

> . . . *a reign of terror that is spreading like an epidemic. It began three days ago in Haifa when Yagil Dahan, captain of the fishing trawler* BATHSHEBA, *murdered his wife and daughter while his son, Chaviv, and an unnamed crew member watched. Authorities believe that financial problems may have contributed to the crime.*
>
> *Then, in Yokne'am Illit, at a high-tech park—called a "startup village" for its number of Research and Development companies—three workers went on a rampage, terrorizing the complex for hours before killing themselves.*
>
> *In Kefar Sava, a similar rampage left over two dozen shoppers dead in a mall; while in Petah Tikva during an exhibition match at HaMoshava Stadium between Maccabi Petah and Hapoel Petah, city rivals, three spectators attacked rival fans, instigating a riot that killed eight people and injured thirty-five.*
>
> *Yesterday, the administrative district at Bat Hefer, a group of workers were taken hostage by armed terrorists, two men*

and a woman. The situation ended in a hail of bullets during which the terrorists were killed, but not before killing seven hostages and one soldier. Another soldier, the leader of the hostage negotiation team, has gone missing.

While authorities have been unable to link any suspects in these grisly incidents, there does seem to be a discernable pattern of violence, and a geographical progression—it appears to be heading toward Jerusalem.

After hearing the narrative of violence, the soldier's spirit rallied and fought to regain control of his body; Ashmedai wrestled him under control. To a passerby, it would have appeared as though the soldier had experienced a gas pang.

"My orthodox boy says the Temple is down this street," Ornasis said, having consulted the student whose body he possessed.

Leaving the shopping district, the three demons fell in step with a great many tourists and religious-types dressed in similar fashion to Ornasis's host body. The sky opened up to them and they found themselves staring at a spacious gathering place in front of a wall constructed of enormous ancient stones. All manner of people were facing it—praying, rocking, reading scriptures, stuffing folded pieces of paper between the cracks.

"The boy says it's the Wailing Wall, or Western Wall of the Temple complex," Ornasis said.

"I see the wall," Lilith said. "Where's the Temple?"

"Tell the boy to lead us to the Temple," Ashmedai said.

Ornasis lowered his head, his eyes glazed has he conducted the internal interrogation.

"The boy says there is no Temple," Ornasis reported.

"Of course there's a Temple—this is Jerusalem," Ashmedai replied. "Hurt him if he refuses to disclose its location."

Ornasis questioned the boy again while Ashmedai interrogated the soldier with whom he shared a body. The soldier refused to cooperate. Ashmedai hurt him until he complied.

"The boy insists there is no Temple, only a temple mount where it once was located," Ornasis reported.

"The girl says the same thing," Lilith added.

"As does the soldier," Ashmedai was forced to admit. "Instruct the boy to take us to the temple mount so we can see for ourselves."

Following the boy's instructions, they took side streets that eventually opened into a spacious area shaded with trees. Passing through it, they climbed steps and found themselves standing upon a vast expanse that featured a golden domed structure.

Solomon's Temple was indeed nowhere to be seen.

"What is this structure?" Ashmedai asked.

"An unholy abomination." The words came from the boy, not Ornasis.

The next instant they were surrounded by twelve armed angels, their weapons drawn, swords as black as night. The boy cried out in alarm and fainted, leaving Ornasis to keep the body standing on his own.

Ashmedai addressed them. "We knew we would find you here," he said.

The angels said nothing. Neither did they lower their swords.

"I am Ashmedai. This is Lilith. And this is Ornasis. I would speak with my prince."

"And your prince would speak with you."

The voice came from above as a being of intense light and beauty descended without touching down. The three demons recognized him.

"My prince," they said in unison.

"Much has happened since the days of your capture," the brilliant one said. "I have much to tell you. You have much to learn."

He approached Ashmedai and placed a hand on the body of the Israeli soldier.

"It is good to see you again, old friend. Once you have been acquainted with the present state of affairs, you will without doubt be enraged, as are we. It is good you are once again with us, for I have a mission that requires your unique talents."

CHAPTER
4

AFTER A WEEK FOLLOWING THE SPECTACLE, I WAS STILL LOOK-ing over my shoulder. I was being stalked. Is it possible to get a restraining order for an angel? He hadn't threatened me, but I'd be a fool to think there wouldn't be some sort of reprisal for messing up a Spectacle.

At the time, with all the attention on the intersection and the intended target, I thought I could do my thing without being noticed. The last thing I'd wanted was to step onto center stage with thousands of angels watching. Been there. Done that. Don't care to repeat it.

But Jana had seen me chuck the tomatoes. Apparently, my stalker angel saw it too. Had he been watching me all along while I was with Jana in the restaurant? I tried to think back. When did I first notice him across the street? I couldn't remember. At the time my mind had been focused solely on the Spectacle activity and the woman and her baby.

Would I do it again? Of course I would. Two lives were saved. The fact that I'd thwarted a supernatural Roman colosseum-style

Spectacle was icing on the cake. But the harsh truth of life is that actions have consequences.

These were my thoughts as I prepared to take a shower for a lunch date with Sue.

The thing that was most unnerving was the persistence of the rebel angel's preoccupation with me. At night, in bed, when I closed my eyes, I saw him, arms folded, leaning against the building. Staring at me. That image was the warm-up act to my usual nightmares. Most nights featured the battle with Semyaza and Belial in Sheol; but when that feature film wasn't playing, it was a rerun of the Emerald Towers.

Gotta love the golden oldies.

I'd moved into a one bedroom, one bath apartment in east El Cajon on Shady Lane. The name of the street pretty much says it all, especially after dark and on weekends. The entire street was a row of one apartment complex after another, people stacked on top of people. You'd sooner find the legendary El Dorado treasure than find a place to park. But it was just a couple miles from Heritage College and I wanted a place conveniently located for Sue to be able to get away from campus, prop up her feet, or take a nap. Other than that, all I needed was a place to crash, a table to set my laptop on, and some walls I could practice walking through.

Going into the bathroom, I closed the door behind me and thought of a conversation starter I'd stumbled upon once while perusing Facebook, the kind authors post to engage readers with topics that rarely have anything to do with their books: "Even when you're the only person in the house, do you close the bathroom door when you take a shower?" Which is right up there with the king of inane controversies: "What is the right way to hang toilet paper?"

As for the shower question: I always close the door. Don't know why, just do. And no, I didn't post my preference on the Facebook thread, which ran ridiculously long with replies.

Stepping out of my slippers, I reached for the shower curtain before slipping off my robe, to start the water. I pulled back the curtain to find an angel standing in my tub.

Wouldn't you know it. My first shower in my new apartment and there's an angel in the tub. I didn't remember my lease mentioning the unit came with an angel.

The manager told me to expect cockroaches, that they were serious about ridding the complex of pests and that if I saw any I was to inform him immediately and they'd send out a guy to spray. I wondered if the spray worked on rebel angel pests.

It was my stalker. He stood there in cloaked form, invisible to human eyes, visible to other angels and Nephilim.

It took every ounce of will power I had, but I managed to suppress the instinct to jump back and scream like a little girl. Of course, this unannounced and inappropriate appearance was not without precedent. Abdiel had a knack for popping in at inconvenient times.

That's not to say I didn't react. I froze, if only for a moment. To cover, I stepped back, pulled open a drawer on the vanity, and reached for a new bar of soap.

The angel watched me intently.

I went about my business, unwrapping the bar of soap, placing it on the bathtub tray, turning on the water, and stepping back to wait for it to get hot. The water gushed out of the faucet and flowed the length of the tub, swirling under the bare feet of the hovering angel. Angels don't touch the ground, not even the faithful ones. To them, all creation is tainted and repulsive.

I was hoping that when it became apparent I wasn't going to acknowledge his presence, he'd leave. No such luck.

Maybe he would leave once I started the shower. I pulled the tub faucet diverter and the water flow sputtered from the shower head then settled into a normal flow, passing right through the angel.

He stood there stoically. Calling my bluff? Would I really disrobe and step into the shower with him still there?

It was my move. Refuse to step into the shower and acknowledge that I was aware of his presence, or . . .

Loosening the tie on my robe, I shrugged it off and stepped into the shower. I don't have to tell you how much nerve it took me to do that. I hadn't showered with another guy since the gang showers in the guy's locker room in high school; I'd never taken a shower with an angel.

The shower spray hit me in chest.

"Really, Grant? You're going to pretend you don't see me?"

I lathered my face and hair.

"Very well," he said. "You probably wonder why I'm here. I want you to know that I had no part in that Spectacle you so ingeniously thwarted. You should also know that it had nothing to do with you. As far as I know, the organizers are unaware of your presence. So if you've been wondering about reprisals, there won't be any. No one knows it was you who threw those tomatoes."

I ducked under the spray and let the water wash the soap off my head.

"You should also know why I was there." He paused. "Grant, I was there looking for you. I've been tracking you for some time now."

I bent over and soaped my legs.

"As you deduced, the target at the Spectacle was the woman and child, the wife and son of a high-level executive at Qualcomm."

I washed my feet.

"Their deaths were intended to be the first domino in an elaborate Spectacle that will take years to play out."

Washing my chest and arms, I proceeded to rinse off.

The angel watched as I completed my shower, drew back the shower curtain, stepped out, and began to dry myself.

"You should know," he said, "that there was a backup plan. Every good Spectacle has one built into it, in anticipation of unforeseen anomalies. Have you seen the news this morning, Grant? There was a multi-car crash on Interstate-15, killing a woman and child."

The news hit hard. I closed my eyes and fought back my mounting rage.

You can't stop us. We've been doing this for millennia.

Semyaza had said that to me years ago.

"Just thought you should know," the angel said.

He disappeared.

With a scream of frustration, I hurled the towel against the bathroom door.

CHAPTER
5

"GRANT! WHAT A LOVELY APARTMENT COMPLEX."

There's something about opening a door and being greeted by a gorgeous woman that never gets old. Sue was stunning in a black summer dress with splashes of white and red. If this wasn't the dress she'd worn when I first met her in the book stacks at Heritage College library, it was strikingly similar. It set my heart to thumping then, and it did the same now. She stood casually with her weight on one foot, a stylish leather satchel slung over her shoulder.

I stepped aside and invited her in.

Crossing the threshold, she casually glanced about my new digs.

"Of course it will look more like home once you get something on the walls," she said.

I'd never been much for decorating. "Maybe you can help me with that," I said.

She smiled sweetly.

"When does the furniture arrive?"

At present I had a used dining table with three chairs, a sofa, a chest of drawers, and a bed. The basics. What more does a guy need?

"You know how it is," I said. "Most places refuse to deliver furniture until after you've bought it."

My attempt at humor fell flat.

"May I use your bathroom?" she asked.

I indicated where it was, though given the size of the apartment that was hardly necessary.

The door closed and I prayed there was no angel in the tub. My luck he'd be visible this time. When I heard no screams, I figured Sue was in there alone.

Earlier, while waiting for her to arrive, I'd debated whether I'd tell her about the Spectacle and my shower companion. I'd decided not to tell her. At least, not yet. She'd been living angel-free since Abdiel dropped in to tell her about my adventure in Sheol. Since then, whenever I brought up the subject of angels, or anything Nephilim-related, she'd grown uncomfortable, so I'd drop the subject.

Of course there was the possibility Jana would say something to her. I made a mental note to call Jana after lunch and tell her my decision to keep Sue in the dark for now. Which raised a new question: Would I tell Jana about my shower buddy? Probably not. I was still operating under the premise that if I ignored him he'd go away.

Sue rejoined me.

"So," I said, "how about Marichiaro's for lunch? Pastrami sandwich with a side of spaghetti?"

"Grant, I just stopped by to see your new apartment. I'm going to have to pass on lunch. I'm sorry." She patted her satchel. "I have a stack of papers to grade. Another time?"

"How about if we order out? The reason I got this place close to the college was so you'd have somewhere to get away and rest, or grade papers. We can eat. You can grade. And I'll be so quiet you won't even know I'm here."

The expression Sue gave me said it all: a tilt of the head, apologetic eyes. No further explanation was necessary, but she gave one anyway.

"Can I take a raincheck? I really need to be alone to do this," she said. "I'm still finding my way with this professor gig. You understand, don't you? I can work through the papers more efficiently in my office."

As a writer I understand deadlines, but I also know what it's like to want to be with someone so much that it aches. I ached; she didn't.

"Sure. We can do lunch another time," I said.

She smiled a sweet "thank-you" smile and placed a hand on my cheek as she walked to the door.

"Thank you for understanding," she said.

The door closed. She was gone. I was alone.

I'd been looking forward to going to Marichiaro's, a small Italian place that had been a favorite after-football hangout when I was in high school. Grabbing the keys to my recently acquired car—a 200,000 mile old clunker with a spoiler that even then put a strain on my bank account—I headed for the door. No reason I couldn't drown my sorrows in pizza and high school nostalgia.

Turning right from Shady Lane, I nearly caught up with Sue at the Second Street signal light. Four cars separated us. The college was straight ahead. My left turn signal was blinking.

Only, when the signal turned green, Sue didn't go straight. She turned left. Then left again— the onramp to Interstate-8.

"Of course, the satchel," I said aloud.

She'd said she was returning to her office to grade papers. So if she'd just come from the campus, why would she bring the papers with her to my apartment?

"She lied to me."

Abandoning lunch plans, I followed her onto Interstate-8.

"Where are we going, Grant?"

My rebel angel stalker appeared next to me in the passenger seat, still in stealth mode.

Startled, I made an unplanned lane change. To cover, I flipped on my turn-signal halfway into the other lane.

"Still not talking to me?" he said. He gazed out the window with a childlike expression. "I haven't ridden in a car since I took a ride in a Model-A when they first came off the assembly line. Things have certainly changed since then."

Now you just smash them into one another to kill people, I wanted to say, but didn't.

"You're probably wondering why I keep dropping in on you," he said.

I concentrated on the road, keeping a discreet distance between me and Sue. I didn't want her to know I was following her.

"You have nothing to fear from me, Grant. I want you to know that."

The last time a rebel angel told me that, he lured me into a trap. *Never trust the devil, Grant,* he'd said, but by then it was too late. I wasn't going to make that mistake again.

"I was one of the spectators in Sheol," he said. "It was impressive the way you held your own against Semyaza and Belial. Even more impressive what you said. Do you realize the impact you made that day? You started a revolution. A splinter faction has formed in Lucifer's ranks. The ramifications are huge, Grant, greater than you can imagine."

Sue signaled a lane change, taking the ramp to south Interstate-805.

I followed.

"Humans aren't the only ones who've been deceived, Grant.

We angels have, too. From the very beginning. You opened our eyes to that."

Sue signaled again to exit the freeway and I knew where she was going. I followed her into Greenwood cemetery. Now that I knew what she was doing, I circled around and approached from a different direction, parking my car so that I could watch her without being seen.

She got out of her car and settled on the grass in the shade of the tree where the professor was buried. She placed a hand on his grave and talked to him. I was too far distant to hear what she was saying.

"Is that Sue Ling?" the angel said. "She's a knockout, Grant."

I couldn't argue with that.

"I thought the woman you were with at the restaurant was Sue Ling, but that was Jana Torres, wasn't it?"

Sue removed papers from her satchel and set to work grading them, all the while carrying on a conversation with the professor.

"I'll leave the two of you alone," the rebel angel said.

He vanished.

For a half-hour I watched her, wrestling with my feelings. Even though the professor was dead, Sue still preferred being with him than with me. Equally disconcerting was the fact that my stalker appeared to be gathering information about my personal life. There could only be one reason for that. He was going to use that information. Once again Sue and Jana were in danger because of me.

That night I tossed and turned in bed, unable to sleep as I played out a dozen scenarios in which I told Sue I knew about her visit to the professor's grave, everything from confronting her directly, to lying—that on a lark I'd gone to Greenwood to pay my respects and saw her there. All of the scenarios ended the same way: Sue getting angry and defensive.

Should I just let it go?

I couldn't help thinking that for Sue the move to San Diego was more about the professor than it was about a career change. The more I thought about it, the angrier I got. Sue's intentions were clear. She didn't want to have anything to do with me, and I doubted she ever would.

In bed I tossed in frustration and caught a glimpse of my stalker. He was standing in the corner of my bedroom, watching me. I pretended to sleep, all the while expecting him at any moment to say something.

I lay there waiting.

After what seemed an eternity, I turned over again, sneaking a peek. He was still there.

This was unnerving. A battle of wills. I wasn't going to give him the satisfaction of knowing I could see him.

I waited longer this time, my anger increasing by the minute. There's something about emotions in the dark in the middle of the night—anger is angrier, fears are greater, and patience is thinner. I'd finally had enough.

Throwing off the covers, I bolted out of the bed and shouted, "What do you want from me?"

My voice echoed off the walls of an empty room.

He wasn't there.

Tired from lack of sleep, I shaved and showered—gratefully alone—my mind focused on getting some writing done. The sales of my book were steadily declining and my finances were on life support. I needed a new book contract, only the idea cupboard was bare. Should I do something historical? The supernatural angle didn't seem to be panning out.

I figured I could go to the library in search of inspiration. I'd considered using the Heritage College library in the off chance I'd bump into Sue, but I wasn't sure I was ready to face her yet, so I settled on San Diego State University.

Dressed and ready, my mind playing with the idea of doing something about the high-stakes drama underlying the U.S. Constitutional Convention in 1787, I emerged from the bedroom.

My stalker was standing in the living room waiting for me.

I was in no mood for this. He'd ruined my night's sleep, and now he was attempting to disrupt my day. I was in a reckless state of mind. I walked straight toward him. If I kept going, I would either run into him or walk right through him—I wasn't sure which. But I was about to find out.

At the last moment, he stepped aside.

That's when I made my move. Going to the hall closet, I walked inside and closed the door behind me. He'd follow me eventually, wouldn't he? If for no other reason than curiosity. Privacy was obviously not an issue for him. After all, we'd once shared a shower. When he did follow me into the closet, I didn't plan on being there.

I stepped through the outside wall, walked back down the breezeway, and through the front door without opening it. As expected, he wasn't in the living room. He had three options if he was following me: Go through the back wall of the closet into my bedroom, exit through the side wall into the breezeway, or retrace his steps and come out through the closet door. Whichever one he chose didn't matter. I was ready for him.

I drew my sword and waited for him to appear.

A moment later, he stepped through the front door.

I swung with all my might.

His sword flashed and with a shower of sparks he blocked my blow. In order to do so, he had to materialize. That was the plan.

He smiled. "You are full of surprises, Grant," he said. He lowered his sword, leaving himself defenseless. "Good, now we can get down to business."

I kept my sword leveled at him. "Who are you and what do you want?"

"I need your help," he said. "You're the only one I can turn to."

"Who are you?" I repeated.

"My name is Nosroch."

"Nosroch. Can I call you Noz?" I asked out of spite, and to get even for all the hide-and-seek games.

"I would prefer you didn't," he said stiffly.

"Great. Noz it is."

He vanished in a huff.

Insolence. My weapon of choice. There's no better way to clear the room of angels, rebel and faithful alike . . . or get you pumped full of demons. But sometimes it's a risk worth taking.

CHAPTER
6

Israeli Defense Forces, Central Command

COLONEL YAKOV AMAR MARCHED INTO THE SITUATION ROOM of Sayeret Matkal, Israeli Defense Forces' elite hostage rescue unit, his jaw set, his unblinking gaze hardened. Reaching the front of the room, he squared his shoulders. A banner hung on the wall behind him: *Born in Israel — Made on the Battlefield.*

The Colonel spoke with staccato precision. "By now, you've heard the news from Alon Shvut."

The mention of the West Bank settlement created a stir among the unit. Alon Shvut had a history, a violent one that clenched the jaw of every Jewish citizen whenever it was mentioned in conversation. The international community considered the settlement illegal under international law—an assessment the Israeli government disputed—making its population of around 3,000 frequent targets of Palestinian attacks.

A few years back, a member of the Islamic Jihad rammed his car into a crowded bus stop and would have killed dozens of commuters had not the vehicle been stopped by sturdy concrete bollards. Jumping out of the car and brandishing a knife, the attacker killed a young woman and wounded two others before a security officer shot him dead.

That same year, three Israeli teenagers were hitchhiking on their way home when they were kidnapped by Palestinian brothers financed by a Gaza terrorist group. With $39,000, the brothers had purchased a used car in Hebron and three M-16 rifles. Israeli Defense Forces mobilized, implementing *Operation Brother's Keeper* to locate and rescue the boys.

For eleven days, all of Israel held its breath as rescue forces searched for the boys, only to find their bodies buried in a field that had been purchased as a dumping ground. Five days later, the kidnappers were caught, hiding in a disused cesspool.

The failure to rescue the boys had left a bitter taste in the mouths of the Sayeret Matkal unit, many of whom were sitting in the situation room now.

"Here are the facts as we know them," Col. Amar said. "At 11:15 this morning, twenty-three children were kidnapped when their bus was commandeered by approximately twelve heavily armed Palestinian terrorists at the Zomet Institute, an interactive learning center run by a group of engineers and Orthodox rabbis who integrate religious faith with modern technology. What has not been released to the press is that three of those children have high profile parents."

Pictures of the three were displayed on a side screen identifying the children, two boys and a girl, and their parents:

Lavie, son of Knesset member Avi ben Tzur
Jonathan, son of Knesset member Orly Mazuz
Shira, daughter of Southern District Court Judge Nachman Shaffir

"At present, we do not know why the terrorists targeted these children. There have been no demands. We have had absolutely no communication with them."

A voice came from the back of the room. "Just get me and my Tavor within range. I'll communicate with them."

This prompted laughter and guttural grunts.

Col. Amar continued: "According to witnesses, when the bus left the center it headed south. A drone flyover has identified it at this location."

The picture on the screen changed, showing an overhead view of a bus parked outside a structure next to a vineyard. A dirt road connected the building to the main thoroughfare.

"Efrat Winery," the colonel said, "is currently closed for renovation. We haven't been able to locate the owners, Lithuanian Jews with no known ties to Hamas or any Palestinian group. They may or may not be inside the winery. But as you can see, other than the bus, there are no other vehicles. On the southwest corner there are piles of sand and gravel, scaffolding, and the usual construction equipment."

The colonel paused, allowing his men a few moments to study the image.

"We don't know why the terrorists chose this location. It's defensible, but they have to know we're not going to just let them waltz out of there, which means they're anticipating a standoff."

"Are the children still on the bus?" one commando asked.

"There has been no activity around the vehicle," the colonel replied, "but we can't discount the possibility that some of the children may still be on the bus, possibly incapacitated."

Possibly dead.

The colonel didn't say as much. He didn't need to; everyone was thinking it.

"We also have to assume the bus is rigged with explosives. We'll know more once we have eyes on the ground."

"What's the plan, colonel?"

"Identify the threat. Neutralize the threat. Get the children out."

"The vineyard," another commando said. "It's the only cover."

"Actually, there's a better way."

All eyes turned to the speaker.

The colonel acknowledged him. "Captain Dorn will brief you on the plan."

Capt. Rogan Dorn made his way to the front, an impressive figure with broad shoulders, a firm jaw, and steely blue eyes.

Col. Amar stepped aside.

Rogan approached the drone photo. "There are two problems with a strike from the vineyard," he said. "One: They'll be expecting it, thus eliminating the element of surprise. Two: Once we emerge from the vineyard, we'll have to cross an open parking lot. While we don't know the extent of their weaponry, even small arms fire could pin us down and give them time to retaliate by killing hostages. They may be looking for an excuse. We don't want to give them one."

The assembled commandos stared at the projection. The vineyard was the only cover remotely close to the building. On the sides and behind the winery there was nothing but open field.

"We will approach at night from two directions," Rogan said. "A diversion in the front parking lot and the main strike force from the rear."

There was a chorus of objections.

One commando stood to answer for them all. "Terrorists are

deranged, not stupid. They'll have eyes on the field. And the distance to cover is easily three times that of the parking lot."

Rogan calmly folded his hands in front of him. He glanced at the only two commandos who weren't objecting, Sokoloff and Harel, his two closest friends. While they had not been briefed ahead of time, they knew Rogan well enough to know he was up to something.

"Hear him out!" the colonel shouted over the objections.

There was a scraping of chairs as the men took their seats. Unfazed by the protest, Rogan approached the map and pointed to the far side of the field. "The main strike force will assemble here."

Crossing the open field would be suicide. Everyone knew it. But, to the man, they had pledged their lives to protect Israel. If that meant crossing an open field under fire to save young Jewish lives, so be it. Rogan knew that.

He signaled the man in charge of the projector. "Put up the overlay," he said.

What appeared to be an ancient map settled atop the drone photo. Parallel broken lines stretched across the field from the point Rogan had indicated, to about thirty meters from the structure. It looked like a garden path lined with rocks.

"Originally constructed by the Hasmoneans, expanded by Herod the Great and the Romans, this is the Biyar Aqueduct, an underground tunnel that once brought water to the Temple mount. This will be our access to the winery."

———————

"Wipe that smug smile off your face," Sokoloff said.

Following the briefing, Sokoloff and Harel approached Rogan at the front of the situation room.

"Leave it to you to find a solution buried in an old book," Harel said.

While the fact that the solution came from an ancient text was surprising, the fact that Rogan had found it was not. On their off-duty hours when the majority of the Sayeret Matkal blew off steam playing sports or frequenting bars to watch sports and hook up with women, Rogan read. His greatest love was the *Tanakh,* the Jewish Holy Scriptures. After that he read mostly history, mostly about the Hasmonean dynasty, mostly Judah Maccabee, the Israelite resistance warrior who led a revolt against the Seleucids and restored the Temple on the 25th of Kislev, 164 BCE. Because of Rogan's fascination with Judah Maccabee, his buddies gave him Judah's nickname, "The Hammer."

Uri Sokoloff was "The Falcon," derived from his Czech last name.

Noam Harel was "The Mountain," also derived from his surname. His first name meant Tenderness, which caused him no small amount of ribbing. While mountain was an apt description of him—he was the tallest and largest of the commandos—there was nothing remotely tender about him.

The relationship between the three men went beyond Israeli Defense Forces and beyond Sayeret Matkal. They had a common heritage. They were direct descendants of King Solomon. And this lineage qualified them for specialized training no other member of the Sayeret Matkal received. Tattoos on their ring fingers, a pentalpha—five interlaced A's—within a circle. It identified them as members of a secret, elite team.

"Dorn, Sokoloff, Harel, in my office."

Col. Amar stood in the doorway of an adjoining room. When the three commandos were inside, he shut the door behind them.

Any lingering levity they'd brought with them dissipated the moment they saw who was waiting for them—the commander of their elite team, who was also the commander of the angelic host, the Archangel Michael.

CHAPTER
7

Israeli Defense Forces, Central Command

THE ARCHANGEL OFFERED NO GREETINGS. HE GOT RIGHT down to business.

"You are familiar with the corridor of terror stretching from Haifa to Jerusalem. We have identified the bloodlust as the work of three notorious demons: Ashmedai, the strongest and their leader; Ornasis; and Lilith. From the information we have gathered, the clay vessels that imprisoned them were dredged up from the bottom of the sea by a fishing trawler. It was King Solomon himself who captured them and consigned them to the deep."

The archangel spoke the name as though it was just yesterday Solomon was king of Israel. Perhaps to him that's how it seemed.

"We do not know their current location, though we suspect they have been reunited with their prince. Having been imprisoned for centuries, they are as wild starving animals and are particularly dangerous. Should you encounter them, do not underestimate them. They are cunning."

"Are they responsible for the abduction of the children?" Rogan asked.

"Unknown, though we can't rule it out."

He held out his hand, in the palm of which was a ring that bore the same image the three commandos had tattooed on their fingers engraved on a red gemstone. Inside the ring was inscribed the name of God.

"Rogan Dorn, you have been chosen to wear the ring," the archangel said.

This was the moment for which they had trained. Rogan caught his breath. He would be the first to wear Solomon's ring on a mission.

He stepped forward. Without hesitation, he took the ring and slipped it onto his finger.

The instant he did, he saw that Michael had not come alone. A dozen angels were in the room with them, invisible to the others, though Rogan saw them clearly. They were armed with gleaming silver swords. Rogan could also see the swords of his two buddies and the colonel, strong and proud, indicators of the intent of their hearts and the depth of their spiritual strength.

Michael said: "Should you encounter Ashmedai, Ornasis, or Lilith, you will capture them, place them in this clay receptacle, and return it to me."

The archangel indicated a clay jar on the colonel's desk.

"Yes, sir," Rogan said.

The Archangel Michael vanished, along with the other angels. Colonel Amar took it from there.

"Let's save those children," he said.

An hour later, as they loaded onto the transport that would

take them to the Efrat Winery, Rogan, a veteran commando, felt the same anxiety he'd experienced on his first Sayeret Matkal mission.

CHAPTER
8

Efrat Winery, Israel

A BOBBING LIGHT SPLASHED AGAINST ROUGH-HEWN STONE and reflected off knee-deep water as Rogan led the Sayeret Matkal main strike force single-file through the ancient Biyar Aqueduct. It amazed him to think that thousands of years ago Israelite workers using crude cutting tools carved this tunnel out of solid rock. Rogan could spend weeks in here, months, studying the aqueduct and its history. Maybe on his next leave. Shoving his personal interests aside, he focused on the mission: Identify the threat. Neutralize the threat. Rescue the children.

Wading through water made for slow progress and determined effort. As team leader, Rogan had faith in the physical condition of his men, that they'd be able to transit the distance of the tunnel and still have enough strength to storm the winery at a dead run if necessary. Each man cradled an IWI Tavor in his arms, holding it high to keep it out of the water. The Tavor, an Israeli Weapons Industry product, was an efficient assault rifle that could switch between semi- and full-automatic mode. It was fashioned for maximum reliability, durability, simplicity of design, and ease of maintenance under adverse or battlefield conditions.

When they had located the aqueduct entrance, they found it sealed by two stone slabs. It took four men each to remove them. What obstacles awaited them at the exit was unknown. Had they the time, Rogan would have led a reconnaissance team to plan every detail to access the passage down to the second. But they didn't have time. Children's lives were at stake and the clock was ticking. They had to move fast with what little information they had.

When they'd entered the aqueduct, there still had been no communication with the terrorists, no demands. Other rescue teams would have set up a perimeter and tried to establish communication. To stall for time. To negotiate. Sayeret Matkal wasn't other teams.

Strike fast. Strike hard. Surprise is everything. Controlled chaos. That's how they trained. That's what they were known for.

Having reached the calculated distance of the tunnel's egress, there was an incline and Rogan waded out of the water. Like the entrance, the exit was blocked, but by a pile of rocks, not stone slabs. Rogan and his men set to work, dislodging stones slightly larger than a man's head, handing them back, commando to commando. A rush of fresh air signaled the breakthrough. Tearing dry brush aside, Rogan crawled out and found himself in a shallow wadi, the sides of which were barely three meters high.

As the remainder of the strike force emerged from the tunnel, Rogan, Sokoloff, and Herel lay against the sandy incline and with binoculars assessed the situation.

There were three armed terrorists guarding the rear of the structure, a small covered patio with white iron tables and chairs. There was nothing fancy about it, probably an eating and smoking area for workers. The meager light of a quarter moon outlined the dark shapes of the guards. Rogan studied them, assessing their battle readiness.

The men slouched; one of them was seated at a table. While they were facing the open field, they were not alert. All three of them were holding their rifles—AK-47s from the look of them— in one hand, a bottle of wine in the other.

"Definitely not professional soldiers," Sokoloff said.

"They're drunk," Harel added.

An uneasy feeling crept over Rogan. It felt wrong. Given the high profile of the victims, he expected a professional force. Was it possible they didn't know who they'd kidnapped?

With the strike force in position, Rogan spoke over the COM to the diversionary force in front.

"We're good to go," he said.

"Copy that," came the reply.

With nothing to do now but wait for the diversionary force to implement the initial stage of the plan, Rogan allowed himself a wry smile as he pictured the events that were about to unfold in the front parking lot of the winery. It was a tip of the hat to the historic raid on the airport in Entebbe when Sayeret Matkal forces approached an airport terminal in a black Mercedes, the kind used by government officials in Uganda. A Mercedes was being used tonight also, but with a twist—

A red Mercedes GT Roadster convertible thundered up the dirt road and into the Efrat Winery parking lot, pulling to a stop near the glass front doors of the showroom. A burly man tumbled out from behind the wheel. He was wearing a cowboy hat, Hawaiian shirt, shorts, and flip flops. A buxom woman with platinum blonde hair remained in the passenger seat.

"Will you look at that!" the man cried with an American accent. "It's closed, sweetcakes!"

He stood with hands on hips staring at the dark building.

The front door opened and a man with a rifle emerged, clearly perplexed.

"You're closed!" Hawaiian shirt cried. "Do you realize we came all the way from Beaumont, Texas, just to taste your wine?"

The terrorist didn't understand a word of English. He shouted at them to go away, waving his rifle for emphasis.

Another terrorist joined him.

"This is unacceptable," Hawaiian shirt shouted. "I want to register a complaint. Do any of you speak English?"

A third and fourth terrorist appeared, ogling the blonde.

"EN . . . GLISH," Hawaiian shirt cried.

One of the terrorists stepped forward. "You . . . go . . . now," he said in broken English. He leveled his rifle at Hawaiian shirt, who raised his hands.

"All right! All right! We'll go." He walked to the driver's side door. "But I have to tell you, you're getting a one-star review on Yelp."

He started to open the door.

"One thing more," he said. "Can any of you give us directions to Bethlehem?"

The code word spoken, four successive shots rang out from the vineyard and all four terrorists collapsed onto the macadam, dead.

The blonde threw off her wig, jumped out of the car—not a woman after all. The two commandos threw open the winery doors and tossed flash-bang grenades into the showroom while the full diversionary force poured out of the vineyards and stormed the building.

———

"Go, go, go!"

The instant the command came over the COM, Rogan signaled three designated snipers who dispatched the guards on the patio with a single shot each. Following Rogan's lead, his team emerged from the wadi on a dead run. They encountered no resistance.

Crossing the patio, they breached the building through an unlocked door. The winery was built on two levels. This was the lower level. Rows of wine casks stretched the length of the room. Seated between the casks were the children, all hugging their knees, probably so ordered by the terrorists.

Between the sounds of the flash-bangs and gunfire coming from upstairs and the sudden appearance of armed men streaming through the doors, the children were wide-eyed and frightened, many of them crying.

"Be quiet and move quickly," Rogan said to them. "We'll take you to your parents."

Half the team moved to secure the room's perimeter while the other half began shepherding the children out the back, across the field, and into the tunnel.

With the operation proceeding as planned, Rogan signaled Sokoloff and Harel to follow him. They had been tasked with locating and securing the three high-profile children. Child by child, they searched each face.

Reaching the end of one row, Rogan turned to his left. He had just started down the next row when he heard Harel call out.

"Over here!"

That same moment Rogan saw three children huddled

separately from the others. An angel was standing over them. He had a black sword.

"Sokoloff! Harel!" Rogan shouted. "I found them."

They couldn't hear him through the din and continued running the opposite direction.

Rogan made his way down the row, never taking his eye off the angel, his thumb touching the ring on his finger reassuringly. He was about to order the angel to stand aside when the supernatural being vanished.

Rogan ran to the youngsters.

They weren't the children he was looking for. He helped them up and led them to the egress point, handing them off to another commando. Turning back into the room, he retraced his steps. Running to the end of the row of barrels, he glanced in the direction he'd last seen Sokoloff and Harel.

They were at the far side of the room. Just beyond them, a couple of terrorists were shoving three children into an adjoining room. Sokoloff raised his weapon, but couldn't get a clear shot. The door slammed shut. Sokoloff and Harel quickly approached, took up positions at the door, weapons ready, and with a silent signal between them, burst into the room.

The door closed behind them.

The instant it did, Rogan saw two angels appear, guarding the door, their black swords drawn.

Invisible to ordinary men, did they know Rogan could see them?

Gunfire erupted on the other side of the door.

Scenarios flashed through Rogan's mind. He'd fought visible angels in training sessions and he felt confident he could hold his own against these two, but a fight would delay him and he needed to get into that room now.

To his left was a hallway. He sprinted down it, flanking the angels.

The hallway shared an adjoining wall with the room Sokoloff and Harel had entered. Rogan placed his hand on it, the hand with Solomon's ring. This he had not done in training, having been taught the powers of the ring, but never having experienced it. At the time he'd argued that training in theory was inadequate. Teaching a recruit the operational specs of the Tavor assault rifle was far different from having him fire one in the field, different still from firing one under battle conditions. His argument fell on deaf ears. The Archangel Michael offered no explanation.

The palm of Rogan's hand brushed the surface of the wall. It was smooth. Solid. Was it really possible to do this? The lives of his men and the children depended on a legend.

Rogan took a deep breath. He pressed his hand against the wall.

His hand disappeared, passing through seemingly solid mass as though it was not there.

Another deep breath and Rogan followed his hand through the wall.

Emerging on the other side, he entered a room lined from floor to ceiling with racks with wine bottles. The three children, frightened, crying, were seated on the floor. The two terrorists lay dead just a few feet distant. Sokoloff and Harel stood over them.

Situation secure.

Or so it seemed.

There was something not right with two of the children, one of the boys and the girl. When Rogan looked at them their faces flickered back forth between that of a child and that of the demon that possessed them.

Before Rogan had a chance to warn his team members, Sokoloff, who had not seen him enter through the wall, swung his

Tavor in the direction of Harel and fired a short burst into his friend; Harel's face registered shock as he flew backward by the impact of the blast.

A cry of horror welled up inside Rogan, erupting into a shout. "No!"

Sokoloff swung around.

His friend's face flickered, one instant Sokoloff, the next instant not Sokoloff.

Hundreds of hours of Sayeret Matkal training kicked in and Rogan instinctively raised his rifle.

"Sokoloff! Stand down!" he shouted.

The face of his friend registered horror, aware of what he was doing, but unable to stop; the face of the demon was one of murderous intent.

Sokoloff's weapon fired in a raking motion as it swung around, shattering bottles and spraying the room with red wine. A bullet slammed into Rogan's shoulder. The next round would end him.

Rogan fired, hitting Sokoloff square in the chest, at this close range penetrating his body armor, blasting him off his feet.

His friend was dead when he hit the ground. The only life remaining in him was the demon which rose out of him and came toward Rogan.

Rogan raised his hand.

"Be still!" he shouted. "I command you, be still!"

The demon froze.

The two demons inside the children, in similar fashion, rose to attack him.

Rogan swung around. "Be still!" he shouted again.

They froze, half in, half out of the children.

With three whimpering children and the floor littered with bodies, two of them his friends, his team members, it took Rogan a moment to compose himself.

The three demons were fixated on the ring, staring at it with a mixture of horror and loathing.

Rogan turned his attention to the first demon.

"Identify yourself," he commanded.

The demon resisted.

Rogan seized it with his ring hand.

"Identify yourself!" he shouted

"I am Ashmedai."

Rogan repeated the command to the other two demons.

"Lilith," said the one.

"Ornasis," said the other.

Turning back to Ashmedai, Rogan said, "Who do you answer to? Who is your prince?"

Ashmedai struggled, refusing to answer.

"I command you. Who is your prince?"

"Nosroch," Ashmedai said against his will. "We answer to Nosroch."

The three demons writhed to break the grip the power of the ring had over them. Again, Rogan ordered them to be still, keeping his ring hand between him and them. He could feel them straining against his grip on them.

The three children were crying, their heels digging into the floor as they pressed against the wall, alternately looking at him and the dead men on the floor. Unable to see the demons, they thought he was yelling at them.

"It's all right," he assured them. "I'm going to get you out of here, but first I have something to do. Trust me, I'm not going to hurt you."

His words had little effect on them. Rogan had to work fast before they panicked and tried to escape. This was going to be tricky enough, impossible if the two demon-possessed children became moving targets.

Slowly, he knelt and lay his weapon on the floor. He shrugged off his backpack and with his free hand pulled it in front of him, opened it, and reached inside. Scooping out the clay jar, he placed it on the ground and removed the lid.

Without taking his eyes off the other two demons, he gripped Ashmedai. The demon struggled and it was all Rogan could do to keep it from breaking his grip. Ashmedai was strong, but the power of the ring was stronger, and Rogan succeeded in getting him into the jar and replacing the lid.

He moved in front of the girl.

"It's all right," he assured her. "I'm not going to hurt you."

But Rogan didn't know that with certainty. Was it painful to have a demon extracted from your chest? Even if it was, he had to do it for the child's sake, like a doctor giving an inoculation, all the time assuring them it wouldn't hurt.

He seized the demon Lilith and pulled it from the girl's chest. The terrified girl slumped against the wall.

Placing the demon in the jar, he repeated the process with the boy who was possessed by the demon Ornasis.

Situation secure.

Rogan sat on the floor facing the children.

"Feel better now?" he asked them.

He gave them time to recover from the trauma, as much as they could in this chamber of death.

"Your parents are worried about you," he told them. "Come with me and I'll take you to some men who will get you safely out of here."

After placing the jar in his backpack and retrieving his weapon, he gently helped the children to their feet. Leading them to the door, he told them to stay behind him as he cautiously opened the door, checking for hostiles.

The angels he'd seen guarding the door were gone. All was

quiet. The hostages had been evacuated. Upstairs he heard the sound of heavy boots on hardwood floors, no gunfire.

Rogan guided the three children down a row of casks. Two commandos were standing at the doorway leading to the patio and the tunnel. He handed the children over to them to be evacuated.

"All secure, sir," one of the commandos reported.

Rogan nodded, finding it difficult to speak, the images of Sokoloff and Harel lying dead fresh in his mind.

"You're wounded, sir," the commando said. "Let me get you a medic."

Rogan looked at his bloodied shoulder. Touched it. Now that the rush of adrenaline was wearing off, he felt the pain.

"I'll get it tended to," he said. "First, there's something I have to do."

He keyed the COM. "Col. Amar," he said. "Capt. Rogan. Meet me downstairs."

Rogan returned to the room where his fallen comrades lay and took up a position outside the closed door. Within minutes he was joined by the colonel.

Rogan handed him the backpack.

"The three demons, sir," he said. "Ashmedai. Lilith. Ornasis."

"Well done, captain," Col. Amar said.

Rogan felt no satisfaction. It was all he could do to keep his emotions under control.

"Their capture came at a high price," he said.

Col. Amar waited for further explanation.

"I'm sorry, colonel," Rogan said.

He stepped through the closed door.

When Col. Amar entered the room where the bodies of Sokoloff and Harel lay, he did so just as Rogan was passing through the wall.

———

The day after the rescue operation, the phone in the colonel's office was answered on the first ring.

"Col. Amar? Rogan."

"Rogan! Where the devil did you go?"

"It was a trap, colonel. The whole operation. Those weren't terrorists at the winery. My guess is they were locals, hired guns promised all the wine they could drink. That's the only explanation I can come up with for the location. Kidnapped children had nothing to do with it. They were pawns. There were angels at the winery, colonel. Angels were running the show. They lured me away from . . ." Rising emotions made it difficult to speak. ". . . from my men, and then into the trap."

There was a long silence. Rogan could hear muffled sounds. The colonel wasn't alone.

"What happened in that room, Rogan. You have two dead soldiers to account for."

"Ashmedai, Lilith, and Ornasis. They played us, sir. They were after the ring. They knew about it. How?"

Another pause.

"You said there were angels," the colonel prompted.

"Black swords," Rogan replied. "The whole operation was to lure me out, to identify the one with the ring and secure it."

More muffled sounds.

"He's with you now, isn't he? The Archangel Michael."

Another pause, this one shorter. "Affirmative. He came for the jar."

"And the ring," Rogan said.

"Rogan, come in. We'll work through this."

"Does he know two men died, two good men?"

"Rogan—"

"The demons possessed those children, colonel," Rogan said. "Sokoloff and Harel had no way of knowing that. Rebel angels distracted me so I couldn't warn them. They didn't have a chance, sir."

"What happened in that room, soldier?"

Rogan took a deep, ragged breath. "Sokoloff and Harel followed the hostiles into the room and took them out. There were two angels posted outside the room to delay me. Instead of engaging them, I entered through an adjoining wall."

"You entered—"

"I walked through the wall, sir. I think I surprised them. I believe the plan was to have Sokoloff take me out the moment I came through the door. When I entered, Sokoloff—that is, Ashmedai—turned his weapon on Harel and killed him and then, realizing I was behind him, swung around to shoot me. Sokoloff didn't want to shoot, colonel. I could see it in his eyes. Ashmedai was controlling him."

Rogan found it difficult to continue his narration as he relived the experience. He began to weep.

"I messed up, sir. I made a rookie mistake. I failed to identify the threat. In that split-second, I thought the threat was Sokoloff. All I could see was his Tavor pointing at me. But the threat was Ashmedai, not Sokoloff. I could have stopped him with the ring, but I didn't. . . . I . . . I fired. I killed Sokoloff, sir."

"Rogan, return to base. That's an order."

"I can't, sir. How can I? My career is over. Once my men learn that I killed Sokoloff, they'll never follow me again."

"At least tell me where you are."

"Negative, sir. The instant I tell you, an archangel will be standing beside me. He doesn't care about Sokoloff and Harel. What are we to them? He only wants his ring back."

"Rogan, I'm giving you a direct order—"

"Ask him about Nosroch."

"What the devil, Rogan? Who's Nosroch?"

"Just ask him, sir. Tell him he'll get his ring back if he tells me about Nosroch."

On the other end of the line there were more muffled sounds.

"Nosroch is a rebel angel, faithful to Lucifer in the rebellion against the Almighty."

"Where was he last seen?"

"Rogan—"

"Ask him where Nosroch was last seen—surely they keep tabs on the enemy."

More muffled sounds.

"In Southern California, San Diego. Watchers spotted him at a Spectacle. What does this have to do with—"

"Tell Michael I'll give the ring back to him, but not just yet. There's something I have to do first."

Col. Amar cursed. His patience had run out. "Capt. Dorn, get your butt in my office this instant!"

"One more thing, Colonel. Tell Sokoloff's family I'm sorry, that I wish it was me who died in that room."

Rogan ended the call.

A short time later he boarded a freighter sailing out of Haifa and tossed the cell phone he'd purchased for the call to the colonel overboard.

CHAPTER
9

WRITERS WASTE TIME LIKE EVERYONE ELSE, FINDING ALL SORTS of attractive distractions, anything to keep them from putting words on screen. Procrastination comes in the usual forms, such as games on a computer or smartphone, solitaire being a perennial procrastinating pleasure; Angry Birds was big for a while, Tetris for the older set. Then of course there is Facebook, Twitter, Pinterest, Instagram, Snapchat, and checking your email. When writers get truly desperate, it's amazing how important washing dishes becomes.

Professional writers are professional procrastinators. For historical writers, research is often used as an excuse not to write. I've been known to watch a two-hour documentary on life in medieval times while researching what sort of shoes peasants wore in the Middle Ages.

Today, while I was supposed to be coming up with a new book topic, I found myself in the research section at San Diego State University, looking up the term "bad penny"—as in the phrase, "A bad penny always turns up."

I found it fascinating (a professional writer's rationalization to justify wasting time) that the phrase had been used as early as the 14th Century in William Langland's famous prose poem "Piers Plowman": "Men may lykne letterid men . . . to a badde peny." Equally fascinating that a bad penny was a reference to clipped pennies, in which disreputable types would cut slivers from pennies, melt down them down into bars, and sell them to goldsmiths.

A person who was a bad penny was one who had a predictable, and often unwanted, way of showing up after an absence, whose presence is unwelcome on any occasion, but whom fate perversely employs to torment you by making said person appear—"turn up"—repeatedly, often at the worst possible times.

Like an angel in a man's shower.

Following his abrupt departure in a huff, Noz had taken to pouting, angel style. He would show up in cloaked form at all hours of the day and night and watch me. He didn't speak to me; I didn't speak to him. He'd watch for a while and disappear. It was annoying—annoying enough to drive me to the reference section to look up the term "bad penny."

"What are you doing?"

Noz appeared suddenly in the seat opposite me at the reference section table. He wasn't cloaked.

I closed the book. "Trying to get some research done," I said.

"Maybe I could help. I've been around for—"

"Millennia. Yeah, I know."

It occurred to me that he was a historical researcher's goldmine. He probably knew what type of shoes peasants wore in the Middle Ages.

I got up and replaced the phrase book in the stacks. He followed me.

"I don't much care for humans," he said.

"There's a news flash."

"It's not easy for me to come to you like this."

His comment had a hook in it. He wanted me to say, "Then, why did you?" But I wasn't biting.

"You intrigue me, Grant Austin. One moment I think you're stalwart and noble; the next, you play the buffoon."

"That's me in a nutshell," I said. "In a nutshell," another fascinating phrase. I made a mental note to look up its etymology next time I needed to procrastinate.

I made my way to the exit. He followed me outside, and as I made my way to the parking structure, I wondered what the passing students would think if they knew that the man walking beside me was an angel, one of Lucifer's lieutenants.

When I climbed into my car, I didn't unlock the passenger door, hoping he'd take the hint. He stepped through the door and into the passenger seat.

"Buckle up," I said.

He grinned. "Concerned for my safety, Grant?"

"It's the law. If a policeman sees that you're not wearing a seat-belt, I'll get a ticket."

He sat there.

"I'm not starting the car until you buckle up."

When he saw I was serious, he put on his seatbelt.

I exited the parking structure and merged onto the freeway.

"I don't think you appreciate the risk I'm taking coming to you like this," he said.

I laughed. "That's rich. It's been my experience that whenever an angel shows up, I'm the one at risk."

"Semyaza," he acknowledged. "His thwarted plan to enlist you since high school is well known among the ranks of angels."

"Yeah, I'll bet it's been an ongoing source of amusement for you."

But I was also thinking of Abdiel banging my head against walls and Belial straining my atoms through membranes.

"We share a mutual adversary in Semyaza, Grant," he said.

That ticked me off. "Really?" I shouted. "That old shtick, Noz? You really need to get a new playbook. Did you take that line out of *101 Ways to Deceive and Torture Humans?*"

He gazed at me in all innocence. "I don't understand your anger, Grant."

"You and I have something in common, Grant," I parodied. "Semyaza is a bad angel, Grant. I hate him too, Grant. But I'm not like him. You can trust me."

Noz still didn't get it.

"That's the line Belial used on me just before he shanghaied me to Sheol."

Noz looked away. "I didn't know that," he said.

He sounded sincere. But so had Belial just before he yanked me through the membrane while taunting me. *Never trust the devil, Grant.*

"I'm an outcast, Grant," Noz said. "A renegade. There are a number of us. Semyaza has been given the task to hunt us down and deliver us to Lucifer."

"A renegade rebel angel," I said. "So, what, that makes you a double rebel angel? A rebel rebel angel?"

"I can see that this is hard for you, Grant Austin. Maybe it was a mistake coming to you."

"If you're looking for sympathy, you've got the wrong guy."

I was hoping he'd disappear. He didn't. We rode the rest of the way to my apartment in silence. At my front door, unlocking the deadbolt, I shut the door in his face. He stepped through it.

Bad penny.

I turned on him. If he wanted a fight, I'd give him one. As is often the case when you're in the midst of an argument, I was caught up in the heat of the moment. The fact that if I goaded him too far he could go all nuclear on me and reduce me to a whimpering puddle of flesh didn't occur to me until later.

"Tell me this," I challenged. "After all these millennia, why now? What could possibly motivate you to turn against Lucifer now?"

"You," he said.

"Me?"

"What you said in Sheol, Grant. You opened our eyes to the truth."

My remembrance of Sheol was that I'd survived it.

"Let me ask you a question, Grant. Do you think it's possible for a rebel angel to regret his role in the rebellion? Is it possible for us to repent and seek forgiveness?"

I didn't have an answer for him. This was a question for the professor, not me.

"That's what we've been asking ourselves," Noz said. "Surely you can see how that would be a threat to Lucifer, and why he would task Semyaza with hunting us down."

"So, why not just do it? Ask for forgiveness."

"It's not that easy, Grant. We made our choice during the rebellion when we sided with Lucifer, and now we await judgment. But now, we can't help but wonder: Is our fate sealed? Can a single act in our past doom us forever even if now we regret that decision?"

"I'm not the one who can answer that question."

"And we're not expecting you to answer it. But you should know you are the one who inspired us to ask it. Not just by what you said, but by who you are. You went to Sheol because your fate is sealed and you want to change it."

"That's different," I protested. "The fate of Nephilim are sealed not by anything we've done, but simply because of who we are."

"You're right, of course," he said. "But still, you seek the Father's grace, His favor, as do we. In that, our goal is the same."

I found myself sympathizing with him. The feeling was short-lived.

"No, no . . . NO!" I shouted. "All of this . . . this . . . bleeding heart stuff. I've fallen for it before. That's what you do, isn't it? You're a liar, a disciple of the father of lies. You twist things around to deceive people. Well, I'm not falling for it this time."

In a calm voice, he said, "What will it take to convince you of my sincerity, Grant Austin?"

To my surprise, inspiration struck and I knew exactly what would satisfy me.

"Touch down," I said.

"I don't understand."

"Sure you do. Angels hover. You refuse to walk the earth. It's tainted to you. Touching it is repulsive. If you want to prove to me that you're sincere, touch down. Wiggle your toes in my carpet."

From the expression of revulsion on his face, I knew I'd scored.

"You are asking the impossible," he protested. "Would Abdiel do such a thing for you?"

"No, he wouldn't," I said. "But the Divine Warrior did. When he rescued me from Sheol, he stood in my apartment, on my carpet, and left footprints. If you want me to believe you, make tracks in my carpet."

"You presume too much."

"You asked what it would take and I'm telling you. That's the price for my believing you."

He looked down at the carpet, then back at me, and disappeared.

"That's what I thought," I said. "Good riddance to a bad penny."

"Why would you say such a thing, Grant Austin? I have just arrived."

The voice came from behind me, startling me. I turned to see Abdiel.

"Grant Austin. You look well."

"Umm . . . give me a second," I said, a hand pressed to my chest. "You startled me."

My heart was doing its flip-flop thing not because Abdiel startled me, which he did, but because he'd just missed Noz. Had he come a second sooner, or had Noz dallied a moment longer, I would have found myself standing between two eternal combatants. That had happened once before with Abdiel and Belial and it wasn't pretty.

"To whom were you speaking?" Abdiel asked, looking behind me.

I considered telling him about Noz, but something stopped me. This was my problem and I didn't want to complicate it by getting caught between two opposing eternal forces. So far Noz was not a threat, just an annoyance.

"I was just trying out some lines," I said.

"I don't understand."

"You know. Lines. Sentences. Writers do that sometimes," I said. "We speak them aloud to see how they sound. What can I say? We're weird."

He looked at me with his trademark stoic expression.

"How . . . how are you?" I said. It was a lame question, but anything to move on. "Better still, how's the professor?"

"He lives in eternal bliss, Grant Austin. Why would you ask after his health?"

"Just making conversation. You know, small talk."

Abdiel stared at me.

"I forgot. You're not one for small talk, are you?" An understatement. "What are you doing here? Do you miss me? Want to walk through some walls together for old times' sake?"

No smirk. No shaking of the head. Nothing. Tough audience.

"I come on a mission."

That got my attention. It also puzzled me. Two years ago when Abdiel came to me with a message from the Father, it was to inform me I was putting the seal of His favor in jeopardy by going to Sheol. When Abdiel appeared to me then, he said, "Fear not." Heaven's way of getting your attention.

"Three demons escaped their imprisonment, spreading terror and death the length of Israel," he said.

"Please don't tell me you want me to do something to stop them."

"I do not. They have already been captured and placed once again at the bottom of the sea."

I hadn't realized it, but my breath had caught in my throat anticipating the worst. Relieved, I gulped a breath of air.

"The man who captured them is believed to be here in your city."

"Man? A man subdued three demons and captured them? That's a formidable man."

"To perform that task, he was given a powerful weapon. The weapon does not belong to him and we want him to return it."

"What kind of weapon? Some sort of heavenly bazooka?"

"This is not the time for levity, Grant. It is a serious matter."

"So if this guy is some sort of renegade, why did you give him the weapon?"

"I did not."

"Someone did," I prompted.

"That is not your concern."

"Yet, you came to ask my help. Sounds like my concern to me."

Abdiel's gaze hardened. I'd seen that gaze before, but I held my ground.

"The man is part of an elite force of soldiers commanded by the Archangel Michael," Abdiel said.

"The top brass himself." I was impressed.

"He has sent me to alert you to the soldier's presence in your city."

"And you think he's here, but you don't know for sure. Interesting. I thought you guys knew everything."

"We are not omniscient, Grant Austin."

"But the Father is," I said. "Why doesn't the Archangel Michael ask Him? Unless . . ." I allowed myself a smile. "You are forever telling me, 'We are pleased to serve at the Father's pleasure,' which means that this mission and this weapon wasn't the Father's mission. Whose was it? Michael's?"

"The Archangel Michael," Abdiel said with emphasis.

"So the Archangel Michael was acting on his own."

"We are angels," Abdiel said. "It should not surprise you that we have free will—otherwise there would have been no rebellion, and you would not exist."

He lost me on that last one.

"Mating with human women and the procreation of Nephilim was an act of free will," he explained.

"And both of them acts of rebellion," I pointed out.

Abdiel didn't like that. His gaze hardened even more. I didn't press it, and I shouldn't have been surprised that the actions of angels, even faithful angels, sometimes fell in gray areas— possibly well-intended, but not always well-conceived.

"So what do you want me to do? Make some calls?"

"Be aware that he is here, that is all. You can see things others can't see."

"And if I do see him? How do I alert you? Whistle? Ring a bell and you'll come running?"

I was pushing things too far and I knew it. I just couldn't help myself. Abdiel and I had a history and I knew deep down—very deep down, subterranean even—he liked me.

"If you see him, do not engage him. He is dangerous, Grant Austin. I will check on you periodically."

"Aww, how sweet. You really do care for me, don't you?"

But he'd already departed.

Wow, Grant. Two angels in one day.

I didn't want to admit it, but I'd missed this. After all I'd been through, most of it dangerous or painful, there was a part of me that had grown bored with human life.

Turning around, my heart jumped again.

The Bad Penny had returned. Twice now I'd escaped disaster by a split second.

"What do you want now?" I asked.

Nosroch didn't reply. His face registered intense pain as though he was being tortured.

I glanced down.

His feet were pressed into my carpet and he was wiggling his toes.

CHAPTER
10

ROGAN SAT ALONE IN A GASLAMP QUARTER BAR, DOWNTOWN San Diego, a corner booth, his back to the wall, stirring the lemon slice and ice cubes in his drink. He kept his mind active. If he let his thoughts wander, they had a habit of returning to his fatal error at the winery and visions of the bodies of Sokoloff and Harel lying twisted and bloody on the floor. In the darkness of the corner booth, he pondered the same question that had occupied him aboard the freighter from Haifa and the airline flights from Turkey to Dublin, Dublin to Boston, Boston to San Diego:

How does one track an angel?

All he had to work with was a name and location which, with the date of the sighting uncertain and angelic ability to transport great distances at the speed of thought, was sketchy at best. But it was all he had to go on.

He needed a lead.

Finding angels, faithful or rebel, was not a problem. He saw them everywhere; on all three flights, at the airports, walking the streets of San Diego. The problem was how to extract information from them. The military method, which he'd used countless times on Palestinians on the streets of Israel—confrontation, intimidation, and physical force if necessary—wouldn't work on this assignment. Rebel angels weren't your ordinary street ruffians. Besides, aggressive tactics would call attention to himself—something he could not do. It would be foolish not to think Michael had dispatched angels to find him.

So what did that leave him? Deception. While he hadn't yet come up with a plan, he'd been observing rebel angels and had some ideas. He noticed that while faithful angels were often seen alone, rebel angels moved in pairs. On occasion he'd seen a lone rebel angel, but always invisible to humans. He'd tracked a pair of them into the bar, one visible, the other invisible. An odd pairing. After observing them a while, he determined the tactic was used for sport.

This was their second bar of the night. The visible one was the charmer with Hollywood leading man good looks, a confident bearing, a perfect smile, and a touch of naughtiness that attracted females like moths to a flame. While he was the straight man, the invisible angel was the joker. He bumped arms to spill drinks on the most embarrassing body parts; tripped men who were trying to act suave; pushed, shoved, and threw unseen punches to start fights. Rebel angels loved slapstick.

Rogan wondered if he could use that against them.

As he was watching the duo perform their routine on a couple of coeds, Rogan's line of sight was blocked by four men who took up position at the end of the bar and ordered beers. They were young, fit, boisterous and from their conversation it didn't take long for Rogan to learn they were Navy SEALs in training. It was all they talked about. It didn't take long for their personalities to emerge. One was the leader; one was the muscle; one was the quiet one; one was the cut-up. They reminded Rogan of himself, Sokoloff, and Harel in younger days. The memories the SEALs prompted were a tonic to his soul, and he found himself smiling for the first time in weeks.

With animated gestures, they were reliving the obstacle course they'd run earlier that day, good-naturedly shoving each other the way buddies do, each one in turn boasting about the obstacles they were best at while their buddies countered with the ones in which they didn't measure up. It was all good fun until Muscle noticed Rogan watching them. He took exception to Rogan's smile.

Breaking from the others, he carried his beer over to Rogan's table and stood over him. His buddies were right behind him.

"Something funny?" he challenged.

Rogan met his gaze. Held it.

"I'm talking to you," Muscle said.

"I heard you," Rogan replied.

To his buddies, Muscle said, "This guy is sittin' over here laughing at us." To Rogan, "It's not polite to listen in on a conversation that's none of your business."

Rogan broke eye contact and stirred his drink.

"Hey! My buddy's talking to you," the leader said.

"Maybe we should take him outside and teach him some manners," Muscle said.

Rogan continued stirring his drink. Without looking up, he said, "Stand down, boys."

"We're not boys. We're men," Cut-up said. His voice was high-pitched, adolescent.

Rogan assessed the situation. Four against one. Muscle was strong, but slow and, from his gait, not yet the master of his bulk. The leader was cocky, the type that ran headlong into a situation before fully understanding it. Cut-up was the scrappy sort, undisciplined. The quiet one was more methodical, analytical, but afraid of spontaneity.

"We'll make this easy for you," the leader said. "Leave now while you can still walk."

"I'll leave when I'm finished with my drink," Rogan said.

Cut-up snatched the drink from Rogan. Sniffed it. "It's soda water!"

"That's what old men drink," the leader scoffed. He took the glass from Cut-up and splashed it in Rogan's face. "There, you're done. Now leave."

"You shouldn't have done that," Rogan said.

"Oooooo, what are you doing to do? Beat us up?" Cut-up mocked him.

"No," Rogan said. "Not today."

He slid to the edge of the seat. Muscle stepped back to allow him room to get out. Exactly as Rogan anticipated.

With a leg sweep, Rogan sent him to the floor; pivoted and smashed the leader in the nose with his elbow; a quick thrust of his fist to the quiet one's throat left him gasping for air, giving the cut-up enough time to recover from the surprise. He lunged at Rogan with a fist that Rogan sidestepped, grabbed his arm, and used the boy's momentum to throw him headlong into the wall. Before any of them had time to recover, Rogan had a foot on Muscle's neck and a chokehold on the leader, using him as a bloody-nosed shield against any further attack.

There was none.

To the bartender, Rogan said, "I'll have another club soda with a slice of lemon. Put it on this one's tab." He tightened his grip on the leader, who nodded his head.

Rogan let him go and offered his hand to Muscle to help him up.

"My name is Capt. Rogan Dorn," he said. "I'm a member of the Sayeret Matkal of the Israeli Defense Force. My friends call me The Hammer. And I'd be honored if you would join me at my booth. I think you'll find we have a lot in common."

"Last call," the bartender cried.

The night had passed quickly for Rogan as he swapped stories with the SEALs and answered their questions regarding Krav Maga, the hand-to-hand combat maneuvers developed by Israeli special forces, occasionally slipping out of the booth to demonstrate.

Rogan liked the young SEALs. He understood them. Mostly, he savored the camaraderie, something he knew he would never experience again with his unit in Israel. No rancor, just fact. His fate had been fixed the moment he shot Sokoloff. One moment he was a soldier in the IDF; the next, he was a rogue angel assassin.

The two rebel angels Rogan had been tracking, having had their fun, had left the bar earlier. It didn't matter. Without a clear plan to extract information from angels, it would be premature to confront them.

The bartender began upending chairs and placing them on tables. Rogan and his friends gathered their things and walked out onto the downtown San Diego street bathed in the light of old-fashioned street lamps. A cool breeze blew in off the bay.

Rogan and the leader walked together with the others trailing them. He had since learned that the leader's name was Williamson, a third-generation SEAL out of Pensacola, Florida.

"You know what I'd like to see?" Cut-up said behind them.

Rogan had also learned Cut-up's name but couldn't remember it at the moment. Strafford? Stafford? Swafford?

"I'd like to see Rogan knock Chief Petty Officer Zapata on his butt."

Williamson explained, "Zapata fancies himself an expert in Krav Maga."

No sooner had the words come out of his mouth when a thought seemed to occur to Williamson, an idea that stopped him in his tracks.

"The war games!" he said.

He turned to Rogan.

"What are you doing tomorrow?"

CHAPTER
11

As Rogan drove across the Coronado Bridge, which was still under construction from its recent encounter with American history, he took advantage of the clogged traffic artery—caused by thousands of military personnel reporting for duty at the naval air station—to imagine what it must have been like on this bridge the day the American president was killed. As had most of the world, he'd read about the assassination and seen video clips from media sources, both factual and speculative. He also knew things about that day the general public didn't know, having been schooled by the Archangel Michael about the supernatural battle behind the historical event.

Alternately leaning out the driver side window and angling his head against the dashboard to look upward through the windshield, Rogan scanned the sky in relationship to the geography to recreate in his mind the events as Michael had described them. Several times the driver behind him hit his horn to coax Rogan along when traffic moved forward.

As the route of the bridge made its characteristic downward sweep into Coronado, Rogan approached toll booths that had been reopened to pay for the costly bridge reconstruction. Entering the island, he drove down quaint streets that were populated by outrageously expensive houses. Leaving thoughts of history on the bridge behind him, he focused on his war games mission.

When Williamson proposed the mission to him, Rogan's initial reaction was to decline. He had a mission of his own. But when Williamson described what was at stake—unit pride and bragging rights—the young seaman struck a sensitive nerve. These were things Rogan understood, values he cherished. Despite his recent actions, he was—and always would be—a special forces soldier at heart. And the chance to be part of a unit again—even unofficially—exerted a powerful tug. And as strong as that feeling was, there was something else. An intuition, a gut feeling that his involvement would, in ways unknown to him now, be beneficial to his own mission.

If nothing else, the exercise would allow him to practice his ring skills. Of course, he said nothing of this to his new-found SEAL buddies.

Williamson had outlined the war games with enthusiasm. Part of a weeklong series of exercises, Rogan's mission was to test base security. The game was simple: the SEALs were tasked with penetrating the perimeter and placing a sticker with the SEALs insignia on the base flagpole; security forces were tasked with preventing the breach. During the exercise, the sticker was to be affixed to their ID and had to be surrendered to security if they were detained.

Attempts to elude security were not restricted to members of a SEALS team. One year a pregnant woman, the wife of a SEAL with an adorable two-year old, tried to walk on base beside an unwitting seaman with a valid ID, attempting to pass herself off as his wife and child. To Williamson's knowledge, no one had ever enlisted the aid of another military force. It was that idea that had stopped him mid-step on the sidewalk outside the bar the night before.

To prepare for the mission, Rogan had memorized a map of the base that he had found online. He'd used Google Maps to familiarize himself with the streets of Coronado, occasionally dragging the map's little yellow man to key locations to get a street view. He also returned his rental car, exchanging it for a Kia Soul; its box-like profile would make it noticeable, key to the plan; while its white color—the most popular color for cars—would allow him to disappear into traffic if needed.

Of course, using his Nephilim skills, he could simply stroll onto the base through fences and walls, but that would violate the spirit of the war games. And while he didn't rule out the use of his Nephilim skills, Rogan not only wanted to succeed in his mission, he wanted base security to know that he had bested them.

The stream of cars approached the main gate of the base and, four blocks distant, Rogan saw something he hadn't anticipated.

"Mahanaim," he muttered under his breath.

He turned down a side street, parked at the curb, got out and walked back to the corner to get a better look.

"This is going to complicate things."

He'd read of a similar occurrence in the Tanakh, but never imagined he'd see one himself. The passage in Genesis described Jacob on a journey when he happened upon one, a passage that was remarkable in its simplicity, as though this kind of thing was a regular occurrence. Jacob had named the place Mahanaim—two encampments: Jacob's encampment and an encampment of angels.

Rogan stared, not at the naval base, but at the sky above it.

There were hundreds of them, faithful angels by the appearance of their silver swords. From their activity, it wasn't an assembly, but a working camp. Angels were coming and going with purpose, ascending and descending. And while Rogan didn't think for a moment that their purpose for being there was to locate him, he had to assume that the Archangel Michael had alerted the post to be on alert for him.

Rogan assessed the threat. While the ring he was wearing gave him special powers, his appearance was that of an ordinary human. He could move about the naval base as long as he didn't do something that would call attention to himself, like be seen drawing his sword or walking through walls, the latter being a key part of his war games strategy.

His instincts told him to walk away. An American naval war game was not worth the risk of endangering his mission to avenge the deaths of Sokoloff and Harel. He owed nothing to the four SEALs in training. He could turn back now. They'd never see him again.

Two things stopped him. The pride of the Sayeret Matkal was on the line. He'd made a commitment to military brothers; the fact that it was an American force was beside the point. And he couldn't shake the feeling that fulfilling this obligation would somehow prove beneficial to him.

Wearing a colorful Hawaiian shirt, Rogan stood on the corner and waited for the flow of traffic onto the base to ease up. Then, returning to his car, he proceeded with his mission. He drove toward the main gate.

The entrance to the base was three lanes wide with security gates offset from the road about ninety meters. The lanes were designated with white paint—left to right: Visitors, DOD, Trucks. A blue line separated Alameda, the public street that ran parallel to the base, with white lettering: US Govt Property.

Rogan drove the Kia Soul across Alameda, across the blue line, pulled to the curb in the truck lane, and waited, the engine running. To his immediate right was a row of palm trees and a three-foot brick wall with a sign: Naval Air Station North Island.

In the visitor parking area just outside the base, he saw a man leaning against the back of a car. He was dressed in tennis shorts and a white shirt, a bag with a tennis racket at his feet. One of the guards at the gate stared at him suspiciously. A moment later a jeep with four armed men appeared from the base, just as a second car with a base sticker reached the tennis player. Greetings were exchanged and the tennis player grabbed his bag and climbed into the passenger seat. The jeep stopped a short distance away.

The car with the tennis player approached the gate. A security guard blocked the way as the jeep swung around and pulled up behind them. The four armed men jumped out of the jeep and surrounded the car, their weapons trained on the driver and tennis player. The armed guard closest to the passenger side door tapped on the window with his automatic weapon and ordered the passenger to roll down his window and show his identification.

The tennis player reached into his back pocket, pulled out a wallet, his ID, and handed it to the guard who checked it. The guard appeared visibly disappointed.

"No sticker," Rogan said.

The ID was returned and the car proceeded onto the base.

Rogan watched as several cars passed him and proceeded normally onto base. He waited. It wasn't long before one of the guards spotted him, walked a short distance from the gate, scrutinized him, then said something into a communications device.

"Here we go," Rogan said.

The jeep with the four armed guards appeared. Rogan waited until they were about forty-five meters away. He threw the Kia into reverse, backed onto Alameda, and floored it. In his rearview mirror, he watched the jeep accelerate to follow him.

Rogan made a sharp right on 6th Street, an immediate left

on Country Club Way, counted four houses, and turned into a driveway that led past the house to a garage on the back of the property, much to the surprise of an elderly man who was watering his flower beds in the front of the house.

Rogan got out of the car.

A few moments later, the elderly man rounded the back corner of the house.

Rogan raised his hands in greeting. "Uncle Mandelbaum! I finally made it!"

The elderly man stopped a safe distance away. "Who the devil are you?" he said.

"I'm Kuni…you know, Fishel's friend!"

"I don't know what you're talking about. Get off my property."

Rogan looked past the man to the street. No jeep appeared. While this wasn't surprising—he was off base, no longer a threat, and the guards had no jurisdiction here—still, it didn't hurt to take precautions.

"Fishel, your nephew," Rogan said.

"I don't know any Fishel," the man said. "Now get off my property or I'm calling the police."

Rogan offered his apologies for the intrusion, insisting he was sure he'd gotten the address right, climbed back into his car, and drove away.

He circled the island to the north side, turned on 1st Street, crossed Alameda, and approached the base again, this time Gate 2. As before, he pulled to the side in view of the gate. To the north was the bay. To his immediate left, a tall bush and a six-foot brick wall.

He didn't have to wait long.

The scene repeated itself. A guard stepped away from the gate.

"That's right," Rogan said, "the white Kia Soul."

The guard ran back to the gate and a moment later another

jeep with armed guards appeared. Opening the car door, Rogan ducked down and rolled to the base of the bush. A second jeep from the main entrance came roaring down Alameda to intercept him.

Rogan checked the immediate area, including the sky. Seeing no angels, he placed his hand, the one with Solomon's ring, against the brick wall, and stepped through it.

On the base side of the wall, there was a gas station. Rogan straightened his Hawaiian shirt and walked past the pumps toward the arched entrance of the commissary and entered the store. Grabbing a cart, he pushed it down an aisle, loading the cart with potato chips, Lucky Charms cereal, Viva paper towels, and Bounce fabric softener. Printed across the top of the back wall was a sign: Thank You for Shopping at Your Commissary.

He passed two men in navy scrubs.

"Let's grab a sandwich at Subway," the taller sailor said.

"But not here," his buddy said. "Let's go to the one by the fitness center."

"There's a Subway right here."

"It's always crowded."

"But the other Subway is all the way on the other side of the base."

"Quit your griping. A little walk isn't going to kill you."

Rogan reached the end of the aisle and positioned himself so that he could see the front doors. Four base security guards entered. One positioned himself at the door; the other three proceeded down the aisles—one went right, another left.

Not until they saw him did Rogan make his move.

Abandoning his cart, he slipped into the garden center, walking briskly to the back wall. He removed the Hawaiian shirt and stuffed it under a bag of fertilizer. Now in a military green t-shirt, he pulled a San Diego Padres ball cap from his waistband and put it on.

Fingering the ring, he approached the wall. Out of the corner of his eye, he saw movement.

An angel.

Visible, the angel was bent over slightly, admiring a yellow orchid.

The angel paid no attention to him, but Rogan couldn't chance walking through a wall with him there.

One of the guards entered the garden center.

A few feet away, a woman with an infant in a stroller was reading the back of a box of grass seed. Rogan dropped down to one knee.

"She's adorable!" he said.

The woman smiled. "Thank you," she said.

"What's her name?"

"Abigail."

"And she's what, a year old?"

"Terrible twos," the mother said.

Rogan glanced in the direction of the angel, silently urging him to move on. He was running out of time.

"Do you have children?" the woman asked.

"Single. But some day."

He glanced again. The angel was gone. He could still be nearby, but Rogan was out of time. He'd have to risk it.

"Well, Abigail," he said. "You have made my day."

The woman smiled.

Giving up all pretense, staying low, Rogan moved quickly until he was out of sight and stepped through the back wall.

He emerged into sunlight and walked quickly, catching up with the two sailors he'd seen in the commissary. He fell in step with them. The guards would be looking for a single man in a Hawaiian shirt, not three men walking together.

"Hey guys," Rogan said. "I'm new on base. Can you direct me to the Subway sandwich shop?"

"We're headed there now," the taller one said. "Where are you from?"

They made small talk as they walked, Rogan fabricating a story about being an army brat, having lived all over the world, most recently Germany. He told them he'd joined the Navy because he knew it would anger his father. Of course, he used adjectives of the baser sort to make it believable.

They stopped once to salute a passing car.

"Lucky you," the tall one said, referring to the vehicle siting. "First day and you get to see Rear Admiral Morison."

Their route took them well north of the flagpole, but close enough for Rogan to see that it was guarded. He wondered if the rules of the game allowed this tactic since the area surrounding the pole was open and it would be impossible for anyone to approach it without being challenged.

He didn't care. He had something else in mind.

When they reached Subway, Rogan excused himself to "hit the head," hoping neither of his traveling buddies had the urge. They didn't. Closing the door behind him and not locking it, he approached a side wall and hesitated.

Already he'd passed through a wall blind, and he was pressing his luck each time he did it, but bold plans required bold acts. He stepped through. His luck held. He emerged between buildings.

His destination was a short walk away. He fell in step behind a small group of sailors heading his direction, then cut over to Vought Street and walked the rest of the way alone until he reached the Training/NAES Admin building. He went inside where two guards were checking everyone's ID for further access into the building. He doubted they'd been alerted to his presence, and even if they had, they'd be looking for a man in a Hawaiian shirt. He checked the registry, found the room he was looking for, and stepped back outside.

Walking around the back of the building, he located an emergency exit and, when it was clear, he passed through the closed door, went up two flights of stairs, found the office he was looking for, and walked past it. He checked the nameplate on the door, opened it, and rushed in, startling the aide sitting behind the desk in the front office.

"Is this the Force Master Chief's office?" he gasped, feigning breathlessness.

"The Master Chief isn't in," the aide replied.

"I know," Rogan said, inwardly relieved. "He's fallen on the stairs and told me come get you."

The aide was around the desk in a heartbeat. "What's he doing back here?" he said to himself, rushing out of the office and down the hallway.

Rogan stepped into the aide's office, through the door into the Master Chief's office, turned to an adjoining wall, and walked into the office he'd targeted. He removed his wallet, peeled off the SEALs sticker, and placed it over the medals of the distinguished, gray-haired Rear Admiral's portrait.

Leaning against the desk, he waited.

More than an hour passed before Rogan heard voices on the other side of the door. He stood and, when the door opened, held out his hand to a startled Rear Admiral Morison. The base commander stared at him dumbfoundedly.

Rogan looked at the sticker on the portrait. The commander followed his gaze.

"Compliments of the SEALs and Israeli Defense Forces," Rogan said.

—————

Rogan stood on the Coronado beach next to Chief Petty Officer Zapata as three helicopters hovered offshore over the water. Three teams of SEALS deployed from the choppers, plunging into the ocean. Combat rubber raiding craft tumbled out after them. Surfacing, the trainees scrambled onto the rafts and paddled furiously toward a rock jetty.

"You Israelis sure know how to poke a hornet's nest," Zapata said, "I'll give you that."

"Standard operating procedure," Rogan replied.

His war games actions had earned him an invitation to observe the training exercise. While he watched the men approach the jetty, he could feel Zapata's gaze sizing him up. Rogan was familiar with the scrutiny. Zapata was a man's man. Though the chief petty officer didn't say it, Rogan knew what he was thinking: *I could take him.*

"Security issued a formal protest," Zapata said. "They argued you failed to achieve the mission objective."

"They were guarding the pole."

"A violation of the rules," Zapata said. "Rear Admiral Morison lit into them something fierce, not for violating the rules, but for failing to guard the commander of the base. He awarded us the win. By the way, the security chief wants to talk to you, find out how you did it."

Standing atop the jetty were training observers, tracking the progress of the teams. Unknown to them, two angels stood with them. Rogan glanced overhead at the invisible encampment. It was as before. He saw no unusual movement. The angels on the rocks were intent on the exercise; they paid him no attention.

The first of the rafts reached the jetty.

"Your guys," Zapata said. "Williamson, Stafford, Adams, and Clay."

Rogan watched as the men attempted to climb onto the jetty. Waves battered them repeatedly, throwing the rubber craft against the rocks. It overturned. Two of the men landed on the rocks, the other two were tossed into the churning sea. While one secured the craft, the other reached to help his buddies climb onto the rocks.

"Williamson will make a good SEAL," Zapata said. "Stafford is borderline."

Once all four men were on the rocks, they hauled the rubber craft up the jetty to the top, where the observers clocked their time.

A short distance away, a news camera crew was recording the exercise while a second camera focused on an attractive brunette holding a microphone who provided commentary.

Zapata followed Rogan's shift of interest.

"Each year the Public Affairs Office invites a local news station to cover this part of the exercise," Zapata explained. "Good public relations for us."

He grinned slyly at the way Rogan was staring at the reporter.

"I can introduce you, if you'd like," he said.

Rogan was already walking toward her. Standing a short distance away, he folded his arms and watched as she finished the wrap-up.

She noticed him and, after giving the cameraman some final instruction, walked toward him and extended her hand. She said, "I'm . . ."

"Jana Torres," Rogan said.

She smiled warmly, accustomed to being recognized.

"Are you a member of a SEAL team?" she asked.

"Honorary member," he said. "I'm Rogan Dorn with the Israeli Defense Forces."

Her eyes quickened, the way reporters' eyes do when they recognize a story.

"Are you consulting with the Navy?"

"I'm not here in an official capacity," Rogan said. "I recognized you from your Laughing Jesus news clips in Israel two years ago."

That pleased her.

Shouts came from the jetty. One of the rubber crafts had overturned, spilling the third training team into the water; waves dashed them against the rocks. Rogan and Jana watched the life and death struggle as the men scrambled for a hold on the slippery surface. Another wave came with force, slamming one of the team members against a jagged surface. He fell limp and slid down, floating lifeless in the water.

With the other team members struggling to survive, two observers scrambled down the jetty to make the rescue. The angels made no effort to intervene.

Reaching the unconscious trainee, the observers signaled to the top of the jetty and a rescue litter was lowered to them on a rope. After securing the trainee in the litter, it was hauled to the top of the jetty where medical crews attended to the man. His team members, having made their way to the top, stood over their fallen comrade.

"I hope he's all right," Jana said.

"It's a dangerous profession," Rogan replied. "It only gets worse from here."

"The voice of experience?"

Rogan didn't reply. Jana read his eyes.

"You've lost men on missions."

Again, no reply.

A pall had fallen over the exercise, on the jetty, on the shore. The camera crew was still filming.

Zapata shouted at them. "Turn that thing off!"

The camera crew looked to Jana for instruction. She nodded and the cameras were lowered.

After several long moments of silence, Jana said to Rogan, "I'd like to interview you, if you're willing."

"I couldn't do that," Rogan said. "But I would like to talk to you. Perhaps over dinner?"

Jana's looked at him to ascertain his motives.

"We could talk about your experiences in Israel," Rogan said. "Things aren't always as they seem."

She smiled. "You sound like someone I know. He was with me in Israel."

CHAPTER
12

Off the Coast of Israel

A PLEASURE CRAFT BOBBED MONOTONOUSLY ON THE WATER'S surface. Levi Reis, a short man with nervous mannerisms, leaned over the rail for the hundredth time, wondering why it was taking so long. Had he not given them precise coordinates? Had he not shown them a sketch of the vessel?

At any moment he expected the diving team to emerge from the watery depths, give him a thumbs-up signal, and hand him the ancient clay jar that would change his life forever. This was the big one. After today, he could quit his job and live the life of luxury he'd always dreamed of. He already knew where he would live and the price of the airline ticket that would take him there.

Dubai. For years he'd spent his evenings turning page after page of Dubai real estate magazines and clicking through Internet images of the city, He'd subscribed to Al Jazeera newspaper to keep up with local news and events. And when he closed his eyes at night, he dreamed of gazing out the window of his First Class seat and watch as Israel—with all its factions, and strife, and violence—grew smaller and smaller until it was just a bad memory.

Any moment now, any moment now, he thought as he watched the air bubbles rise to the surface.

All of his adult life, he'd lived alone on a pittance of a salary as a nameless clerk at the Department of Antiquities. His brother, Nathan, a navy diver in his younger days, had fared no better as the owner of a produce store. With a wife and daughter, Nathan barely earned enough to keep his creditors at bay. Then, one night, while they were drinking at a local bar, Nathan introduced him to Vang, a buddy of his from the navy, also a diver. They approached him with, in their words, "the opportunity of a lifetime."

Levi was skeptical. Vang was of the seedier sort, and as the plan was presented to him, his impressions of the man were confirmed. Vang was an operative in black market antiquities. He was looking for an inside man, someone with Department of Antiquities connections who had access to archaeological information. Levi's initial inclination was to tell them he wasn't interested, but when Vang described the kind of money that could be made in the black market, together with Nathan's vouching for his friend, Levi told them he'd see what he could do.

Their first operations were small, low risk, but profitable. Then, three days ago, Levi came across a memo on a colleague's desk. The risk was minimal, but the potential payoff set Levi's head spinning.

A new girl in the office, secretary to one of the lead archeologists, had left a high-profile operation unattended on her desk. Levi saw his chance and pounced on it.

A black crown of a wetsuit broke the surface and Levi's heart lodged in his throat.

The diver removed his mask. It was Nathan.

"Did you find it?" Levi cried.

"It's not down there," his brother replied. "Are you sure you have the correct coordinates?"

"You saw the memo. I took a picture of it with my smartphone. Of course, they're correct."

"I don't know what to tell you," Nathan said. "Let's call it a day and try again later."

"There is no later," Levi wailed. "An exploratory team is scheduled to arrive in the area tomorrow."

His fingers drummed on the railing as his dream of Dubai began to fade.

Just then Vang emerged and Levi braced himself for an argument he knew as coming. Somehow he had to convince them to make another attempt.

Vang's hand rose out of the water clutching a clay vessel.

Levi reached for it. Vang ignored him, climbing aboard the craft with it tucked securely under his arm. Again Levi reached for it and Vang shot him a glance that made him back away.

One-handed, Vang removed his tanks. The three men stood in a circle, their eyes fixed on the vessel.

"It doesn't look ancient," Nathan said.

Vang shook it. He shook it again. "It's empty," he said.

"It can't be empty," Levi cried. "The memo . . ."

"Don't believe everything you read."

The voice startled them and they turned to see a strange man standing on deck. No, not standing, hovering. Beside him was the new girl, the office secretary. But, how? She, too, was hovering.

"And it's not empty," the man said.

A dart of light shot from his hand and the clay jar shattered.

Levi saw his brother's eyes grow wide with alarm. Vang's eyes, too. An instant later, he felt something hit his chest with force, penetrate him as a powerful presence seized control of his body and invaded his mind. Horrified, Levi was powerless to stop it. He tried to scream, but his voice was choked to silence.

With voices not their own, the divers and Levi spoke in unison:

"My prince," they said.

"You failed me," the angel said. "You underestimated Capt. Dorn."

"It won't happen again, my prince," Ashmedai said.

"See to it," the angel said, "or you will spend eternity possessing rats and vermin."

CHAPTER
13

A DAPPLED PATTERN OF LIGHT AND DARK GREEN BLANKETED the ground, blurry shapes that swayed gently side to side from a coastal breeze, bringing the pattern to life. Small bunches of flowers were scattered nearby. Sue Ling looked positively beatific sitting on the grass, her legs folded under her, wearing a bright red, white, and blue silk summer dress that hugged her knees. This was the perfect place for a picnic date—if it wasn't a field of graves and if the bunches of flowers hadn't been placed there by mourners and if I hadn't tracked Sue down to find her.

She was speaking softly to the grave. I couldn't hear what she was saying and I didn't want to hear it, so I stood a discreet distance away until she paused. The thought occurred to me that the conversation might not be over; that the professor might be talking to her now, and she listening. That may sound crazy to average folk, but when you've been where I've been and seen what I've seen, a conversation between a woman and a dead man is low on the scale of weird.

Sue glanced up, startled by my presence.

"Grant! What are you doing here?"

Her tone was hostile, as though my being there was a violation of her right to speak to dead people.

"I tried calling you," I said. "But your cell was turned off."

"Did it ever occur to you that it was turned off for a reason?"

"Then, I went to the college."

"You what? Why would you do that?"

"They said you'd called in sick."

Obviously a lie. The hole I was digging myself into was getting deeper and deeper. I played the concerned boyfriend card.

"So I went over to Jana's thinking I could make you chicken soup or run to the drugstore for you."

I should have stopped there, the compassionate act took some of the starch out of her anger. But, as usual, I kept talking.

"When you weren't there, I called Jana and she said she thought you'd gone to work."

"You called Jana?" she said, bristling.

She reached for her bag and pull out her cell, checking the messages.

"Great. Three calls. She must be going out of her mind wondering what happened to me. Thanks a lot, Grant."

"Hey! I was worried too."

Again with the concern, only this time it didn't have the same effect. She blew my concern of the water when she said—

"How did you know to look for me here?"

Just like that the tables were turned and I found myself on the defensive. Time to come clean.

"The other day, when you came over to the apartment. . . . after you left . . . I followed you."

"Grant Austin! You've been stalking me?"

"You lied to me!"

My voice rose to a volume unsuitable to the location. My

outburst earned me disapproving stares from two elderly ladies visiting a nearby grave. I dialed it down.

"You said you were going back to the college," I said in my defense. "With our lunch plans canceled, I went out to grab a bite to eat and saw you turn onto the freeway."

Sue was smart enough to piece together what happened after that.

"How many times have you spied on me here?"

"How many times have you come here?"

That was unkind and I regretted saying it.

"I followed you that one time," I backpedaled, "and came looking for you today."

She straightened her dress, refusing to look at me.

"May I?" I asked.

She glanced up to see me motioning to the ground and gave an indifferent shrug.

I sat on the grass with the professor between us.

After a lengthy uncomfortable silence, I ventured forward. "You have to let him go, Sue."

"What if I can't?"

"Don't you think I miss him, too? There's not a day goes by that I don't wish I could go to his house and ask his advice about something."

"With all due respect, Grant. It's not the same for you."

She had me there.

I struggled with my next thought. I'd told myself I wasn't going to tell her this. I knew it would hurt her. But now, here, I felt she needed to know, even if she used it to end our relationship.

"Do you know how much this hurts me, Sue? The fact that you prefer spending time with a dead man rather than spending time with me."

There it was. The professor and I awaited her answer.

Sue wiped away a tear.

"I thought by returning here, to San Diego," she said softly, "being close to all the places that reminded me of him, I'd find a measure of peace."

She fell silent.

I didn't know what to say. And for once in my life, I did the smart thing and said nothing.

I looked around. For being a place of the dead it really was beautiful. A man and what appeared to be his teenage daughter and adolescent son approached a headstone. The kids placed flowers on the grave.

Sue was looking at them, too.

"There's an angel beside them," I told her.

Sue glanced away. Maybe I shouldn't have told her.

"They will always be part of my life," I said.

"Believe me when I say I've given that a lot of thought, Grant. Not just the way trouble of that sort seems to find you—"

Like in the shower. I still hadn't told her about Noz.

"—but what will happen to you when . . ." her voice broke. "Your death will be a thousand times more painful to me. I know the professor's at peace. But the thought of you . . ."

Her voice trailed off. She couldn't bring herself to acknowledge my future life as a demon, having been denied heaven.

"So where does that leave us?" I asked.

Sue leaned forward and placed her hand on the grass, an intimate gesture.

"I can't just forget him," she said.

"I'm not asking you to." I placed my hand on top of hers.

She glanced at me. Our eyes met and she turned her hand upward, interlacing her fingers with mine.

"Did you know that Jana's got herself a new fella?" she said. "She wants us to meet him at dinner tonight."

CHAPTER
14

"THE TANAKH, THE JEWISH VERSION OF WHAT YOU CALL THE Old Testament," Rogan said, unable to take his eyes off the woman seated beside him at the table.

She was more beautiful in person than she was on television. But then, maybe it was that she didn't smile when reporting the news. Did she know the power she had over men? He'd do anything she asked for that smile.

"Really? That's what you do for recreation, read the Old Testament?" Jana said.

They were seated at an upscale restaurant beside a wall of windows overlooking San Diego Bay. Sailboats glided effortlessly across the water. On the wharf, couples walked hand in hand, mingling with tourists in shorts and sandals. The sun had just dipped behind the peninsula on the far side of the bay, leaving the sky painted with brilliant orange hues.

Rogan laughed. "Is that so strange?"

"For a military man? A little."

"It helps me keep life in perspective," he said.

Conversation lulled as they gazed out the window at sunset, the water, the bay bridge.

"I crossed the bridge this morning," Rogan said, "quite exciting to be at such a historical location."

Jana nodded. "When people go to Dallas, they want to see the bookstore depository. When they come here, they want to see the bridge."

Rogan's mind retreated to the news reports he'd seen of that day.

At his urging, Jana recounted her experience on the bridge on that fateful day, all the while Rogan found himself wanting to tell her about the unseen battle, what really happened.

Their waiter appeared and asked if they were ready to order. Jana explained they were waiting for another couple to join them.

Rogan checked his watch.

"Is your friend always this late for his engagements?" he asked.

I looked at my watch and wondered what was taking Sue so long.

"Are you about ready?" I called to the back bedroom. "We're running late."

"Relax, Grant," Sue called back. "We're going to be fashionably late. It's our gift to Jana."

"I don't understand."

"We're giving her some alone time with her date."

"And she knows this?"

"It was her idea."

Ten minutes later, when Sue made an appearance, I didn't care how long it took her to get ready. It was worth it. She was stunning. Her hair was up, revealing a pale, slender neck; she was wearing a simple, sleek, black dress that clung seductively to her every curve. It was a constant wonder to me that a woman so beautiful could be interested in me.

As we entered the restaurant a short time later, with her arm linked in mine, as everyone's head turned our direction, I assumed that they were thinking the same thing.

At the table, Jana and her friend stood to greet us.

"Rogan, this is Sue Ling, my former college roommate and best friend."

The man took Sue's hand gently which she'd offered to him.

"My pleasure," he said.

I didn't like the way he looked at her, a little too friendly for my taste. The fact that his shoulders were broad, his face ruggedly handsome and swarthy. That he spoke with an Israeli accent didn't help.

"And this is Grant Austin," Jana said. "The friend I wanted you to meet."

I extended the obligatory hand.

The moment his eyes met mine, they hardened. His face turned to stone. When he gripped my hand, he squeezed hard enough to make my knuckles crack. After what I consider an appropriately long time, I tried to pull my hand back. He held onto it with his vice grip for several uncomfortable moments before letting it go.

"I take it you're not a military man," Rogan said, taking his seat.

"That's something I've never been accused of," I said, keeping things light.

"It would do you good. One of the first things the military teaches you is discipline; how to be on time."

"I'm afraid that's my fault," Sue said, sweetly.

Mercifully the waiter arrived and took our drink orders.

Conversation turned to the usual small talk. Jana told us how she and Rogan met while she was reporting on the SEAL training exercise. Rogan asked Sue if she was also a reporter, which gave her an opportunity to tell him a little about her life as a college professor.

"And Grant's a writer," Sue said, shifting the conversation to me.

"A Pulitzer Prize winning writer," Jana added.

Rogan wasn't impressed, which didn't surprise me. I could count the number of military men who'd told me they'd read my book on one hand, and have four fingers left over.

"Grant and Sue were with me in Israel," Jana said.

That opened the door to sharing our experiences following the Laughing Jesus from location to location, leaving out the supernatural parts, of course. Rogan listened without expression. When we were finished, he said:

"I never understood his no-show at the Geneva conference. Everything seemed to be leading up to that event. Why abandon the mission once all your forces are in place?"

Jana and Sue looked at me for a cue as to where to go from here.

I shrugged good-naturedly. "Apparently he got recalled by the home office."

"How would you know that?"

Rogan's tone was hostile; the challenge unmistakable. I'd tried to be genial, but I'd had enough.

Meeting his gaze, I said, "I have my sources."

From there, dinner went downhill. Whenever Jana or Sue spoke, he was warm and congenial. Whenever I said something, he was disparaging and rude. The tension between us took all the flavor out of our overpriced meals and the evening couldn't end quickly enough for me.

When the check came, over Jana's objections I insisted on

paying it, even though it was going to put a serious dent in my bank account, which was already on life-support.

As we were leaving, the girls excused themselves to go to the ladies' room, which was tucked away in a quiet corner. The instant they were gone, Rogan grabbed my shirt and slammed me against a wall.

"What are you?" he demanded.

The pressure against my chest made it hard to breathe.

"What's your problem? I told you. I'm a writer."

"Not good enough. I've never seen anything like you."

Having pinned me against the wall with his left forearm, he placed his right hand against my chest.

"Be still!" he said.

"Like I have a choice."

He stared at my face, looking for something but not seeing it, which seemed to anger him even more.

The hand against my chest pressed harder and, to my horror, passed through my shirt, my skin, and into my ribcage. I could feel his hand searching for something, as though he'd lost his car keys and couldn't find them.

He gripped my heart and squeezed until I almost passed out.

"If you don't mind," I struggled to say, "I'm still using that."

He withdrew his hand.

"I see demon in you," he said, "but no flickering. Where is it hiding?"

I was beginning to understand, but only beginning.

"How is that possible?" I asked. "And flickering. What flickering?"

"Answer the question."

"It's not hiding anywhere," I said, dropping all pretense. "I'm part demon, part human. I'm Nephilim."

He released me, taking a step back. The hostility gone, he

looked at me bewildered, as someone would if they happened upon a creature that was supposed to be extinct.

"Nephilim," he said.

"In the flesh. How did you do that with your hand?"

He was breathing hard. "We need to talk," he said, still unable to grasp what was standing in front of him.

"Talk, fine," I said. "As long as you keep your hands to yourself."

CHAPTER
15

I took Sue back to Jana's apartment. She had an early class the next morning. Rogan and Jana wanted to hit a couple of hot spots. At least that's what Jana said. After the way he acted toward me at dinner, knowing what I know about Jana, I suspected she would be the one generating the heat.

So when Rogan met me at our agreed-upon location, naturally I was curious as to how a member of the elite Israeli Sayeret Matkal fared against the formidable femininity that is Jana Torres.

For our meeting I had chosen somewhere I felt confident no one could overhear our conversation.

The crunch of gravel announced his presence, and as he approached, I observed he wasn't limping and there were no noticeable bruises or abrasions.

"I see you survived Jana," I said.

"She's loyal to her friends," he replied wryly. "Apparently the two of you once dated?"

"In a different lifetime," I said. "Were you able to smooth things over?"

"I told her we had a little heart to heart while they were in the restroom and that we came to an amicable understanding."

"Heart to heart. Very funny," I said, rubbing my chest.

"We're going out again tomorrow night."

He gauged my reaction to determine if I still had romantic feelings for Jana. To say that his stature—who am I kidding? His muscles—intimidated me would be an understatement.

"Did you tell Jana you were meeting up with me tonight?" I asked.

Rogan circled to his right. I countered, step by step. When he saw what I was doing, he grinned. It was clear the intimidation thing was one-sided.

He perched casually on the edge of an air conditioning unit.

"If I had," he said, "she would have insisted on coming with me to protect you. Is it true you stopped an angelic Spectacle with three tomatoes?"

"You told her I was Nephilim?"

"I had to know if you were being honest with me."

"Didn't she question how you knew?"

"She knows I have a sensitivity to the supernatural. That's why she wanted me to meet you. Tomatoes, Grant? Hardly a Nephilim's weapon of choice."

"Sensitivity to the supernatural? Not exactly how I'd describe sticking a hand in in a man's chest," I countered.

"Just answer the question."

"I wanted to keep a low profile," I explained. "Besides, there were thousands of them and only one of me. As it turned out, it didn't matter. They killed the woman and her child later that afternoon."

Rogan lowered his head in thought.

"Why meet here?" he asked.

I walked to the edge of the roof of the Emerald Towers. The

whole of San Diego stretched out before us, horizon to horizon: the downtown lights, the bay, the bridge, the airport.

"See that ship down there? The World War II aircraft carrier? That's where I was standing when the F-18 Hornet strafed the bridge."

I didn't ask if he was familiar with the events of that day. The whole world knew about it.

"Did you know that Jana was on the bridge?" I asked.

He nodded.

"I was helpless to do anything to stop it, to save her. Worse, I was informed that everything that was happening was because of me."

A realization sparked in Rogan's eyes. "You could see the heavenly battle!"

Even now I could see it, feel it. Every horrific moment.

"Why you?"

"From my high school days, they had been grooming me. Everything that happened that day was to impress me with their power."

"Who was grooming you?"

"Semyaza, one of Lucifer's lieutenants."

"Because you're Nephilim," Rogan said, understanding.

With a suddenness that startled me, he pushed himself away from the air conditioning unit and into the center of the roof with an expression of amazement. He knew where he was standing.

"That was you? The Archangel Michael told us about the tribunal of angels. In this place? That was you?"

"You're on speaking terms with the Archangel Michael?" I said.

"The commander of my team."

It was my turn to smile. To think that an archangel was telling people about me. Imagine that.

"You stood face to face with Lucifer himself!" Rogan exclaimed. "I never would have guessed you had it in you."

As much as I was enjoying the adulation, I had questions of my own.

"Are you Nephilim?"

"No. Fully human," he said.

"So how is it you can—"

Rogan stretched out his hand to show me a ring.

"I am a blood descendant of King Solomon."

I blinked. "As impressive as that is, it doesn't explain your abilities."

"This is Solomon's ring, given to him by the Archangel Michael. It gives me the same power it gave him, the power of Nephilim."

That explained a lot, but it also raised a lot of questions.

"You can see angels?" I asked.

"Yes."

"Walk through walls?"

"Yes."

"What about membranes?"

The question stumped him.

"Dimensional portals."

"That was not part of our training," he said. "You?"

"I've done it. With help."

"What do you mean, with help?" Rogan prompted.

"Abdiel. The angel who trained me."

"Abdiel. I don't know him. Did he also train you to fight with your sword?"

"Trained? No."

"But you've fought angels."

I grimaced at the memory. "And lived to tell about it."

"Who? Where?"

There was a glint of professional interest in the military man's eyes.

"Michael didn't tell you about that?" That was disappointing. "The usual. Semyaza and Belial, battle to the death."

"So that's how you know about Belial."

At his insistence I gave a blow by blow description of the battle in Sheol and its outcome.

"You've met the Divine Warrior," he said looking at me a little differently.

I'd scored some points with him and I have to say it felt good. To me Rogan was the total package, a special forces soldier with the power of Nephilim. Plus, he knew things I didn't know, and it irked me that Abdiel had been holding out on me.

"That chest cavity search you did on me," I said. "You were looking for a demon."

"You can't see demons?"

"Not only can I see them, I know what it's like to be possessed by them."

My comment troubled him.

He spoke slowly. "We had a mission."

He cleared his throat and in solemn tones narrated the rescue attempt that ended with the death of his two friends and the capture of the demons responsible. I thought of the professor and empathized with Rogan's pain.

"I tracked their prince here," he said, "the one who masterminded the trap. And I will not rest until I stand over his grave."

"You're going to kill an angel?"

"The death of my friends will be avenged."

"And you know for certain he's here."

"Maybe you can help me with that," he said. "His last known location was a Spectacle in San Diego, possibly the one you thwarted."

"They weren't exactly wearing name tags," I said.

"Have you ever heard of a rebel angel named Nosroch?"

As I drove home, I reviewed the pieces to the puzzle and was ready to solve the game: the elite soldier with the ring on the Emerald Towers for the win. Rogan was the rogue soldier Abdiel warned me about. The question was, what was I going to do about it?

For the moment, nothing. First of all, I wanted no part of angel games. Abdiel admitted that Solomon's ring was part of an unsanctioned angelic scheme. Had it been sanctioned by the Divine Warrior I would have turned on Rogan in a heartbeat. Second, Rogan did not appear to be a threat to me, or Jana and Sue. On the contrary, given his feelings for Jana, I got the distinct impression he would come to her rescue should the occasion warrant it. And third—and this was a big one—if Rogan was right about Nosroch, he was definitely someone I wanted on my side.

On a personal note, with the absence of the professor, it felt good to have someone with whom I could talk to about Nephilim things, a kindred spirit with a working knowledge of spiritual warfare.

So, for the time being, I'd keep Rogan's secret. I only hoped it wouldn't come back to bite me.

CHAPTER
16

You would think being a physics professor, Sue would appreciate precision machinery. You would be wrong if her choice of cars was any indication. She's an "all I want is something that gets me from point A to point B" car aficionado. So when she moved out here from North Carolina, she had a student drop her off at a local car lot after class. Within the hour she was back on campus for her next class, having purchased a 2003 Saturn Ion with 225,000 miles.

Who buys a car in an hour? It boggled the imagination.

Granted, my car was no better, but at least I'd agonized over the purchase for twenty-four hours. Besides, I wanted better for her, something reliable. The thought of her breaking down on the freeway or at night twisted my gut into a knot.

Then, this morning, the Saturn—the car she'd had for less than a month—failed to take her from point A (Jana's apartment) to point B (the college). It wouldn't start. The good news was, she wasn't on the road at the time. So she hitched a ride from Jana to work and I picked her up after her final afternoon class.

She wasn't the only one hitching a ride. As we got into the car at the college parking lot, I noticed we'd picked up an uninvited passenger. Bad Penny himself was sitting in the back seat. He was in invisible mode so Sue couldn't see him.

Wouldn't you know it, driving down the hill to my apartment Sue started getting affectionate. It wasn't anything that would make a minister blush—she kissed me on the cheek and caressed the back of my neck, running her fingers through my hair—but it definitely wasn't the kind of thing she would do if she knew an angel was watching.

I glanced into the rearview mirror. Noz smiled and gave me a thumbs up. I tried not to roll my eyes.

A block from my apartment, I pulled into a corner convenience store. I was all out of ginger ale, Sue's soda of choice. She also asked me to get her some Advil. As I climbed out of the car, I said:

"Sorry about your Saturn, Sue, but look on the bright side: It'll give us some time alone."

I emphasized alone, hoping Noz would take the hint.

"That's nice, Grant," Sue said. "But if you don't mind, I'd like to take a nap and try to shake this headache."

When I returned with the soda and pain reliever, Noz was still in the car. So much for taking a hint. At the apartment complex, he followed us inside like a puppy dog.

While Sue went to the kitchen to get a glass of water for the Advil, I closed the drapes in my bedroom for her.

At the bedroom door, she said, "Don't let me sleep longer than an hour." She gave me a sweet peck on the lips. "I really appreciate this, Grant. Renting a place close to the college where I can unwind was very thoughtful."

She eased the door shut behind her, leaving it open just a crack.

Noz was waiting for me in the living room.

"We need to talk, Grant," he said.

I shushed him, pointing to the bedroom.

"Then let's go someplace where we can talk."

I shook my head.

He vanished.

"Good," I said, because after talking with Rogan the night before I was dreading my next encounter with Noz, even though I knew it was not only inevitable, but necessary.

At the Emerald Towers when Rogan asked me if I'd heard of Nosroch, I wasn't exactly forthcoming. That's not to say Rogan's information about the rebel angel didn't cause me alarm. It did. But that didn't mean I was ready to jump onto Rogan's blood vengeance bandwagon. The idea of a frontal assault on an angel struck me as suicidal. Before committing to open warfare, I needed more information; about Rogan and his experience with angels, and about Noz and his real intentions given this new information.

With Noz gone and Sue in the back bedroom, I settled into a chair, picked up a research book on the middle ages, and read the same paragraph three times, finding it difficult to concentrate.

After five minutes Noz appeared again, this time in visible form.

"She's asleep now," he said.

I slapped the book shut and stood. "You were in there watching her?"

"How else would I know when she was asleep?"

"Noz, you can't just—"

"My name is Nosroch."

"What you did is inappropriate. You can't just watch a woman while she's sleeping."

"We do it all the time."

"That doesn't make it right."

He stared at me like I was being unreasonable.

"I need to know where I stand with you," he said. "Do you trust me now?"

Had he asked me that question before I met Rogan I probably would have given him the benefit of the doubt, as foolish as that sounds.

Don't trust the devil, Grant.

"You said you'd believe me if I wiggled my toes in your carpet," he said.

"It's not that simple."

"You set the conditions."

"Semyaza clothed himself in flesh for four years," I replied, "and we both know how that turned out."

It was obvious he was frustrated with me. He had reason to be, but I didn't care.

"Never go home with your heroes," he said to no one in particular. "They're not the same once you see them in their boxer shorts."

"What's that supposed to mean?"

"You're not the person you were in Sheol."

"Sorry to disappoint you."

He stared at me a long time. "What will it take to convince you that I mean you no harm?"

"A lifetime. Trust is earned. It takes more than one grand gesture."

"I don't have that kind of time."

"That's a laugh," I said. "I'm the one with the short lifespan, you're immortal."

"Have you not heard anything I said?" he cried. "Semyaza and his cohorts are hunting us down to force us to take an oath of allegiance to Lucifer."

In my mind I could see it, having experienced the same kind of tribunal atop the Emerald Towers.

"And if you refuse, what will they do to you? Fill you with demons? Execute you?"

"Angels can't die, Grant."

Now I knew he was lying.

A History of Angel War," I said, "and I quote: 'Do angels die? As surely as light can be extinguished. Anything created can be uncreated. Where injury or loss or death are absent, there can be no war.'"

"Abdiel," Noz said. "We'd heard he'd sung our history to your professor. He shouldn't have done that."

"To quote the big guy again: 'We are pleased to serve the Father.' Meaning, it wasn't his decision. He was acting under orders."

Noz didn't respond.

I felt vindicated. Now I knew he was trying to deceive me.

"The passage you quoted is accurate," he said somberly. "It is possible for angels to die. However, it does not tell the whole story. It is also true that no angel has died since the rebellion."

"The war in heaven," I said for clarification. "When Lucifer and a third of the angels attempted a coup."

The sadness that came over Noz was palpable. I have seen a lot of angels in a lot of situations, but I have never seen one so positively . . . dim.

"It is a fearful thing to see an angel die, Grant Austin. The loss of our brothers on both sides was great, their deaths are felt keenly even to this day. Accordingly, both the faithful and rebel forces—though we continue to battle—have an understanding. We will never again kill one of our kind."

"Touching," I said with pure sarcasm. "Pardon me if I don't shed any tears. But it seems you have no trouble killing humans . . . for sport."

I had him dead to rights. Pun intended. He knew it. I knew it. And it frightened me. I expected him to cast aside this whole charade, hover a few feet above my carpet—ablaze with light so brilliant it would force me to my knees—and proclaim: I AM NOSROCH. TREMBLE BEFORE ME.

My eyes scanned the ceiling for what I knew would most certainly follow. . . . demons, which made me the dinner entree *du jour.*

All of a sudden my verbal victory didn't seem so satisfying.

Only, no demons appeared on the ceiling and Nosroch didn't ignite with radiance. If anything, he appeared even smaller.

"Do you watch the news, Grant?" he said softly.

"Um . . . yeah, sometimes."

I didn't know where he was going with this. Was I going to be the lead story tonight on the six o'clock edition?

"A local man is on trial for killing three cyclists and injuring five more."

"Another one of your Spectacles I suppose."

"We are not responsible for every bad thing that happens in this world, Grant. He was—what do you call it?—DUI."

"Driving under the influence."

"He was a broken man standing before the judge, having admitted his role in the deaths. He regretted his actions publicly, repeatedly, saying he wished he could change places with those he'd killed. His admission of guilt fell on deaf ears. The families of the victims refused to forgive him; the judge told him he was without excuse.

"Grant, in the war of the heavenlies, I am that man. Under the influence of misplaced loyalty, I have done unspeakable things. I wish I could reverse the course of history, but I can't. I cannot make restitution to the families of those I have killed or injured. And when I stand before the Judge of Judges to account for my actions, I will do so as a broken angel."

Had he been an actor I would have given him an Oscar. His performance touched me, but is that what it was, a performance?

Had we not just survived one the greatest performances of all time in the Laughing Jesus? I wanted to believe Noz, but my past experiences with his kind was furiously waving a red flag.

We've been doing this for millennia.

"So you're saying that given the opportunity, you would give your life in exchange for those you have killed?"

"I would."

"What happens when an angel dies?"

"He is obliterated into nothingness, wiped from reality, not just in the cosmos, but in the heavenly realm."

My thoughts returned to Sheol, the grand realization that Lucifer had not only deceived the world, but his own followers. And the motive behind it.

"So, in essence," I said, "you are doing exactly what Semyaza wants you to do, pledging your allegiance to Lucifer."

"After all I've said, how can you—"

"Isn't Lucifer's argument that your punishment is too severe, that if the Father were just He would annihilate the heavens and the earth and start over? You aren't breaking from him, you're admitting he's right and aligning yourself with his grand plan."

"No, Grant, that's not what I'm saying. The Father's creation, even though it is warped by sin, is a wonder to behold. Neither do I speak for anyone else. I'm confessing that for my sins, I and I alone deserve to die. Is that not the first step in human salvation?"

CHAPTER
17

ROGAN AND I STOOD ON A CORONADO STREET CORNER LOOK-
ing up. It was 1 a.m.

"How long have they been here?" I asked.

"I thought maybe you would know," Rogan replied. "They
were here when I arrived."

The angel encampment over the naval air base was fascinating;
reassuring and troubling all at the same time—reassuring to know
that the good guys had established a formidable presence over my
city, troubling because military outposts are placed in potential
war zones.

"Has anything changed since you first saw it?" I asked.

Rogan shook his head. "Activity level is the same as it was
before, and that was in daytime. Do angels require sleep? R&R?"

"Couldn't say. But I do know Abdiel has a habit of popping
into my bedroom at all hours of the night, so they clearly don't
have time zones." Noz did this too, but this was no time to bring
him up, whatever his intentions.

My thoughts spun off in a different direction. An individual's
sword was an indicator of their intentions and spiritual strength.

Noz's sword was black as the ace of spades like all the other rebel angels. But hadn't Belial told me Lucifer required all of the rebels to keep their swords black as a sign of solidarity? Was Noz keeping his sword black to hide his identity as a member of the anti-Lucifer splinter group, or was it black because he was still evil?

"Are you coming?" Rogan said, already halfway across the street, heading toward the naval base.

"Do you have a pass for me?"

"Who needs passes?"

He stepped through the perimeter brick wall.

"Great. We're entering a naval base illegally," I said. "This will look good on my record, right below the line describing how I got bit by a guard dog and arrested for climbing the White House fence."

Stepping through the wall, I caught up with him.

We entered the base from the south side. The lights of the runway were to our left. A helicopter flew low overhead. We walked purposefully as though we were acting under orders. That might fool base security, but angel encampment security was a different matter. While Rogan appeared as human, I had Nephilim written all over me. We kept a look-out for angels but had no idea what distance was safe. Could I be spotted from above? I felt like I was a neon sign, flashing: *Nephilim Nephilim Nephilim.*

It didn't help that our destination was on the far side of the base, an unavoidable complication. To approach from the north would mean coming in off the bay, which was much riskier.

The base streets were relatively quiet, but not empty. A military base this size never sleeps, and there was enough foot traffic so as not to attract attention to ourselves.

Rogan led me to the back side of the physical training center.

"Wait here," he said.

Without waiting for a reply, he stepped through a wall.

I waited. One minute . . . two . . . five minutes. I was feeling increasingly conspicuous. How long should I wait? Then what? Go in after him, or retrace our steps off the base?

Rogan's sudden appearance startled me even though I was expecting it.

"Clear," he said.

"What took you so long?"

"Just being thorough. You don't want surprises, do you?"

I followed him through the wall into the training facility, down a corridor, and into a large, dark room not unlike a recreation center minus the basketball hoops. He flipped on the lights.

"Should security come," he said, "we go through that wall."

I looked in the direction he was pointing.

"If we get separated," he added, "make your way to the street corner where we entered. I'll meet you there."

I couldn't help but admire his military skill. He'd scoped out the territory, assessed the situation, and formulated a plan, far different from my usual rushing headlong into a situation and reacting blindly to whatever I encountered.

It had been Rogan's idea to train together, and since my relationship with Abdiel had been infrequent following the professor's death, I took him up on it, though I had to admit the thought of sparring with a member of Israeli special forces was daunting. Compared to him I was the proverbial ninety-eight-pound weakling.

When we considered training locations, we had both agreed my apartment was too small for the exercise. I'd suggested the rooftop of the Emerald Towers, thinking it would give me a psychological boost. He pointed out that training in the open would make us visible to anyone of the supernatural persuasion. The training center on the naval base was his idea. If we got caught, he was certain his connection with the SEAL team was strong enough to earn us a free pass. Still, it was best not to get caught. Hence, the escape plan.

Standing on floor pads, we faced each other.

"How much training have you had with swords?" he asked.

"No training, just experience. I broke up a fight between Abdiel and Belial in my former apartment, and I already told you about the battle with Belial and Semyaza."

"Impressive," he said.

Maybe so, but the memory of the experience didn't feel impressive.

"You?" I asked.

"No battle experience. But I have sparred with the Archangel Michael."

Great. The commander of all angelic forces. I was doomed.

"Well, let's see what you've got," he said, stepping back. His sword appeared, broad and glistening silver.

I raised my arm and my sword appeared, dingy gray as though it had been sitting in the back of my closet for years.

The question of who would strike the first blow was answered before it was asked. He swung. Gripping my sword with both hands I blocked the blow and my arms nearly buckled even though he was obviously holding back.

Each time our swords connected there was an explosion of sparks.

He advanced. Another blow. I retreated. Another arm-buckling block.

I was beginning to think this wasn't such a good idea.

"Keep your guard up," he said.

"I'm trying!"

He advanced, blow after blow, and it was all I could do to fend him off, my arms getting weaker and weaker. He backed me off the mat.

"Good," he said, returning to center.

Good? He thought that was good? I was ready to call it a night.

"Now you attack," he said.

He raised his sword in defense.

"All right," I said, "but I don't want to hurt you."

"I can take care of myself."

I'd meant it as a joke. He was all business.

I swung, tentatively.

He blocked the blow with ease.

"Put some muscle behind it!"

I swung harder. He parried the blow effortlessly.

With my next attempt, I gave it all I had.

He sidestepped. My blow found nothing but air and I stumbled, off balance. He grasped my arm with his free hand, pulled me forward, pivoted, swung his leg around behind me, and the next thing I knew I was flying head over heels. I landed on my back with a thud that knocked the breath out of me.

I stared up at him standing over me.

"Interesting move," I gasped.

"When you're fighting for your life there are no rules," he said. "You have to anticipate everything."

"I'll keep that in mind. But you can't do that to an angel, can you?"

"They won't be expecting it."

He offered his hand and lifted me to my feet.

"Let's go again," he said. "This time remember: Always keep your balance."

I readied my sword.

"Attack," he said.

I swung. He parried. I swung again. He sidestepped and this time I was ready for him. Keeping my balance, I stepped forward, turned, and attacked.

"Good," he said, blocking the blow.

With each swing I was gaining confidence, swinging harder and harder, forcing him back.

That's when he did something I wasn't expecting. He stopped retreating and attacked. His swing was horizontal. Not only was I not prepared for it, my sword was out of position and my side was exposed.

Committed to the blow, he couldn't stop it in time and his eyes grew wide with concern.

Instinctively, I protected myself.

His sword passed through me.

He stepped back.

"How did you do that?"

"A little trick I learned while trying to stay alive," I said.

"Show me."

I explained that it was no different than passing through walls.

He lowered his sword. "Let me try," he said. "Attack."

It was clear he wasn't going to make an attempt to block the blow.

"Um . . . I don't know if this is a good idea."

"Do it!"

I'd never swung a sword at a defenseless opponent and found it difficult to do.

"All right," I said. "On the count of three."

"Just swing the sword, Grant!"

I swung.

My sword passed through him.

"Outstanding!" Rogan shouted excitedly. "Again."

For the next several minutes we swung our swords at each other's bodies never once making contact, laughing like fools.

That's when we were surrounded. Not by base security. By angels.

There were five of them, their silver weapons drawn.

"It was the clash of swords that gave us away, wasn't it?" Rogan glanced around, assessing the situation as he spoke. "You saw it even though we're in a building. We'll have to keep that in mind."

Rogan and I lowered our arms and our swords vanished.

The five supernaturals had a military bearing. They didn't speak. Were they too assessing the situation, or were they waiting for someone?

"We're no threat to you," I said.

Only once had I seen Abdiel come close to a laugh. The angel who appeared to be in charge had that same expression on his face. Apparently he found my assurance absurdly humorous.

"Do you not recognize him?" Rogan said, pointing at me. "When was the last time you saw an actual Nephilim? That's the famous Grant Austin."

All five of them took a closer look.

Which gave Rogan the chance he wanted. With their attention distracted, he split between two of them, ran to the nearest wall, and disappeared.

Two angels followed him. Three stayed with me. I found perverse pleasure in the numbers. Was I the greater threat? The greater treasure? What did it matter. I liked either of those scenarios.

"Grant Austin."

I recognized that voice.

"Hello, Abdiel."

He hadn't arrived alone. An angel of equal intimidating size and demeanor stood beside him.

"Where is Capt. Dorn?" the other angel said.

The fact that he asked meant that, at least for now, Rogan had managed to give his pursuers the slip.

"I don't know," I said. "He left rather abruptly."

"You will show reverence to the Archangel Michael," Abdiel said.

The commander of the angelic forces himself. His presence completed the trifecta. I'd met the Divine Warrior, Lucifer, and now the Archangel Michael. Under different circumstances I might have asked for his autograph.

"I have heard of his insolent tongue," Michael said.

"No insolence intended," I said.

If it was just Abdiel, I would have indulged myself. But even I have enough sense not to be smart-mouthed in front of someone's superior.

"The fact that Rogan used me to make good his escape, and left me behind, should indicate to you that I was not part of his plan."

"How do you know Capt. Dorn?" Michael asked.

"A mutual friend introduced us."

Thinking I was being flippant, the archangel bristled, or rippled—it's hard to put supernatural reactions into words—his displeasure.

"Again, no insolence intended," I insisted. "He met a friend of mine. She introduced him to me."

"What were the two of you doing here?" Michael asked.

There was no use denying what we were doing. It had set off angel alarms.

"We discovered we have abilities in common," I said. "We were training together."

"To what end?"

He was really straining my self-control now. To what end? Did he really ask me to what end? Did he not know that Semyaza and the entire rebel force wanted to make demon chowder out of me?

Swallowing the sarcasm, I said, "While I can't speak for Capt. Dorn, my goal is training for survival."

"You are familiar with how Capt. Dorn gets his Nephilim powers?"

"Family blood and the ring of Solomon."

"Are you aware the ring does not belong to him?"

"He told me you gave—"

"That he is absent without leave from his unit?"

I blinked, surprised. "He didn't tell me—"

"That he fled his country with the ring and that he is eluding me to keep from returning it?"

Having been cut off twice, I didn't respond.

"Well?" Abdiel prompted.

"Oh, it's my turn to talk now?"

"Answer the Archangel," Abdiel said sternly.

"I know you gave him the ring," I said. "I didn't know it was to be returned. And I didn't know he was AWOL."

"Has he asked you to—"

"I also know," I interrupted him, my frustration getting the better of me, "that I am not Rogan's keeper, neither am I his personal secretary, or his attorney. If you want to know why Rogan is here and what his plans are, I suggest you talk to him. Now, if you're going to smite me, just do it and get it over with."

The Archangel Michael gave me a look I couldn't quite decipher, then disappeared, taking the other three angels with him.

"You shouldn't have spoken to the Archangel that way," Abdiel said.

"I didn't appreciate being interrogated like an adversary," I said, adding, "but you're right. I apologize."

"Does your apology extend to me?" Abdiel asked. "Did I not warn you to stay away from Capt. Dorn?"

"With all due respect, I refuse to be dragged into what is clearly a personal matter between Rogan and the Archangel Michael."

"Heed my advice, Grant Austin. Capt. Dorn is on a vengeful

path that has dire consequences. Now prepare yourself. I will take you home."

"Wait, my car is—"

When I awoke I was alone and lying flat on my back in the middle of my living room, feeling the usual effects of being strained through a membrane portal. I had the distinct feeling that Abdiel's Uber service was less a kindness and more a punishment for the way I spoke to an archangel.

CHAPTER
18

"ROGAN, HOW DID YOU ESCAPE THE ANGELS?"

While lying on the carpet last night, attempting to recover from Abdiel's disassembling of my atoms, my cell phone rang. It was Rogan, making arrangements for our next meeting. When I say arrangements, I don't mean the usual time and place. He'd outlined a plan worthy of a Sayeret Matkal undercover operation that included a Starbucks, a restroom, a trolley ride, an Uber, and a soup kitchen designed to elude any angels that might follow me.

That's when I asked him how he got away from the pursuing angels on base. He said he'd tell me later.

This was later.

"With all the open space on the base," he said, "I knew they'd be looking for a man running. So, instead of passing through the wall, I hid inside it. They went right by me. I stayed in the wall all night and walked off the base the next morning."

While it was clever, I was hoping for something more spectacular, some kind of Nephilim maneuver of which I was unaware.

"Wait a second. You called me last night," I said. "You called me while you were in the wall?"

"I had time to kill. But enough about that, let's focus on today's mission."

We were standing on a corner, downtown San Diego, in the business district. It was a typical day with people in all manner of dress, from suits to delivery shorts, all going about their usual activity. We spoke in quiet tones so as not to attract attention. Words like *angels* and *demons* will do that.

"Are you telling me Abdiel never trained you to extract demons?" Rogan asked.

"He was too busy banging my head against walls," I said replied offhandedly, getting to the question that was bugging me. "You know he told me to stay away from you, don't you? Why didn't you tell me Michael wanted the ring back? Why didn't you tell me you were AWOL?"

"Would it have made a difference?"

"Of course it makes a difference," I said. "You're not the one who was interrogated last night by an archangel."

"If it makes such a difference, why are you with me today in defiance of Abdiel?"

It struck me that he wasn't the only one with secrets, but I wasn't ready to tell him about Nosroch yet. So I kept my answer simple.

"I'm not Abdiel's to command," I said.

"Then what's your problem, Grant? You have your archangel, I have mine."

Apparently he was ready to move on, which was fine by me. He slipped his backpack off his shoulder. Reaching inside, he pulled out a clay jar with a lid.

"Once a demon is captured," he said, "you have to contain it. I picked this one up in Old Town."

If you were looking for clay jars, that's where you'd find them.

Old Town was the historic site of the first Spanish settlement in San Diego, now a popular tourist attraction.

"Why clay?" I asked. "Why not something more modern, like Tupperware?"

"It has to be clay," Rogan said, giving no reaction to my attempt at humor. "That's what Solomon used. It makes sense when you think about it, made from the dust of the earth, the same substance that humans are made of."

"But that doesn't make sense," I said. "Demons slip in and out of humans at will."

Rogan paused in thought. "All right, it doesn't make sense," he said, "but this isn't the time for metaphysical discussions. This was how I was trained and I can tell you from personal experience it works."

He had a point. If it worked, who was I to argue?

Rogan returned the jar to the backpack and slung it over his shoulder.

"You do know how to recognize a demon-possessed human, don't you?" he asked.

"Can't say that I do. I've always been the one possessed."

His eyes narrowed. By the way he looked at me, he had more than a professional interest in my admission. "What was it like to be possessed by a demon?" he asked.

"Demons. Plural. Not something I'd care to experience again."

For several long, uncomfortable moments, he stared at me.

"Let's circle back to that at a later time," he said. "I want to hear about your experience. For now, you need to know that recognizing demon possession is as easy as seeing swords."

Of all the things he could have said, why did he have to say that? I didn't want to tell him how long it took me to see swords. Apparently, it had come easily to him. But then the power of Solomon's ring gave him full Nephilim powers. I was only part

Nephilim. What came easy to him was difficult for me. What if it took me just as long to learn how to capture demons?

"You see it in their faces," he continued. "They flicker back and forth between the person's face and the demon as they appeared when they were human."

My mind went back to the reading I'd done about the Divine Warrior and the passage where he encountered a man possessed by a legion of demons. The Divine Warrior would have seen hundreds of faces flickering on the man's head.

"Jesus cast demons out," I said. "Why don't we just do that?"

"Good question. The Archangel Michael explained that to us," Rogan said. "A good example is when the Divine Warrior cast the demons into a herd of swine. He did it to demonstrate to people who cannot see demons that he had power over them. For our purposes, it's best to capture the demons so that they cannot possess anyone else."

"That makes sense," I said. "Step me through the process."

He nodded. "Once you see the demon, you command it to be still. That immobilizes it. Then, you reach into the person possessed, grab the demon, and place it in the clay jar and seal it."

My hand rose involuntarily to my chest. Thanks to Rogan I had experience with that, too.

"What if the jar breaks?" I asked.

"Exactly what you'd expect. The demons are freed. Solomon cast the jars into the ocean to keep that from happening. Admittedly, not a full-proof method, but better than just leaving the jar lying around."

"One more question," I said. "Why here?"

When Rogan told me we were going demon hunting, for some reason I thought we'd be going to homeless camps, or neighborhoods that were notorious for gang activity. Instead, we were in the high-rise district of downtown San Diego with law offices, banks, and insurance companies.

"I thought that was obvious," he said. "These buildings have the highest density of demon activity. Are you ready?"

I wasn't, but didn't want to admit as much to him.

Rogan selected a black glass skyscraper popularly referred to as the Darth Vader building. He led me into the law firm's spacious lobby to a padded bench close to the elevators where we had a good view of people coming and going. It wasn't long before an efficient-looking woman in a beige skirt-suit approached us.

"May I help you gentlemen?" she asked.

"We're waiting for someone," Rogan said curtly.

"But thank you, anyway," I added.

"If I can be of any assistance," she said and walked away.

Rogan was intently studying the faces of two men in suits headed for the elevators.

"There's a limit to how long we can loiter here," I mentioned. "Security will think we're casing the place."

"It won't take long," he said. "See that man on the left?"

I looked and saw the hollow-cheeked face of a man in his forties, nothing more.

A pang of panic shot through me, not only because I couldn't see a demon, but out of fear of what Rogan would do next. He wasn't going to go up to the guy right here and thrust his arm into the man's chest, was he? They might do that sort of thing in Israel, but in San Diego reaching into a man's chest in public is frowned upon.

The men passed us. Rogan sat back.

"Just asking," I said, relieved, "but why not that one? Too small?"

Rogan stifled a laugh. "We're not fishing, Grant. We don't throw the small ones back."

It was mid-morning and business in the bank was modest. The morning rush was over and it was too early for lunch.

"Tell me how many demon-possessed people you see," Rogan said.

I've always hated pop quizzes, especially when I was unprepared. I didn't want to admit to him that I couldn't see what he saw. It wasn't for lack of trying. I'd hoped that being able to see swords, which came easily to me now, would mean I was also able to spot demons.

Anticipating Rogan's displeasure over my failure, I shook my head. "I don't see any," I confessed.

"Neither do I."

Trick question. If there's anything I hate more than pop quizzes, it's trick questions.

A man in a fitted gray suit entered the lobby through the front doors. He was talking on his smartphone and heading toward the elevators when he passed us.

Rogan locked onto him like a guided missile. "Here we go," he said.

I stared at the man's face, not caring that it was rude. I was desperate. No flickering. I saw nothing but a clean shave.

We fell into step behind him.

At the elevator he pushed the Up button and kept talking into his phone. "I don't care what she says. She's on her way out. I've seen to that." He paused. "No. No! Just do what I tell you. File the paperwork."

The elevator doors opened.

The man stepped inside and pushed the button for the 24th floor.

We followed behind him and Rogan pushed the button for the 23rd floor, causing the man, who was still talking on the phone, to do a double take. I wondered what was on the 23rd floor that he found odd we would go there.

The elevator doors closed.

The instant they did, Rogan grabbed the man and slammed him against the back of the elevator, pinning him against the wall with his left forearm, cutting off his breath so he couldn't cry out.

The man's face was a mix of fear and anger, and all human. I only saw one face, one human face.

From the look of him, he probably worked out, may have even taken some martial arts classes, because he tried some moves, but every move was anticipated and blocked by Sayeret Matkal training.

The elevator dinged at the second floor and the doors opened for a young woman cradling a stack of papers. Her face registered alarm.

"Rogan?" I said.

"Deal with it," he snapped.

"Sorry, miss," I said, punching the close doors button frantically, "you'll have to take the next one."

The elevator doors closed.

Rogan raised his ringed hand to place it against the man's chest.

The man's eyes fixed on the ring and the demon inside recognized it and knew what was about to happen. Throwing the man's head back, twisting his features, stretching his mouth agape so wide I thought the man's jaw would surely dislocate, with a voice as deep as a well and as rough as rocks, the demon spewed all manner of vile curses and threats. With extraordinary strength, the demon shoved Rogan away.

But Rogan was equal to the task. Planting his feet like a wrestler gaining leverage, he leveraged the man against the wall and slammed his hand against the man's chest.

"Be still!" he commanded.

The demon wailed and struggled.

"Be still!" Rogan shouted again.

The demon ceased its struggle.

"Grant, my backpack. The clay jar."

Unzipping the backpack I retrieved the container as Rogan was reaching inside the man's chest, whose eyes—who could blame him?—were as big as saucers.

Rogan extracted the demon, his forearm straining with the effort.

The creature was hideous and I did my best not to think that someday I would look just like it.

I removed the lid to the clay jar and Rogan placed the demon inside.

The man in the suit passed out. Rogan backed away and the man slumped to the floor.

"Just as well," he said.

"Won't he tell people what we did to him?"

"Would you?"

Rogan checked the lid on the clay jar. He needn't have. I'd made double certain it was on tight. He placed it in his backpack.

The elevator dinged and the doors opened to the 23rd floor.

"Freeze!"

Two security guards in a shooter's stance leveled guns at us.

With a jerk of his head Rogan signaled me to follow him. We stepped through the back of the elevator, emerging in a copier room where a woman was feeding papers into the machine. When she saw us appear through the wall, she screamed. Loose papers flew everywhere.

"Sorry," I said as we ran past her.

We made a circuitous route down corridors, through walls,

down stairs, through one final wall on the ground floor, and onto an adjoining sidewalk.

"Where are you parked?" Rogan asked.

"Horton Plaza."

"Which direction?"

I pointed west. "It's just a matter of time before the police are alerted," I said.

"We can elude the police," he said. "Our greater concern is angels. Now would be a good time for one of those membranes. Do you think you can find one?"

"Find one? Possibly. Step through it? I told you, I've never done it on my own before."

"It's time to man up, Grant," he snapped. "If you see one, tell me."

Turning on his heel, he set off at a brisk pace. I fell in behind him, feeling like a failure of a Nephilim.

We took a zig-zag route toward Horton Plaza, one block north, two blocks west, three blocks south, then west again. When we were within sight of the parking structure, we saw a police cruiser. We doubled back, around a corner.

Halfway down the block Rogan asked, "Are they following us?"

I glanced over my shoulder as the cruiser rounded the corner. "They're behind us," I said.

"Look for angels," he said.

I glanced around. "Two. Across the street."

If the news bothered Rogan, he didn't show it. He was in full commando mode.

"Rebel or faithful?"

"They have silver swords."

"Are they looking at us?"

"No. They are preoccupied by a group of teenagers."

I picked up the pace, resisting the urge to check on the police cruiser again.

Rounding the corner, Rogan was nowhere to be seen. I scanned the length of the street, both sides. No Rogan. There was a coffee shop on the corner. Had he gone into it?

The entrance was back around the corner. I turned to retrace my steps when a hand shot out of the wall and grabbed me, not pulling me through the wall, but into it. Rogan lifted a finger to his lips, indicating quiet.

This was a new experience for me. I'd never stood in a wall before. We could hear everything a couple was saying at a table in the coffee shop. They both had a Southern drawl.

"What's so special about an old Navy ship?" she said.

"It's the *MIDWAY*. It's a historic aircraft carrier," he said.

"You promised you'd take me to Sea World."

"We can still go to Sea World."

"But it would only be half a day," she complained. "Half a day isn't enough for Sea World."

As we listened to them argue, I wondered what they'd do if they knew we were listening to them. I thought of the saying, *If these walls had ears,* and wondered if the person who coined it was thinking about angels.

After what seemed a suitable length of time, we stepped back onto the sidewalk. The coast was clear. No police cruiser. No angels. From there we made our way to the parking structure without further incident.

I never did find out if the couple went to the *MIDWAY* or Sea World.

CHAPTER
19

"What have you been up to this morning, Grant?"

Sue sat casually on the sofa, shoes off, her legs folded beneath her. When she arrived at my apartment, I'd been checking the website of a local news station to see if Rogan and I had made the headlines. We hadn't. I closed the laptop.

I couldn't get the image out of my mind of the man slumped on the floor in the elevator. Surely, he knew he'd had a demon in him, didn't he? And those around him—coworkers, family— had to have noticed a difference in his behavior. How would he explain it to them? As I envisioned him lying there, I noticed one other thing that was telling. Throughout the ordeal he never once let go of his cell phone.

"Grant? Are you listening to me? I asked you about your morning."

"Oh, you know," I said. "The usual."

"Have you found a topic for your next book?"

It took all the self-control I could muster to keep a straight face. Between the constant appearances of Nosroch, sparring with

Rogan, and hunting demons, I hadn't had a writer's thought in weeks.

"The search continues," I said.

"Don't worry. You'll come up with something."

Her faith in me, while comforting, was unfounded. How had my life become so complicated? It was a house of cards that could come crashing down at any moment. I was trying not to dwell on all the secrets I was keeping, aware that any one of them, if known, could lead to disaster. I wondered what she'd think if she knew I was having conversations with a rebel angel, or if she found out I was hunting demons with Rogan. I also wondered what Rogan—or Abdiel for that matter—would do if they found out I was conversing with Nosroch. I wondered what Nosroch would do if he learned I was training with an elite member of Sayeret Matkal with the powers of a Nephilim who was determined to kill him.

"Tell me about your day," I said, shifting the topic of conversation away from me.

Sue settled comfortably on the sofa and described her concern for some of her struggling students, both academic and personal; her frustration with petty faculty politics; and the burden of a heavy workload. I couldn't help but be envious of her new life free from the supernatural.

"Oh, by the way," she said. "Jana called. She invited us out to dinner with her and Rogan. I told her we'd love to join them. Is that okay?"

"My schedule's clear," I said, as though I had control over it.

"I thought we'd go to that Mexican restaurant over by the mall. Apparently, Rogan is quite taken with south of the border cuisine." She got up and stretched. "Now, if you don't mind, I think I'll take a nap. Then you can drive me back to Jana's and I'll make myself beautiful for tonight."

"That won't take long," I said.

She smiled. "Aren't you sweet."

Picking up her shoes, she went to the bedroom.

With an hour to kill, I sat at the table in front of my laptop. Motivated by guilt over Sue's comment regarding my writing, I opened the computer and clicked on the IDEAS file. The document names of four prime suspects lay before me. My thought had been to take a second look at them and see if any appeared more promising to me than they had last time I'd viewed them.

Ten minutes later I found myself still staring at the screen, not having clicked on any of them. My mind kept drifting back to my failure to see the flickering faces of demon-possessed people.

"Am I interrupting?"

It was Noz.

"How long have you been standing there?" I asked.

"Long enough to know something's troubling you."

I closed the laptop. It seemed the whole world and heaven were conspiring against my writing career.

"Have you thought about—"

I held up a hand to stop him. Walking down the hallway, I pulled the bedroom door closed, but not all the way. I didn't want the sound of the latch to wake Sue.

"Another nap?" Noz asked.

"You haven't been in there watching her?"

Noz frowned. "That was uncalled for, Grant."

I disagreed, but let it pass. "What do you want now?

"The same thing I've wanted since we first met. Have you given thought to our last conversation?"

"For the sake of argument," I said, "let's say I believe that you're sincere. I still don't know what you want from me. A character reference?"

"We are both charting unknown waters, Grant. You contend

that you don't deserve the same judgment that awaits the angels that have rebelled, since, while their offspring, you never participated in the rebellion. So you are petitioning the Father to bless you and all Nephilim with His favor, or at least give some indication of your eternal future since the salvation that has been extended to humans is not available to you. Is that a fair summation?"

"Go on," I said.

"I, on the other hand, along with others, regret our part in the rebellion and wish to repent. We, too, seek the Father's favor."

"Actions have consequences, Noz. Your punishment fits the crime. Why should you get a free pass?"

"It's called grace, Grant. It's not something we deserve, but something we hope for. The Father showed His grace to humans who have sinned; we humbly ask the Father of grace to do the same for us."

I half-expected the ghost of the professor to rise in protest.

I protested for him. "The Father sent His son to die on the cross for the salvation of humans, is that what you're asking? For Jesus to die for your sins?"

Can angels cry? If not, Noz was close to it.

His voice trembling, he said, "Grant, you have no idea how deeply that remark cut me. We would never ask the Father to make such a sacrifice again. We would rather perish. You must remember, we have known the Father more intimately than you. Accordingly, we place our faith in His infinite wisdom and mercy. When we stand before His judgment, all we ask is that He take our contrition into consideration."

"I still don't know what that has to do with me."

"You wish to stand before the Father and receive an answer to your petition. It would be an honor if I were able to stand beside you to make ours."

"Hold it right there. I'm not going to Sheol with you, Noz. I don't care if it is the only access to the King's Highway and heaven."

"The King's Highway is closed, Grant. Belial was lying to you."

"But I suppose you're telling me the truth, the whole truth, and nothing but the truth."

"Not exactly."

I have to admit, I wasn't expecting that. "So you are deceiving me."

"No deception. I just haven't told you all of my reasons for seeking you out."

"Of course you haven't. All right, let's hear it."

My tone was defensive, and why shouldn't it be? I had every right not to trust a rebel angel asking for favors.

Nosroch sensed my hostility. He paused, as though he was having second thoughts about what he'd come to say.

"Despite your lack of trust in me, Grant, what I saw in you at Sheol, I see in you now."

"So you no longer see me standing here in my boxer shorts."

"I regret saying that. It was spoken out of frustration. I know you to be a noble soul, Grant, otherwise I would not ask this of you."

With this buildup I sensed his request was going to be a doozy.

Noz proceeded. "I have told you the effect your speech in Sheol has had on many of us who formerly sided with Lucifer," he said. "We weren't the only ones. Many of the demons who were there were similarly influenced."

This was too much. I hadn't yet wrapped my mind around the thought that there were rebel angels who wanted to repent. Now he was telling me there were evil demons who wanted to repent, too?

When I petitioned the Father on behalf of all Nephilim, in my mind I imagined how they appeared thousands of years ago in human form, as I am now in my time. My plea was for justice for a race of beings that fell between the cosmic cracks. If I thought of the ungodly creature Rogan and I had just captured, of the demons Semyaza had loosed on me . . . the whole thing fell apart.

Noz said, "You are aware that the natural state of spirits of Nephilim is to be clothed in flesh, and that being deprived of bodies causes them constant torment."

"I'm also aware," I countered, "that they torment what they possess."

"I won't argue what we both know to be true. There are some, having lived in pain for centuries, who have been driven mad; others, who are evil, having aligned themselves with the powers of darkness, inflict pain and suffering for what they perceive is the Father's injustice."

"Get to the point, Noz."

"There are still others, those under my charge, who retain a measure of who they once were as Nephilim. In life they were good men, men of renown who, even now as demons, desire to reclaim what they once were. One of them is my Nephilim son, Elihu."

I folded my arms impatiently.

"I propose that my demon son possess you, that you get to know him, allow him to convince you of the sincerity of our repentance."

"You want me to be possessed by one of your demons?"

"My son."

"Voluntarily?"

"Yes."

"No."

"Think about it, Grant. What better way to convince you we mean no harm, to convince the Father that your petition—"

"I said, no."

Noz gave me a fatherly look, the kind that indicates he's disappointed in you.

"To quote Gomer Pyle," I said, "Fool me once, shame on you; fool me twice, shame on me."

"I was hoping by now you would have come to trust me."

"Do you really want to know what I'm hearing, Noz? The same old refrain. 'Grant, I'm giving you the opportunity of a lifetime, everything you've ever desired.' That's what Semyaza told me. 'Grant, I'm on your side. I can take you to the heavenly throne room where you can present your petition directly to the Father.' That's what Belial told me. I'm not falling for it again. Do your worst, Nosroch, but I will never consent to be demon possessed."

"It's about time you stood up for yourself, Grant!"

Sue's voice startled me.

I swung around to see her storming from the bedroom.

"Sue, stay back," I cried. "You don't know who this is."

She walked past me.

"Nosroch," she said.

"You're not afraid of me?" Noz said.

"You're not the first angel I've met."

"Of course. Abdiel," Noz said.

I attempted to step around her, to put myself between her and the rebel angel. She moved forward, not letting me.

Her gaze fixed on the rebel angel, she said. "At least twice now Nosroch has appeared to you to enlist you in his agenda. I heard every word."

"You were supposed to be asleep. Noz, you told me she was asleep."

Sue closed the distance between her and Nosroch. With folded arms and fire in her eyes, she said to the angel, "I think you should leave."

Nosroch met her gaze, the two of them standing toe-to-toe like combatants in an arena. I couldn't help but notice Sue's sword. Normally a soft lavender shade, it shimmered silver with righteous indignation.

Noz disappeared.

For a long moment I stared at Sue's back, as still and hard as a statue. When she turned, she began gathering up her things with a fury, her purse, her leather satchel. She swung around and strode past me toward the bedroom to get her shoes.

Without looking at me, she seethed, "When were you going to tell me about Nosroch, Grant?"

The question wasn't so much a query as it was a condemnation. Dozens of replies came to mind, all of them sounding like an adolescent who'd been caught doing something naughty.

I followed her into the bedroom just as she was coming out, slipping on her shoes as she walked. I could feel waves of anger emanating from her when she passed.

"Sue, slow down. Let me explain."

"I don't even want to look at you right now, Grant," she said, opening the front door. "Take me home. Unfortunately, we have a dinner date, remember?"

CHAPTER
20

WHEN WE ARRIVED AT THE RESTAURANT SUE STILL WASN'T speaking to me.

On the ride to Jana's apartment, I tried several times, all of them unsuccessful, to break through the stony wall of silence she'd erected between us. Now that she knew about Nosroch, I wanted to tell her everything, even about Rogan—our demon-hunting experience downtown, how demons had killed his buddies Israel, how he was determined to hunt down and kill Nosroch, their prince. But as much as I wanted to tell Sue everything, I knew I couldn't without revealing Rogan's Nephilim abilities. So as much as I wanted to come clean, the closest I could come to it would be a dusty version of the truth.

At Jana's apartment, while Sue changed for dinner, I paced and stewed, trying to come to terms with a partial revelation. As it turned out, while she got ready, she'd been doing some thinking herself . . . on how to make the wall between us higher and thicker.

We rode to the restaurant in silence.

The others had arrived before us and were already seated at the table. As usual, diners in the surrounding tables and booths were nudging each other and pointing at the local celebrity.

Rogan and Jana rose to greet us and we sat at the table, boy-girl-boy-girl, which placed Rogan and I opposite each other. Complimentary chips and salsa had already been served.

While Mexican food had been an essential part of our diet for three of us, it was a relatively new experience for Rogan. Sue had told me he liked it, and he immediately demonstrated that her comment was an understatement. He began wolfing down the chips and salsa. When the standard single-chip dip into the community salsa bowl proved too tedious, he picked up the bowl, held it under his chin, and shoveled the red chili salsa with gusto, signaling the waiter for more when the bowl was empty.

When the novelty of Rogan's enthusiastic dining antics wore off, Jana turned to Sue.

"Rough day?" she asked.

"I'd rather not talk about it," Sue said, purposely not looking at me, which was, in couples-speak, her way of saying that I'd been a jerk.

"Grant, how was your day?" Jana asked, none too subtly.

"I've had better," I said.

Rogan looked up and grinned, thinking I was making a veiled reference to my inability to see demon-possessed people.

Conversation lagged as we made a pretense of looking at the menu, the only sound being Rogan's chomping on chips. The waiter arrived and took our drink orders, giving us a slight reprieve from the awkward silence. The girls ordered margaritas, Rogan chose a Mexican beer, and I got a diet Coke.

"What's good here?" Rogan said, returning to the menu. Jana and I were in agreement that he should try a combination plate to get a taste of several items: a taco, a cheese enchilada, and a tamale with rice and beans.

After the waiter returned to take our order, it left us with no further diversions to avoid the strained mood at the table.

"Grant," Jana said, "you should show Rogan around the city. Balboa Park. The zoo. Old Town."

"I've been to Old Town," Rogan said.

I stifled a grin. What he didn't tell her was that he'd gone there to get a clay jar to capture demons.

"Jana, why don't you tell us about your day instead?" I said, thinking that was the safest topic. "Are you working on a story?"

She gave a sad smile. "It was an emotional day," she said.

"Emotional good or bad?"

"Both. I did a story on Rady's Children's Hospital, the Neuro-Oncology program. I met the cutest little girl. Her name is Savannah. She's currently undergoing radiation treatment for tumors on her spine."

Tears filled Jana's eyes as she spoke.

"She's such a sweetheart, and a trooper. And her parents are remarkable. You can see how much they love Savannah just by the way they look at her. Of course, Savannah has lost all her hair. But despite being consigned to a hospital bed, despite the ordeal, the discomfort, the pain, she's such a happy little girl. No one should have to live with that kind of pain, especially a child. She should be playing with her friends, running barefoot in the park."

When Jana spoke of living in pain, I could feel a pair of eyes boring through me.

"Savannah stole my heart," Jana said. "Her parents too. They've done nothing to deserve this. Yet they've chosen to be there for each other, and to live life with love and hope."

Our order arrived and we began the routine of unwrapping utensils from cloth napkins and surveying our meals, deciding where to begin.

Rogan attacked his combination plate with gusto and Jana

used his preoccupation with a cheese enchilada to mouth to me, "Have you told him who you are?"

My reply was to cut my carne asada.

"You know, Grant," Jana said, "Rogan's something of a Bible expert."

"Not an expert," Rogan said without looking up from his plate. "I read the Tanakh."

"Isn't that interesting, Grant?" Jana said. "You know, Rogan, Grant's had a couple of excellent Bible mentors, among them a notable professor—Sue worked closely with him—and another world-renowned authority with an extensive resume. Grant read his unpublished history on the supernatural. Why don't you tell Rogan about it?"

"I've done a study of Jesus as a Divine Warrior," I said, sidestepping Jana's ploy. "Wrote a book about it. But I'd much rather hear about Rogan's studies. Do you have a favorite topic?"

"While I read the Tanakh every day," Rogan said, "a favorite topic of interest to me is in what you would call the intertestamental period—the time between the Old and New Testaments—specifically the history of the Maccabees."

"Are you familiar with Nephilim?" Jana asked him.

That got his attention. For the first time since our plates arrived, he looked up.

"Genesis 6," he said. "I'm familiar with the passage."

He was fingering his ring. He had sensed that this was more than polite dinner conversation.

Then, with a twinkle in his eye, he said, "I have done a study on demon possession. Fascinating topic, both Old and New Testaments. Grant, do you think it's possible for demons to possess humans in modern times?"

"I suppose it's possible," I said, challenging him with a glance.

"Interesting," Jana said. "Aren't there angels in both the Old and New Testaments? Whatever happened to them? People don't talk much about them these days."

"Great question," Rogan said. "Grant, why do you think that is?"

"Well, I can't speak for everyone," I said. "Billy Graham wrote a book on angels with examples of modern-day encounters. From what I understand, it sold pretty well."

While we bantered back and forth, dancing around Jana's none-too-subtle attempt to draw me out, Sue sat sullenly, her hands in her lap. She never touched her meal.

When the dinner was over and we got up to leave, Sue approached Jana.

"Are you and Rogan going out?"

"I drove," Jana said. "I'm going to drop him off and go straight home."

"Can I ride with you?"

As we were walking out, Jana came up beside me. She said, "Whatever you did, Grant, tell her you're sorry."

CHAPTER
21

LATER THAT NIGHT, AFTER RETURNING TO MY APARTMENT from the restaurant, I tried calling Sue. She didn't take my calls. At first I cursed Caller ID for the snitch that it is, longing for earlier days when people answered the phone not knowing who was calling. Then, I decided to use it to my advantage. If she knew it was me calling, maybe repeated attempts would wear her down. After the fifth attempt, my phone rang. It was Jana.

"She doesn't want to talk to you. Quit pestering her."

"You're the one who told me to apologize to her. How can I apologize if she won't talk to me?"

"Give her time, Grant."

There was so much Jana didn't know. She didn't know that the rebel angel who had followed us out of the restaurant after the tomato-tossing Spectacle hadn't gone away after all, that he had shown up at my apartment, and for Sue's sake I had to catch her up to date.

"Jana, this is important," I said. "I need you to listen to me."

"Grant, I don't want to hear it. I'm not going to get in the middle of an argument between you and Sue. Stop calling her.

And don't do that guy-thing by thinking you can come over here and stand outside my apartment and badger her into talking to you tonight."

"Jana, you don't understand—"

But I was talking to my phone. Jana had ended the call. Worse, she'd preempted Plan B, going over to her apartment and standing outside until I wore Sue down. I tried calling Jana back. It went straight to voicemail. I tried calling Sue. Straight to voicemail.

The guy-thing Jana warned me about seemed to be the only option left. Then I remembered who I was dealing with. Two strong-willed women, and I wouldn't put it past either one of them calling the police on me, which would mean spending the night in jail.

I didn't sleep at all that night, and in the morning considered calling Rogan and cancelling our morning training exercise, but that would mean giving him a lame excuse, because to tell him the real reason, I'd have to tell him about Nosroch. Then it occurred to me that, for my sake, I needed to keep our appointment. If I cancelled, I'd sit around all morning and stew. Training would give me something to do and get my mind off Sue. Besides, I needed the training.

That's when my cell phone rang. It was Rogan.

"Grant, instead of demon hunting, let's do that membrane portal thing. Where should I meet you?"

"If it's all the same to you, I'd like to stick with demon hunting," I said. "I need the practice."

"How many demon possessions did you see in the restaurant last night?"

My silence was admission that I hadn't seen any. Another trick question?

"There weren't any," I said.

"You're guessing."

I smiled. I'd guessed right. "Admit it. There weren't any."

"There were three."

Suspicious, I stuck to my guess. "You're trying to trick me."

"Am I? There was one two tables to my left; one at the booth in the corner; and one entering the restaurant as we were leaving. It would be a waste of time hunting them if you can't see them."

He had me. "All right. We'll do the membrane thing."

"Where should we meet?"

I knew of three places, but one was the naval base beneath the angel encampment. And while Rogan probably wouldn't hesitate going there again, I didn't want to risk it.

"There's one where the professor lived and one at my old apartment where Belial took me to Sheol. But we can't just knock on someone's door and ask them if we can use their membrane portal."

"Why not? I'm pretty good at talking my way into places."

"Maybe you can do that in Israel, but in California, people don't invite strangers into their homes."

"Then where?"

"While I can't be certain, there's one other place I can think of that might have a membrane portal."

We agreed to meet there.

"Oh, and Grant? You were right about the restaurant. There weren't any demons there."

The wind off the ocean whipped our shirts and pant legs. A familiar view stretched out all around us: the Point Loma peninsula and ocean to the west, the mountains to the east, and the downtown high rise buildings surrounding us.

"Why the Emerald Towers?" Rogan asked. "We're rather exposed, aren't we?"

"With all the angelic activity that has occurred here," I said, "it seemed the most likely place,"

"You're the expert," Rogan conceded.

"Let's get something straight," I said. "I'm no expert. Trust me on that."

"You're the one with experience traveling through membrane portals."

"Never on my own. I've always had help."

That didn't faze him. "Just tell me what you know. We'll figure it out."

Easy for him to say. He had full Nephilim powers.

"What do we do first?" he asked. "How do we find a membrane portal? What do we look for?"

"You don't see a portal, you feel it," I said.

He cocked his head. "Are you sure? Just because you can't see them doesn't mean they can't be seen. You can't see demons in humans. Can angels see membranes?"

I thought back to the professor's living room. Abdiel knew exactly where to find the membrane.

"I don't know," I said, "possibly, but even if it's possible to see them, how can I teach you to look for something I've never seen? I told you, I'm not an expert."

"Fair enough. So what does a membrane feel like?"

"It's a soft spot between dimensions."

"So we're feeling for something soft in the air? That doesn't make sense, Grant."

"Stop thinking like a human. We're Nephilim."

"Excellent point, Grant. Show me."

Extending my arms, with open palms I felt for a membrane. When I didn't feel one, I took a few steps and felt again. For the next several minutes the two of us walked around the top of the

Emerald Towers looking like blind men searching for a way off the roof.

"Is this one?" he said.

I certainly hoped not. Rogan was standing at the edge of the building, his arms extended. If he had found a membrane we'd literally have to take a flying leap to go through it.

I felt where he was feeling.

"No," I said, relieved.

"Are you sure?"

If I told him I felt one, I don't doubt for a second that a member of the Sayeret Matkal would take a running jump off a skyscraper to go through it.

"I'm sure," I said.

We kept looking.

"Here," I said.

He stood beside me and felt. His eyes widened in wonder.

"Grant, you're brilliant!" he cried.

But I didn't feel brilliant. This was the easy part.

"What now?" he asked.

"Hold your horses, cowboy," I said. "This isn't like walking into a department store. It's more like stepping through a screen door that rips your atoms apart and reassembles them on the other side. Each time I've done it, it's taken a while to recover."

"Don't worry about me. I've been challenged physically before."

I'd forgotten who I was talking to, a man who prided himself on enduring physical pain.

"Where will it take us? Are they like wormholes linking two locations?" he asked.

"I don't know. I don't think so." The last time I'd gone through one I'd ended up in my apartment. I doubted there were wormholes in the cosmos that were doorways to my apartment.

"Then how? Do we just think where we want to go and it takes us there?"

"Yes, Rogan. We clap three times, make a wish, and jump."

He looked at me dryly. "Really?"

"No! I don't know. Maybe."

"What if we stick our head through first to see where it goes?"

"I don't think it works that way."

"But you don't know."

Rogan approached the soft spot, stuck out his neck and leaned forward. When nothing happened, he did it again. He looked ridiculous.

"Okay, maybe not," he conceded. "Show me what you did the first time you entered a membrane."

Standing in front of the membrane, I remembered Abdiel's instructions. I had just walked through a wall for the first time, so walking through a membrane was similar, only more difficult. Extending my hand, I felt it. There was definitely a membrane here. What if I was successful? Where would I end up? More importantly, would I be able to come back?

This was insane.

For a few moments I wrestled with my male ego and common sense. As usual in these instances, male ego won. I couldn't back down now.

I stepped forward and the world around me blurred. I tried another step and felt a resistance, tried to push forward, more resistance. It was like the time I got my arm caught in a door, half in, half out, and I panicked. I tried to back out. Couldn't. I tried again. I was stuck. An image of a tombstone flashed in my mind: HERE LIES GRANT AUSTIN. HE GOT STUCK HALFWAY BETWEEN HERE AND NOWHERE.

Mustering all my strength, I backpedaled. The membrane gave way suddenly and the next thing I knew I was on my backside.

"Outstanding!" Rogan shouted. "Where did you go?"

As before, my body felt as though it had been ripped apart. Staring up at a cloudless sky, I waited for strength to return to my limbs.

"I didn't go anywhere," I said. "The resistance was too strong. I backed out."

"You disappeared completely!" Rogan said. "Let me try."

He stood where I'd stood. With his ringed hand, he felt the membrane. There was no hesitation in his next move. He leaped forward . . . and landed on the gravel three feet in front of where he'd started. Undaunted, he circled around and tried again.

What if he was successful and managed to step through the membrane and couldn't come back? How would I explain to Jana that I'd lost her new boyfriend?

As it turned out, it was an unrealized fear. Despite repeated efforts, all Rogan managed to do was jump back and forth on the gravel.

"There's got to be something more to it," he said. "What aren't you telling me?"

"It's like walking through walls," I said. "Maybe that will help."

But it didn't. After thirty minutes we took the elevator to street level. While I was still feeling ill effects from the experience, I also felt good about myself. Despite our failure, I'd at least managed to step into the membrane. Progress. One other thing—finally, I'd found something I was better at than Rogan.

CHAPTER
22

HITCHING UP HIS BACKPACK OVER ONE SHOULDER AND A duffle bag with freshly clean laundry over the other, Rogan reached for the front door and entered the lobby of Hotel West on Broadway. He strode past the night clerk who was dozing behind the counter while a reality show played on the television behind him. There were two antiquated elevators in the lobby, but only one was operational. Once inside, he punched the cracked and yellowed button for the second floor.

When the elevator doors opened, he made his way down a dingy corridor to his eight foot by eight foot room. He tossed the duffle bag to the foot of the bed. Then, shrugging off the backpack, he removed a sealed clay jar and placed it against the wall with six other jars before collapsing onto the bed fully clothed. He slept deeply despite the car horns, racing engines, loud conversations, and drunken swearing from the street below.

Rogan awoke at 4 a.m. without an alarm. He began his normal

morning routine of calisthenics—one hundred push-ups, one hundred sit-ups.

His room was what you would expect of a $50-a-night hotel in a city world-renowned as a tourist destination. Stained carpets and walls were the establishment's decorating motif. The furniture—a wooden-slatted twin bed, a scarred desk and chair, a ten-inch flat screen TV bolted to the wall, and a closet that was little more than a cubby hole—was sufficient for his needs. There was an overhead fan and a window without a screen.

When he'd first arrived, he'd spent his first day at the hotel, after a trip to a local ninety-nine-cent store to purchase disinfectant and Febreze, cleaning the room with a military diligence that would make a drill instructor proud. Just because you lived cheap didn't mean you had to live dirty. Likewise, he cleaned grime and black mold from the small sink, toilet, and shower of the communal bathroom down the hall. While many tourists—looking for an inexpensive place to stay in an expensive city—checked out within thirty minutes of their arrival, giving the inevitable one-star review on Yelp, Rogan wasn't so easily offended. He'd spent the night in worse places than this.

Having completed his calisthenics, Rogan hit the road, running his usual ten miles along Harbor Drive next to the bay, after which he returned to the hotel and stood in line in the hallway for his turn in the communal bathroom.

Fresh from the shower and wearing clean clothes, he completed his morning routine by turning his attention from the physical to the spiritual. He sat at the desk and, in a chair that rocked with one leg slightly shorter than the others, read from the Tanakh.

His days followed a usual routine. For breakfast, he drank orange juice from the container and ate two energy bars as he started his work day by turning on the television, scanning the news channels for local stories that to most people were ordinary human tragedies, but to those attuned to the realm of the spirit were rebel angel Spectacles or crimes caused by demons. After sundown he roamed the downtown streets hunting demons. When he captured them, before confining them to a clay jar prison, he forced them to identify their prince. He had yet to find one under Nosroch's command.

This morning was going according to routine when, with the third click of the channel remote, he saw a familiar face. Jana Torres was reporting from the airport.

". . . was scheduled to land at San Francisco International Airport has just landed here at Lindbergh Field."

The image on the television screen switched to a view of the aircraft sitting in the middle of the runway. Jana spoke over the live shot.

"The doors are opening. Next, the inflatable emergency evacuation slides should deploy. Good. The front. Now the rear. I see them, there, at the rear hatch, the first passengers are emerging."

There was chaos at the exit as the passengers pushed and shoved and punched each other to get off the plane. Some managed to slide down; others in their haste lost their balance and tumbled down. Jana gasped as one woman was shoved through the exit door and missed the slide completely, hitting the tarmac with a sickening thud. She didn't move.

"Oh! That poor woman," Jana exclaimed. "Emergency vehicles are reaching the plane now. I hope she's all right."

The chaos in the plane extended onto the runway as passengers who made it safely down slides began running in every direction. Security vehicles began corralling them like stray cows on an old west cattle drive.

Jana was back on the screen, stepping away from a monitor. She was reporting from the terminal. A TSA security screening queue was behind her.

"Our apologies for the loss of that live feed. Apparently airport authorities have ordered our cameras out of the boarding area for security reasons as they handle the situation on the runway, but we will stay right here and continue our coverage of this bizarre incident at San Diego airport and United Airlines Flight 207 out of Boston."

A talking cheese cracker appeared on the screen as the station went to commercial. Rogan positioned the unsteady desk chair directly in front of the television. The news story interested him. First of all, it was Jana reporting. The next time they met up he could score points by telling her he'd watched it. On the other hand, the odd nature of the story suggested it might be a rebel angel Spectacle.

Jana was back on the screen.

"In case you're just joining us," she said, "here's what we know so far. United Airlines Flight 207 departed Boston's Logan International airport this morning at 6:00 a.m. Eastern Time nonstop to San Francisco with a scheduled arrival at 9:40 a.m. When the flight was over Denver's air space, the pilot contacted air traffic control and informed them he was diverting to San Diego. When air traffic control asked him if he had an emergency onboard, the pilot reportedly replied, 'I just don't feel like going to San Francisco today.'

"Air traffic control ordered him to resume the scheduled flight plan, but he refused. When they attempted to contact the co-pilot, the pilot informed them that he was unavailable. Two F/A-18 fighter jets were scrambled to intercept the aircraft. According to reports, the pilot refused to make radio contact with them, but waved to them in a friendly manner. Escorted by the F/A-18 fighter jets, the plane was permitted to land here at San Diego, but was ordered not to approach the terminal. It came to a stop where you see it on the runway. Shortly after landing, passengers were seen banging on the windows and crying. One passenger held a sign up to the window that said, *For God's sake, help us!*"

Jana touched her ear and listened for a moment.

"I have just received word that we have a couple of video clips that have been posted on social media by passengers onboard Flight 207. Please be advised that what you are about to see may be disturbing to some viewers."

A smartphone video appeared on the screen of a female flight attendant addressing the passengers. Behind her the co-pilot was attempting to jimmy the door to the pilot's cabin.

"Please remain calm," she said. "We are making an unscheduled landing at San Diego airport. There is no cause for alarm. Capt. Harrington, bless his heart, is merely keeping his promise to take me to Donovan's restaurant for a romantic dinner. Isn't he sweet?"

Hearing the announcement, the co-pilot wheeled around in a rage and began shouting at the flight attendant, furious that she was seeing Harrington behind his back. The shouting escalated to name-calling. When she began mocking his earlier love-making performance, he slapped her. She hit back and threw canned sodas and liquor bottles at him. A male flight attendant approached the co-pilot from behind and cold cocked him with a champagne bottle, dropping him to the deck.

That's when things got bizarre.

An air marshal appeared in the video coming up the aisle, ordering the male flight attendant to drop the bottle. The flight attendant refused and the air marshal drew his weapon and repeated the command. The flight attendant dropped the bottle, formed his hand into a gun—like children do on a playground—and pointed it at the air marshal, ordering him to lower his weapon. When the air marshal stood his ground, the male flight attendant shouted, "BANG!" and the air marshal dropped dead.

At first, passengers thought it was a staged drama. Some laughed or clapped half-heartedly; others commented loudly that it was in bad taste. A male passenger in an aisle seat closest to the marshal nudged him with his foot. When he didn't move, a second male passenger rolled him over. He checked for a pulse and cried, "He's really dead!"

That set off a general panic among the passengers.

In gunslinger fashion the male flight attendant sauntered down the aisle toward the fallen air marshal blowing imaginary smoke from the business end of his finger gun. The male passenger straddling the air marshal lunged for the flight attendant's hand.

"BANG!"

The flight attendant fired a second imaginary bullet. The male passenger slumped lifeless onto the dead air marshal.

A second video clip aired of the male flight attendant walking down the passenger cabin aisle posing trivia questions to passengers. If they answered incorrectly or refused to answer, he shot them with his finger gun. The passenger would clutch their head, some their chest, and die.

Rogan was out of the chair loading an empty clay jar in his backpack as a visibly shaken Jana appeared on the television screen. Ever the pro, she quickly regained her composure.

"Airport authorities have detained the pilot, co-pilot, and two flight attendants and have sequestered the passengers for questioning."

Rogan was at the door on his way out. What Jana said next, pulled him back to the television.

"As unbelievable as this incident was, it's not the only bizarre airline incident within the last twenty-four hours. Earlier today on Air France Flight 1321 from Tel Aviv to Paris, the pilot informed passengers that an earlier commercial flight over Turkey had been shot down and he was taking evasive maneuvers. He sent the Airbus into a steep dive, banking left and right, and at one point flying the aircraft inverted. The maneuvers were so violent flight attendants were hurled against the ceiling and the bar trolley went flying the length of the plane. Passengers were screaming and crying and when the plane finally landed at Charles de Gaulle airport, the interior of the plane was covered in vomit. The report that an earlier flight had been shot down was erroneous.

"On another flight, Delta 119 from Paris to Boston, while the aircraft was midway over the Atlantic Ocean, a passenger was discovered dead in her seat. Following procedure, the cabin crew moved the deceased woman to the back of the aircraft and covered her with a blanket. Minutes later another person was found dead from unknown causes. He was moved to the back of the plane, covered, and strapped into a seat. Because the flight was full, the passenger that had been in the rear of the plane was moved to the dead man's seat. A short time after that, another passenger was found dead; then another, and another. Flight attendants enlisted male passengers as pallbearers to carry the dead down the aisle as row after row of back seats was filled with bodies and living passengers moved forward. By the time they landed at Logan International airport, there were twenty-four dead passengers strapped into seats in the back of the plane."

Rogan sat transfixed, staring at the television screen. Behind Jana, the first passengers from United Airlines Flight 207 began appearing. They looked like shell-shocked victims coming out of a war zone. Jana moved to intercept two young women who were leaning heavily against each other as they walked.

But Rogan's attention was on the man behind them. His face was flickering. Rogan pressed closer to the television for a better look at the man, but the cameraman zoomed in on Jana and the young women, cutting him out of the scene.

Rogan grabbed his bag and raced out the door.

His hotel a few blocks west of the news station, Rogan hurried there and paced on the sidewalk while he waited for Jana's news truck to return. His original inclination had been to catch a taxi to the airport, until he saw the demon-possessed man on the television screen. By the time he got to the airport, the man would be gone.

When he'd paced an hour and still no news truck, he went inside and spoke to the woman at the reception desk.

"A friend of Jana Torres," he described himself when she asked how she could direct him. "I've been watching her broadcast from the airport and it's important that I see her. Do you know when she's returning to the station?"

The receptionist, a woman in her mid-thirties wearing a black pinstripe coat and skirt, who gave every appearance of being able to handle the crazies that came through the news station doors every day, sized him up. She liked what she saw but remained guarded.

"How is it you know Ms. Torres?" she asked.

Simple enough question, but it stumped him. He'd said friend—did she want a description of their relationship? That was not her business and he was about to tell her so when he thought, "Grant Austin, I know him too; as well as Jana . . . and Sue . . . I can't remember her last name."

At Grant's name, the receptionist smiled. "Do you have identification? It's required to sign you in."

"Not necessary," Rogan said, "I can wait outside. If you can just tell me when she'll be back."

"Unless you're going to talk with her on the street, she'll have to sign you in, too. Why not do it now and save her the trouble?"

Rogan produced his Israeli Special Forces ID. "Oh my," the receptionist said, impressed. She wrote down the necessary information on a sign-in sheet.

"Right this way, Capt. Rogan," she said, emphasizing the *Captain*.

She led him through a door and down a corridor. They passed the broadcast studio with cameras, anchor desks, and backdrops, which he could see through a window in the door.

"You can wait for Ms. Torres in her office," the receptionist said. "The news crew left the airport a short time ago. You shouldn't have to wait longer than twenty minutes."

Rogan noted the time. He sat in a chair in front of Jana's desk and, while he waited, he took in the room. Like Jana it was professional but complicated, with a system of notes and stacks of papers and folders that made sense to her. On the wall behind the desk was a corkboard with several pictures pinned to it. Her and Sue. Her and Grant. Her and Grant and Sue. He felt a twinge of disappointment that he didn't see a picture of him, even though they hadn't known each other long enough for there to be a picture of him there.

"Rogan! What are you doing here?"

He jumped out of the chair. "I saw your broadcast from the airport. We have to talk."

She dropped a bag she was carrying on her desk.

"Can it wait? I'm doing a report on the noon news."

"I just need to see the footage from the broadcast. It's important."

His tone of voice was enough to convince her of the urgency of his request.

"All right," she said, giving him a concerned look. She reached for the office phone on her desk. Punched two numbers. "Richie? Jana. Can you come to my office right away?"

She hung up the phone just as a young woman poked her head in the doorway.

"Miss Torres, they need you in makeup."

"Tell them I'm on my way." Turning back to Rogan. "What's this about?"

"I think I recognized someone," Rogan said. "One of the passengers."

Jana's eyes quickened.

A man in his mid-twenties in jeans and a Batman t-shirt appeared in the doorway. He stepped aside as Jana was already halfway out the door.

"Richie, this is Capt. Rogan Dorn. He needs to view footage from this morning's broadcast." To Rogan: "Richie is an assistant tech in the video department. He can help you. After the newscast we can talk."

Jana hurried one way down the corridor, tech Richie led Rogan the opposite direction to a room filled with monitors and computer terminals. The tech slid into a chair behind a monitor.

"What do you want to see?" he said.

"The footage when the first passengers are coming out of the terminal."

Richie reached for the mouse and began clicking.

Jana's frozen image appeared on the screen holding a microphone, the same one Rogan had seen earlier.

"Play that," he said.

The image came to life.

Rogan leaned forward, his eyes narrowing as the man appeared. He watched intently until the man was out of view.

"Can you run it back and play it again?"

Richie moved the mouse, clicked, dragged, and footage repeated.

"Stop it there!"

A click and the image froze.

Rogan's gaze hardened. The man's face had definitely flick-ered. He'd hoped that by stopping the image, he could see the demon's face. No luck. The still image showed only the man.

"Is there any more footage of the passengers?" Rogan asked.

"Let me see," Richie replied. As he put the mouse through its paces, he said, "We had a second camera crew in the terminal."

Another video appeared on the screen showing a long corridor. Passengers were coming out of a room. Two girls appeared first, then behind them, the man. This clip was longer.

Rogan stared at the monitor as the man approached and walked past the camera. Rogan's pulse quickened, not only because of what he saw on the man's face, but on the faces of two other pas-sengers behind him. A male and a female.

Giving Richie two "well done" pats on his shoulder, Rogan left the room and the news station.

CHAPTER
23

NORMALLY I'M NOT ONE TO PACE, BUT I HAD TO KEEP MOVING to keep my energy level up after a second sleepless night. Now I knew how a convict felt confined to a prison cell, even if mine was my living room. All I could do was wait, a prisoner of Sue's timing.

Give her time, Grant. But how much time?

Earlier this morning I'd risked a text, offering to take Sue to work if her car was still in the shop. She didn't text back.

I'd considered going to the college.

Again, Jana's voice echoed in my head. *And don't do that guy-thing by thinking you can come over here and stand outside my apartment and badger her into talking to you.*

I checked the clock for the hundredth time. Sue would be finished with her classes by now. Would she come over?

As a writer I went to great lengths seeking alone time. I treasured it. I did my best work when I was alone. But I'd never felt so alone as I did right now.

There was a soft knock on the door.

"Grant?"

The door opened and Sue poked her head in.

"Sue, we—"

"—need to talk," she said, finishing my sentence.

She came in and set her satchel beside the door. An incredible urge swept over me. I wanted to take her in my arms and hold her and never let her go, but her demeanor was stand-offish, guarded.

"Sue, let me begin by saying—"

"Is Nosroch here?" she asked.

Because Sue's work with the professor involved the supernatural, I sometimes forgot she couldn't see the things I saw.

"No. We're alone," I said.

She approached me and took my hands in hers. I saw no anger in them and my heart surged with hope that we were going to work through this.

My cell phone rang. I ignored it. To answer the phone meant letting go of Sue's hands and, right now, that was not an option.

Sue looked at me, amused. "Are you going to answer it?"

"They can leave a message."

One, two, three more cycles of the ring tone then, mercifully, it fell silent.

"Sue, listen—"

She pressed her fingers against my lips. "Ladies first," she said.

She took a breath. "Grant, keeping Nosroch a secret hurt me. The first time I overheard you, I didn't say anything, thinking you were waiting for the right time to tell me. But then several days passed and you said nothing, and the longer I waited, the angrier I became."

"Why didn't you say—"

Again her fingers pressed against my lips. This time she held them there to prevent any further interruptions.

"I wondered how many times Nosroch had visited you when I wasn't here. And I began imagining the two of you meeting day after day, doing who knows what while I was at work. It was obvious you hadn't been getting any writing done."

I cringed. She was right about doing who knows what while she was at work, wrong about who I was doing it with.

She continued. "Then, listening to the two of you the other day . . . the casual nature of your conversation, it sounded like you and Nosroch were best buds. You never talked to Abdiel that way."

True. It's hard to chat casually with someone who has all the warmth and wit of an English butler.

"Listening to the two of you frightened me," Sue said. "Then, when he asked you to allow yourself to be possessed by one of his demons—"

"I turned him down!" I protested, though I had to pull her hand away from my mouth to do it.

"That's not the point, Grant! How could you let things get so far that he felt he could make such a proposition? Don't you see what he's doing? He keeps pressing, a little more each time, and you keep letting him come back. Grant, he's one of Lucifer's men! That will never change!"

"I'll admit I've—"

"I'm not done yet," Sue interrupted. "What hurt me most was that you couldn't tell me you'd been contacted by a rebel angel. I can't help thinking that if the professor were here, you would have confided in him. Which makes me wonder if—when it comes to spiritual matters—you've ever thought of me as anything other than the professor's assistant."

We stood barely a foot apart; her shoulders slumped, her gaze lowered, and me feeling sufficiently chastised.

"I know you have feelings for me, Grant. But I don't think you respect me."

It was my turn to speak. Softly, I said, "Sue—"

Nosroch appeared. "Have I come at a bad time?"

"Yes!" I shouted in frustration, turning on him. "Of course you've come at a bad time. You always come at a—wait, no, this isn't a bad time. I'm glad you're here. This is a good time. You couldn't have picked a better time."

Nosroch took my theatrical reversal stoically. Honestly, I don't think anything humans do shock them anymore. Sue, on the other hand, was looking at me as though I was the victim of verbal autocorrect.

I motioned for her to give me a little latitude. I approached Nosroch with the swagger of a district attorney.

"Sue thinks I've been too familiar with you," I began. "She fears you've been leading me down the garden path."

"Let me set aside your fears," Nosroch said to Sue. "We have not walked in any gardens."

"She thinks you're trying to deceive me," I explained. "I agree with her. While I wasn't certain of this before, now I have proof of your deception and I'm glad Sue is here so she can witness the unmasking."

Nosroch shook his head. "But I am not wearing—"

That's when my next book project came to me: *Idioms for Angels,* or possibly the more generic, *Idioms for Idiots.*

"Grant," Sue interjected. "You have a point to make?"

"Yes, the unmasking. I have proof that Nosroch has been lying to me from the day we met."

For having just been called a liar, Nosroch was remarkably calm.

"Proceed," he said.

I proceeded.

"You have demons under your command, is that not correct? Demons who call you their prince."

"It is the nature of our order to have demons placed under the command of an angel. The proper mode of address is for a demon to call his handler, prince."

"And these demons do whatever their prince tells them to do."

"Correct."

"Can demons initiate actions of their own free will?"

Nosroch's eyes narrowed. "Grant, you have something you want to say. Say it."

"Can demons initiate actions of their own free will?" I insisted.

"They cannot."

I had one last arrow in my quiver. I let it fly.

"I know about Ashmedai, Lilith, and Ornasis. I know what they did in Israel. The reign of terror. The children they kidnapped. The two soldiers they killed. Their ultimate capture."

From the look on Nosroch's face, I concluded I'd scored a bullseye.

"How do you know this?" he asked.

"That's irrelevant," I said. "It's true, isn't it?"

"Those three demons are very powerful. You say they were captured. You're certain?"

I nodded.

Sue stepped closer. She was concerned. "Grant, what's going on?"

Nosroch mused, "I haven't heard those names since the days of Solomon."

My cell phone rang. I raised my hands, exasperated in the face of constant interruptions.

"It could be important, Grant," Sue said.

I checked the Caller ID. "It's Rogan," I said. "I'll call him back later."

I shoved the phone back into my pocket.

"Stop the pretense, Nosroch," I said. "I know those three demons are yours. When they were captured, they identified you as their prince, which by your own admission means they're under your command. You initiated that attack." I turned to Sue to drive my point home. "He's been lying this entire time."

"They're not my demons, Grant," Nosroch said.

"They called you their prince."

"Demons lie when it serves the purpose of their prince."

"You're saying you have nothing to do with them?"

"Ashmedai, Lilith, and Ornasis are not mine to command," Nosroch said. "I am not their prince."

"Then who is?"

"Semyaza."

The last arrow in my quiver proved to be a boomerang; it had circled around and struck me square in the chest. Maybe it was the way Nosroch spoke Semyaza's name, or maybe it was just hearing Semyaza's name spoken, but somehow I knew Noz was telling the truth.

Nosroch himself was not unaffected. He was visibly shaken. "Ashmedai, Lilith, and Ornasis . . . Semyaza is closing in on us. Why else would he instruct them to use my name?"

"Grant . . ." Sue clutched my arm, frightened and with cause. "Semyaza!"

"His finding us was inevitable," Noz said to no one in particular.

He could have gone all day without saying *us*.

CHAPTER
24

THE SUN HAD DIPPED BELOW THE HORIZON, LEAVING THE SKY ablaze with orange hues over an azure ocean that stretched from horizon to horizon. An invigorating breeze blew off the water as we strolled down the shoreline with wet sand beneath our feet. We'd taken off our shoes and carried them in one hand, clasping each other's free hand between us. Sue's flesh felt warm and relaxed. It was the perfect ending to a very long day.

So this was how ordinary people lived. I could get used to it given the chance. I was tired of being Nephilim. Like Pinocchio, I longed to be a real boy.

Thoughts of Semyaza's imminent threat tried to tag along. I kicked them aside. All I wanted right now was to dwell in the moment.

"That was impressive the way you confronted Noz with your knowledge of those three demons," Sue said. "How did you know about them?"

"Let's not talk about that now."

"I think we should, Grant. Or do you still not trust me?"

"I trust you. You know that."

"That's just it. I don't know."

"I'm trying to protect you."

She released my hand.

"Do you know how demeaning that is?" Sue protested. "I'm not a helpless maiden for you to shut away in a tower. Apparently, in your mind it's always been you and the professor with me standing on the outside looking in."

How ironic. All this time I'd been envious of Sue's relationship with the professor. It had never occurred to me that she was envious of my relationship with him.

"What can I do to convince you that I trust you?" I said.

"Be honest with me. You're not writing. So what have you been doing? Has Abdiel been training you?"

To lie or not to lie? That was the question. All I had to do was tell her about Rogan and we could get past this and return to hand-holding on the beach.

"I want to be honest with you," I said, "but I can't tell you what you want to know."

She looked away, hurt.

"Trust goes two ways, Sue. You need to trust me. There are some things I can't tell you because it's not my information to share."

"So you are working with someone."

We walked on, apart. I wanted to put this behind us, to hold her hand again.

"It frightens me to think that Semyaza is back," Sue said. "I should warn Jana."

Given the fact that Jana had once dated that miscreant when he masqueraded as Myles Shepherd, it seemed a wise precaution. And I needed to tell Rogan he was wrong about Nosroch, that Semyaza was the prince to Ashmedai, Lilith, and Ornasis. But how could I do that without revealing that I'd been interacting with Noz?

By now stars were appearing overhead. A weariness pressed down on me like a heavy blanket. As much as I wanted to be with Sue, I was feeling the effects of lack of sleep.

"Do you think there's any truth to Nosroch's request?" Sue asked.

"The demon thing? Why would he ask if he wasn't prepared to do it?"

"But that's just it. It's not exactly standard procedure, is it? Why ask your permission? Why not just order his demon to possess you?"

"Are you saying I should consider it?"

"Of course not! It's just that it got me thinking. He said it was his son, Elihu, a former Nephilim."

"There are no good demons, Sue. Trust me on that."

"No exceptions?"

"What are you getting at?"

We walked in silence to the gentle sound of the surf lapping the shore as Sue gathered her thoughts.

"This isn't the first time I've thought about this," she said. "In fact, I've thought about it for a long time. Nosroch merely brought everything to the surface. He said his son had been a good man."

"What else would he say? Grant, I have a vicious evil demon I want you to try on for size?"

"Men of renown. That's what he said. It's a quote from the Bible describing the Nephilim of old."

"Not the first time a tempter has quoted the Bible."

Sue stopped walking. "Grant," she hesitated, "I have entertained the idea of voluntarily being possessed by a demon."

"You can't be serious."

Tears filled her eyes. "I can, and I am, if the demon was you."

My inevitable fate.

I couldn't believe what she was saying, that she would willingly share her body with me.

"The thought of you in perpetual pain with no place to rest is unacceptable," she choked on her tears. "And I don't think you'd hurt me."

I wanted to believe I wouldn't. But never having been a demon, how was I to know?

"And the two shall become one flesh," I said. "Literally."

She laughed shakily and brushed aside a tear. "I thought of that too," she said. She took a deep breath. "Turns out it was nothing more than the fantasy of a lovesick female. Once my mind started working again, I realized it was impossible."

"Why is that?"

"I'm already possessed."

She laughed at my dumbfounded expression.

"All Christians are," she said.

The light came on. "The Spirit of God, of course," I said.

We resumed walking.

"You called yourself a lovesick female."

"You noticed," she replied with a smile. I took her hand.

"But that whole sharing one body thing . . . that would be weird."

"Totally weird."

"I'd know everything you were thinking, everything you'd ever done, your deepest secrets."

"Let's move on," Sue said.

"I'm not sure I can. Nobody's ever offered to share their body with me. That's not the kind of thing a guy can forget."

She gave my hand a squeeze and, for the moment, all was right with the world.

———

Sue and I ambled through the apartment complex hand in hand. Unlike my complex, with apartments stacked on top of one another like building blocks, Jana's unit was an array of luxury bungalows separated by well-manicured lawns, colorfully lit flower beds, and a central park-like area with benches and a waterfall.

As we reached the front door, Sue dug in her purse for the key, found it, and looked up at me. We'd arrived at that storied goodnight moment portrayed in romance novels and movies where everything else melts away and the only thing remaining is a man and a woman and the enchantment of love. And, of course, the kiss.

"It was a lovely evening, Grant," Sue said. "Thank you."

I'd been anticipating this moment since we left the beach. It wasn't as though we'd never kissed, but our relationship had been strained to the point of breaking and it seemed presumptuous to think that all was forgiven after one moonlit stroll on the beach. Truth is, I was afraid . . . afraid of how I'd react if I attempted to kiss her and she turned away.

I risked it.

I placed a hand on her cheek.

She closed her eyes and, instead of pulling away, leaned into me.

As I drew closer, her eyes opened and met mine. Her gaze was warm, tender, inviting. Our lips brushed, tentatively.

She placed her arms around my neck and pulled me close.

I embraced her. The warmth of her lips, her body pressed against mine, was one of those glorious moments in life you wish could last for an eternity.

But life isn't kind and I felt Sue pulling away.

She placed a warm hand on my chest. "Good night, Grant."

As I walked back to my car, I reveled in the moment, only to have the shrill sound of my cell phone ruin it. It was Rogan.

"Grant, where have you been all day?"

"I've been busy."

"Have you seen the news?"

"Like I said, I've been busy."

"Well, get your head out of the sand. We've got trouble."

He told me about Jana's broadcast from the airport, about the two international flights and the local flight from Boston—in nauseating detail— and how he confirmed that three demons had deboarded the San Diego flight, that he recognized them.

"Grant, it's Ashmedai, Ornasis, and Lilith. They're here in San Diego."

"What? I thought you took care of them."

"I did."

"Are you sure it's them?"

"Grant, I know what I saw."

"Maybe it's just a coincidence, the three flights. There are thousands of flights a day, tens of thousands."

"It's not a coincidence, Grant. Tel Aviv to Paris, Paris to Boston, Boston to San Diego. It's a signal. They know I'm here and they want me to know they're coming for me."

As much as I wanted to, I couldn't come up with a sound argument to refute his conclusion. A vomit-filled plane, a flying morgue, a diverted flight turned game show with sudden death. Subtle, they were not.

"Where are they now?" I asked.

"Unknown. I wanted to give you a heads-up. If they know I'm here in San Diego, chances are good they know about you."

Of course they did; Semyaza was their prince. A chill went through me.

"So what do we do?" I asked. "How do we track them down?"

"If I know Ashmedai, we won't have to. They'll announce their presence soon enough."

"I was afraid you were going to say that."

"And Grant . . . if your phone rings? Answer it."

Just when I was thinking I'd finally get a good night's sleep.

CHAPTER
25

THE NEXT MORNING I AWOKE JITTERY AND UNEASY. MY SLEEP had been fitful, repeatedly bolting up in bed alarmed, knowing that Semyaza was lurking in the dark corners of the room. Each time as my vision cleared, the dark corners proved only to be dark corners.

Fortifying myself with cup after cup of black coffee, I did my best to act as though it was a normal day, hoping that acting so would make it so. I showered, shaved, and gathered up my laundry for a trip to the laundromat, a chore I could put off no longer. I rummaged around my loose change saucer for quarters to feed the machine.

"I would speak with you, Grant Austin."

Quarters went flying.

"For the love of all that is holy, Abdiel! I wish you wouldn't do that!"

"But I would speak to you. And I am holy."

"Couldn't you just text me?"

"I don't understand."

Taking a deep breath to still my racing heart, I said, "What do you want to speak to me about?"

"I came to warn you."

A little advance warning that you were coming would have been a good start, I thought, but said, "Warn me about what?"

"We believe Semyaza may be nearby."

My heart started racing again.

"When you say nearby. . ."

"Close."

"How close?"

"In this geographic vicinity."

Close enough. "Do you know why he's here?"

"Given your shared past," Abdiel said, "we cannot rule out the possibility that it has something to do with you. But do not fear. I will be nearby, in the geographic vicinity."

"Good to know," I said. But it wasn't, not with Nosroch and Rogan also in the geographic vicinity.

"I will take my leave of you now," Abdiel said.

"Do me a favor. Next time you stop by could you give me a heads-up?"

"For what purpose would I lift your head upon arrival?"

"A little advance notice."

"Angels don't give advance notice."

"So I've noticed. Thanks for the warning, Abdiel."

A moment later I was alone. Getting down on my hands and knees, I started picking up quarters.

"Are you praying?" Noz asked.

"For crying out loud!" I cried, grabbing my chest.

"Interesting prayer, Grant," Noz said. "You appear agitated. Is something wrong?"

"Let me ask you something, Noz," I said. "Is it possible to put cow bells around angels' necks? Or maybe install some sort of spiritual deadbolt so I can have a little privacy?" When he didn't answer me, I said, "Abdiel stopped by. You just missed him."

If there had been any levity in Noz, it was gone now.

"What was his message?" Noz asked.

"What makes you think he delivered a message? He might have just stopped by to say, 'Howdy.'"

"The message, Grant."

"He warned me that Semyaza was here. In his words, 'In the geographical vicinity.'"

"He has confirmed what I feared," Noz said.

"There's more. I can't tell you how I know this, but Ashmedai, Lilith, and Ornasis are also in the geographic vicinity."

"But you told me—"

"Somehow they escaped."

Noz looked away, contemplating. "Things are moving more quickly than I'd anticipated," he said. "We must accelerate our planning. It is fortunate that I am here. We have much to discuss."

"What?"

"I need your help, Grant," he said.

"To do what?"

"To plan a Spectacle."

CHAPTER
26

"Have you and Grant patched things up?" Jana asked.

"We're good," Sue replied. "It was just a misunderstanding."

The two friends strolled casually down the main artery of the Fashion Valley open-air mall, past name-brand upscale stores: Bloomingdales, Abercrombie and Fitch, Coach, Emporio Armani, and Gucci. They each carried a bag with new shoes, an outing they'd gone on regularly since college. When Sue had moved to North Carolina, it was her shoe-shopping excursions with Jana she'd missed most.

"Do you mind me asking what the disagreement was about?" Jana asked.

"He was just being Grant, trying to protect me."

"Protect you? From what?"

Sue realized the conversation had started down a road she couldn't go down. Jana didn't know about Noz.

"It was nothing, really," Sue said, hoping to put the conversation to rest. "I overreacted. You know how it is when men tell you you can't do something."

"Now you've piqued my interest. What did you want to do?"

Sue laughed dismissively. "I'd rather not say. It's personal."

"This just keeps getting better," Jana said rakishly. "Something you wanted to do with him? Or even better, to him?"

"Nothing like that," Sue said with a smile. They were no strangers to the intimate details of each other's lives. Her eye caught something in a display window. "Oh! I like those."

She stopped to admire a pair of platform wedge sandals.

"So you're really not going to tell me?" Jana said.

"How are things going with you and Rogan?"

Conceding that Sue wasn't going to tell her, Jana checked her watch. "Things are going well enough. He's letting me help him pick out some new clothes."

"So you're playing with your Ken doll," Sue smirked.

"Oh, trust me, Rogan is built much better than Ken."

They continued on their way. A warm Saturday sun was directly overhead and a cool breeze kept the temperature pleasant.

"How well do you know him?" Sue asked.

"When we're out together, he treats me like a lady. Of course he has that reserved military bearing. We haven't gotten into his personal life. Why? Do you know something? He's not married, is he?"

"It's nothing like that. It's just that . . ."

"It's just that what?"

"I think Grant is training again. You know . . ." she leaned closer and whispered, ". . . the Nephilim stuff."

"With Abdiel?"

"That's just it. I don't think so."

"You think it's Rogan?"

"That's the impression I get."

Jana smiled. "Grant lifting weights with Rogan. That's something I'd like to see. But why wouldn't he tell you?"

"He said it's not his information to tell. But I don't think they're working out. It has to do with demons and it scares Grant."

"Demons?" Jana stopped, lost in thought.

"What?" Sue asked. "What do you know?"

"Yesterday Rogan came to the newsroom. He wanted to see footage related to that incident at the airport."

"What was he looking for?"

"He left before I could ask him. But trust me, I'm going to find out."

Rogan approached them wearing khaki pants and a military green t-shirt.

"Sue," Rogan greeted her. "Jana didn't mention you'd be joining us."

"I'm not," Sue said pleasantly. She hefted her bag. "I have what I came for."

Sue and Jana exchanged a glance. Before leaving she leaned close to Jana and whispered.

"Have fun dressing Ken," she said.

Jana and Rogan sat at an outdoor table for two at a coffee shop along the mall's main artery. She'd ordered chai tea; he an espresso. Shopping bags of men's clothing from a half-dozen stores nestled at their feet.

"I really appreciate this," Rogan said. "It'll feel good to wear stylish clothes again."

Jana performed her usual tea ritual, which required two cups, one filled with hot water. In the empty cup she poured two packets of sugar and a long squeeze of lemon, which she'd brought in a baggy, and which she prepared every morning for just such occasions. She stirred the ingredients. Adding the tea bag, she poured the hot water, let it steep to the count of seven, then removed the tea bag.

Rogan watched with fascination.

"There is a way you can repay me," Jana said.

"Oh?" Rogan smiled. "Name it."

"You can answer a few questions."

"All right. Maybe I can save you some time. No, I'm not married and don't have a girlfriend. No, I'm not a serial rapist. And yes, I find you attractive."

"I suppose you think you're charming," Jana said. "Does that sort of thing work on Israeli women?"

Rogan's smile—which was indeed charming—faded.

"Why did you leave the news station so suddenly?" Jana asked.

"You were busy. I didn't want to—"

Jana's chair scraped as she pushed away from the table and gathered her things to leave, her tea untouched.

"Jana, wait. . . ."

"I don't play silly relationship games, Capt. Dorn," she said. "If you want me to stay, be honest with me."

Rogan's eyes narrowed. This was obviously a man who was not easily intimidated, nor was he one to be manipulated by feminine wiles. Jana wouldn't have been surprised if he let her walk away.

"I thought I recognized someone," he said.

It was a start. Jana sat down.

"I take it we're not talking about an old friend."

"Someone very dangerous."

"I'm listening," Jana said.

"Who's listening? The reporter or a friend?"

"I'll let you make that choice. I'll agree to whichever you decide."

"Fair enough," Rogan said. "I choose friend, but if the reporter wants to listen too, I won't object."

"Understood," Jana said.

Rogan took a sip of espresso before continuing. "The man I recognized killed two of my men in Israel."

Jana reacted to the news, but managed to maintain a professional demeanor. "You're certain it was the same man on the airport footage?"

Rogan hesitated. "His appearance was different, but I'm certain he's the one."

Jana studied him. He was telling the truth, but he was hiding something.

"What does this have to do with Grant?" she asked.

"Grant?"

"Just answer the question."

"Is that really what you want to talk about, Jana?"

"All right," she said, getting down to business. "It's obvious the things that happened on those three flights were supernatural, either demons or a rebel angel Spectacle. You said the man you saw on the footage appeared different. Which leads me to believe it might not be the man you're looking for. So, here's my question: Was it the demon you're looking for?"

Rogan sat back in his chair and studied her. He fingered his ring.

"You're remarkable," he said. "It was foolish of me to think that after all you've been through, you wouldn't recognize supernatural forces at work."

Jana ignored the compliment and waited for an answer to her question.

Rogan leaned forward, resting his forearms on the table. He looked at his ring.

"There's something I should tell you," he said.

Jana's cell phone rang. She checked Caller ID.

"It's the station," she said. "Sorry, I have to take this."

She listened, then was standing and gathering up her things. The call ended without any polite niceties. She slipped the phone into her pocket.

"I have to go," she said. "There's been a shooting at an elementary school."

"Let me go with you."

At the request, Jana paused to look at him. He was scooping up his bags.

"I'll stay out of your way," Rogan promised.

"Sorry," she said. "It's against policy. I can drop you off at the station."

"At least fill me in. What's the situation?"

Jana was already walking briskly toward the parking structure.

"I've already told you everything I know," she said over her shoulder.

CHAPTER
27

"GRANT. PICK ME UP AT MY HOTEL. ASHMEDAI JUST ISSUED AN invitation."

I stood in front of a two washing machines at the laundromat; one chugging away on my whites, the other on my colors.

"What do you mean invitation? Are you sure it's them? Are you in danger?"

"Just get over here as fast as you can."

Rogan ended the call.

I stared at the machines, listening to the sloshing. Was there at least time to let them get through the spin cycle? I really didn't want to plunge in up to my elbows, fishing in dirty water for my clothes, and then carry a dripping wet basket to the car.

But Rogan's call sounded urgent.

Grumbling over the inconvenience, I reached for the lid. It was locked.

"Oh, come on!"

I tried the other lid. Locked.

No matter how hard I lifted, pried, or rattled the lids, they wouldn't give.

A matronly woman watched from a few washers down.

"They're locked," she said. "You have to wait for the cycle to finish."

Several rejoinders to her statement of the obvious came to mind, none of them kind.

Snatching up my empty basket I threw it into the trunk of my car and headed downtown.

Thirty minutes later I pulled up to Rogan's hotel. He was waiting for me at the curb with a bulging backpack slung over his shoulder and a clay jar under his arm.

Putting the backpack and jar in the rear seat, he climbed in.

"What took you so long?"

I was in no mood to offer an excuse. Apparently, he didn't want one anyway. He was in full military mode.

"Do you know where Madison Elementary School is?" he said.

I did. It was a mile from the laundromat which I'd just left.

"My old alma mater," I said.

"Good . . . good," he said. "That's useful."

"Are you sure it's them?"

"Positive. It's the Efrat Winery all over again. They targeted a bunch of kids knowing it would get my attention."

As I jumped on the freeway and headed back down Interstate 8, he filled me in, starting with Jana's phone call from the station and ending with a lurid description of three . While he was waiting for me to pick him up, he'd scanned news channels on the television. According to one report, shots were fired at the school. It was on lockdown and a SWAT team had been dispatched.

"We need to make a stop," Rogan said. "Where is the closest military surplus store?"

"No idea," I said.

"I thought you grew up in this area."

"We grew up in two different worlds, Rogan." I handed him my smartphone. "Google it."

He punched in the search command. Scrolled down.

"There's one on Main Street in El Cajon. GI Joe's."

I chuckled.

"Is that important?"

"It sounds like a store for little boys who never grew up. GI Joe was a toy action figure and a Saturday morning cartoon."

"That information isn't relevant," he said. "Restrict your comments to the mission."

Got it. No humor. While he may be model Sayeret Matkal material, he definitely wouldn't fit in with the slinging one-liner superheroes Spiderman and The Avengers.

"So, what's the plan? Are we going to pick up a carton of hand grenades?"

"Do you think they have ordnance? We could use some smoke grenades."

I glanced at him sardonically. He wouldn't recognize a quip if it exploded in front of him. Time to get serious. "Not likely," I said. "Even fireworks are illegal in California."

"Just as well. Loud noises would alarm the police. We don't want bullets to start flying."

No argument here. "You still haven't told me the plan."

"I don't have one yet. Just get me to the store."

While Rogan was calm and methodical, I was a jittery mess. Already I'd failed at hunting your average unsuspecting demon. These demons were ruthless killers who toyed with their victims. Plus, there were three of them and only two of us. And, if that wasn't enough, not only were they expecting us, they were luring us.

I waited in the car while Rogan went into the surplus store.

He came out with a second backpack, a pair of binoculars, and a parabolic listening device.

"Get me as close to the school as you can," he said.

I headed toward Madison Avenue. Ten minutes later I was pulling to the curb a block away from the school where a barricade had been set up. Jana's news van with satellite dish was a short distance away with several other news vans in an area cordoned off for the media.

Rogan jumped out of the car. "Wait here," he said. "It's best if Jana doesn't see you."

I watched as he approached the barricade. Rogan stood there for a few minutes taking in the scene. Her back to us, Jana was talking with her crew.

Rogan whistled. She turned and walked toward him. She didn't appear pleased to see him. After grousing that they were too far away for me to hear what they were saying, I realized there was a listening device on the passenger seat beside me. I picked it up, but before I could figure out how to work the thing, Rogan was walking back to the car.

When he climbed in, he noticed the earbud cord dangling from my ear and grinned.

He reached over. "You turn it on here," he said.

I handed the device to him. "What did she say?"

"There are three of them. A mother and her boyfriend entered the school through the security gate. A janitor met up with them. He had smuggled a gun on campus. There are three dead. The principal, vice-principal, and a security guard. A second security guard is missing. The school went on lockdown and apparently the three forced their way into a classroom. She doesn't know which room. SWAT has set up a command post in the park."

"Kennedy Park," I said, "just past the school."

"SWAT is attempting to make contact, but so far they haven't succeeded."

"How did you explain your presence here?"

"I told Jana I wanted to see her in action."

"And she bought it?"

"It's Jana. She's suspicious, but I'll deal with her later. We need to get closer to the park. Is there some way we can circle around? What's down that street?"

He pointed across the road.

"Only one way to find out."

I put the car in gear and turned left. Halfway down the street, I turned right, then right again, thinking I'd found a way. No such luck. It was a cul-de-sac.

"Close enough," Rogan said.

He handed me the second backpack and told me to put the clay jar in it. He took his backpack, the binoculars, and the listening device and walked toward the house at the end of the street. I followed behind thinking he was going to knock on the door.

This should be interesting, I thought.

Instead, he walked through a side gate that had a sign on it.

Beware of Dog.

Halfway through the yard we startled a sleeping Doberman. Rogan kept walking as the dog bounded toward us, snarling and barking. At the last second, Rogan stepped through the fence. I was right on his heels and the Doberman was right on mine.

Two backyards later, Rogan paused to assess the house that separated us from Madison Ave. Without comment, he handed me his backpack and the listening device. He glanced up at the roof, leaped, grabbed hold of the edge. and pulled himself up.

"Toss me the gear," he said.

I did as instructed.

"Now you."

I laughed. "Get real," I said.

"Toss me your bag," he said.

I tossed it up to him, but there was no way I was going to be able to—

Rogan lay flat on the roof and reached down for me.

"Come on, Grant, we don't have all day."

He wasn't kidding.

I jumped. Our fingers touched.

"Is that all you've got?" he chided. "Put your legs into it. My grandmother can jump higher than that."

I tried again and got no higher. It was high school physical education all over again: me and the school jock.

Looking around, I spotted a My Little Pony child's stool. Standing on it, I jumped and Rogan grabbed my wrist and pulled me onto the roof.

"Stay low," he said.

We crawled to the peak of the roof and the SWAT command post came into view. Using the binoculars and listening device, Rogan eavesdropped on their operations.

"The children are in the third classroom of the third wing," he reported.

Mr. Lippman's room, I thought. *My fourth grade classroom.* But that information wasn't relevant to the mission. I stuck to the mission.

"There's a corridor that runs the length of the school," I told him. "As you're entering the school there are four wings of class-rooms on the left."

"Snipers can't get a clear shot into the room," he reported. "The curtains on the windows are drawn."

Even if they could get a clear shot it wouldn't do them any good. Kill the host and the demon would simply take another body. SWAT didn't know who they were dealing with.

"What are those buildings beyond the main campus?" Rogan asked.

"Portable classrooms. Overcrowding."

"And that structure in the park?"

The Little League field. "It's a refreshment stand."

Rogan dropped the binoculars, the parabolic dish, and pulled out the earbud.

"We have to move," he said.

Grabbing his backpack, he ran down the roof and leaped, landing on his feet like a cat. I inched my way toward the edge, taking care not to slip.

"Toss me your backpack," Rogan said, "then jump."

I tossed the backpack. Didn't jump.

Instead, I sat down, scooted forward until my legs hung over the edge, then jumped.

"Let's go! Let's go!" Rogan snapped. "What's the fastest way to that refreshment stand? Can we take the car? Is there another road out of here?"

"Not that I know of," I said.

"Then we run."

He threw my backpack at me and took off running, disappearing through a brick fence.

I ran after him.

"What's the hurry?" I called out. "It's not like the demons are going anywhere."

"SWAT is putting eyes in the room," he said over his shoulder. "A fiber optic cable through the air conditioning unit. They estimate fifteen minutes. We have to be in and out before that camera is inserted."

We approached a side street—I think it was Terra Lane; I once knew a girl who lived there, a cheerleader—that connected with Madison Ave. It was barricaded at the intersection.

"How much farther?" Rogan cried, entering another backyard.

"Half a block. Fourth Ave. It intersects the park and the high school."

The same high school where Semyaza—aka Myles Shepherd—had revealed himself to me in all his hideous glory a couple years earlier.

We'd reached an unincorporated part of El Cajon and ran through a field of goats. At 4th, we turned right and crossed Madison Ave. flanking another barricade at a crosswalk. We slowed so as not to attract attention, which was a relief to me because I was winded. But we were wasting precious time.

Skirting the edge of the park, we turned in on a walkway that passed tennis courts, a soccer field, and then the Little League baseball field. We stepped through the wall of the refreshment stand. Standing next to a popcorn machine and shelves of candy, we paused long enough for Rogan to lay out a plan of attack.

"Is there a back door to the classroom?" he asked.

"Only one door," I told him. "The far side is a wall of windows."

"Here's what we'll do," he said.

He told me how Sayeret Matkal had used a red Mercedes as a diversion while the main strike force stormed the winery from a different direction.

"You're the red Mercedes, Grant," Rogan said. "They're not expecting you."

The plan was for me to enter the room through an adjoining wall while he approached from the opposite adjoining wall. I would enter first to draw their attention. Once their attention was focused on me I'd give a code phrase and he'd surprise them from behind.

A sound plan, only I was feeling less like a red Mercedes and more like bait.

"You're forgetting," I said, "I can't tell who's demon possessed and who isn't. What if they've changed bodies?"

"We'll assume they haven't," Rogan said. "If they have, I'll alert you when I enter. You attack the one closest to you. I'll take out the other two."

We were also assuming I'd be able to capture a demon, something I hadn't done before. But I had to try, didn't I? Children's lives were at stake.

But there was one more obstacle separating us from the room, the SWAT team. To get to the adjoining rooms, we were going to have cross open areas without being seen, hopefully without getting shot.

"Any questions?" Rogan asked.

Questions? No. Doubts? I was full of them.

I shook my head.

"Then, let's do this," he said.

CHAPTER
28

ROGAN AND I SPRINTED THROUGH THE REFRESHMENT STAND wall, across a cement walkway, through a chain-link fence, and into the closest portable classroom. So far, so good. There were no shouts of alarm.

We crossed into the next portable classroom and, without stopping, into the fourth room on the fourth wing. Here, we split up. Rogan would go straight across. I would go down the wing two classrooms before crossing.

As I passed through the classrooms I was surprised how little they'd changed since I attended elementary school; the noticeable difference between then and now being whiteboards instead of chalkboards and the stack of Chromebook computers on the shelves. In my day NASA had computers, not kids.

Crossing the open area between the fourth and third wings would be the biggest challenge. You could bet SWAT would be in position to target the door of the occupied classroom which meant they would almost assuredly see us. I looked out the window. It was clear. Then, I saw Rogan sprinting toward the third wing.

"You! Stop!"

Rogan disappeared through the wall of the classroom.

I lowered my head and ran as fast as I could.

"There's another one!"

The sound was coming from above. I glanced behind me to see a SWAT team on the roof of the fourth wing. I fully expected to be shot in the back. However, no shot came as I penetrated the wall.

I could only imagine the response of their superiors when the SWAT team reported seeing two men with backpacks running through walls.

I stood in the empty classroom staring at the final wall, a whiteboard with a list of spelling words: brook, drink, phone, ache, wealthy, bottle, lunch. Anger welled inside of me. This was what should be today's challenge for the children in the next room, not death and vengeful demons. Add to that, their survival depended on a writer who had the misfortune of being born Nephilim. Abdiel should be here protecting them, and Michael.

Memories flashed of the Spectacle at 4th and Broadway, downtown San Diego, as four faithful angels watched stoically as a mother and child were targeted for death, forbidden to interfere by the rules of engagement of an eternal heavenly war. How do you explain their lack of intervention to the families of the children in the next room?

My pulse quickened. What lay beyond that wall? A bloodbath?

Taking a deep breath, I prepared myself for the worst possible scenario and breached the wall.

The first thing I saw were two adults lying dead in their own blood. From their clothing it appeared to be the janitor and the mother. The classroom desks had been jammed into the far corner. The children were hunched under them, frightened and shivering. Two more adults—a young female teacher and the missing security guard—were crouched near the door. The boyfriend, dressed in jeans and a black t-shirt, stood over them, his back to me. He held a gun.

I looked for flickering faces, hoping that the urgency of the moment would somehow kick into gear the skill that eluded me. No such luck.

A slight blonde girl dressed in pink jeans and a princess pullover was the first to notice me. She was closest to me under the desks. My sudden appearance startled her. I pressed a finger to my lips, signaling her to keep quiet.

Crawling out from under the desk, she ran toward me and I feared she'd wrap her arms around me, restricting my movement. She pulled up short, just out of arm's reach.

"Look what we have here, Ashmedai," she said with a voice too mature for her age.

The boyfriend turned around. "The Nephilim," he said with a wicked grin. "What a fortunate turn of events. We were coming for you after we dispatched the troublesome Capt. Dorn. Our prince will be pleased. He is eager to add you to his cadre of demons."

"Oh yeah?" I said, unable to come up with a witty comeback. "Well, I have just one thing to say to your prince." Time for the code phrase. "It'll be a cold day in hell before I let you harm these children."

Nothing happened. No Rogan.

I balled my sweaty hands into fists.

"A cold, cold day in hell," I said louder. "So very, very cold."

Ashmedai in the boyfriend's body looked at me like I was insane.

"I can't tell you how *cold* it will be."

Rogan stormed through the wall like a raging linebacker and tackled the possessed boyfriend to the floor. The gun went flying across the room. Pinning him to the ground, Rogan took in the room.

"The security guard," he shouted, "and the girl standing in front of you. You take the girl, I'll get this one and the guard."

He slammed his hand against the boyfriend's back.

"Be still!" he shouted.

I looked at the girl in front of me. She was what? Nine? Ten years old? So innocent. The thought of reaching into her for a demon was unthinkable.

She smiled at me sweetly, took two steps and shoved me with incredible strength, sending me flying backwards. I slammed against the wall.

She came at me. I raised a hand.

"Be still!" I shouted.

She stopped.

Regaining my footing, I grabbed her arm.

"Ow!" she cried. "You're hurting me!"

"Be still!" I shouted again.

But something was wrong. Her arm was soft and weak.

Rogan was extracting the jar from his backpack. "She's not in the girl any longer," he shouted.

I released the girl.

"Then where?"

Rogan didn't reply. He had his hands full with Ashmedai.

"The Nephilim can't see us!" Ashmedai shouted.

Great. Now everyone knew my inadequacies.

"Leave her alone!" The teacher was coming at me from across the room at the same time the security guard was going after Rogan from behind.

"Rogan! Behind you!" I cried.

Rogan looked up.

"In the woman," he yelled, just as the security guard grabbed him and pulled him off Ashmedai, breaking Rogan's grip on the demon.

The teacher was nearly on top of me.

"Be still!" I shouted.

"Please don't hurt me," the teacher said, close to tears.

"Looking for me?" the girl said with a voice not her own.

This was insufferable. How was I going to capture the demon when it kept jumping between hosts?

Rogan brought the security guard down with a leg sweep and was on his feet, positioning himself to take on two demons at once.

"Stay back!" I shouted at the teacher, hoping to isolate the demon.

As I did, the little girl leaped onto my backpack and began clawing at my face. I grabbed her arms, fully aware that the real threat was the demon inside her. I could feel it clawing through my back, trying to get inside of me.

Was it possible to perform a demon-ectomy on oneself? What choice did I have but to try?

I slapped my hand against my chest and shouted, "Be still!"

It worked! The clawing stopped. But what next? Reach into my chest and extract it?

That's when I saw flickering. The teacher's face! There was definite flickering! I hadn't stilled the demon, it had fled the little girl.

The suddenness of my attack caught the demon off-guard. With the little girl still on my back, I flung the teacher against the wall, pinning her with my hand.

"Be still!"

The demon froze. Without releasing the pressure against the teacher's chest, I lowered the little girl to the ground and told her to hide under her desk. She scampered away, joining her classmates.

I turned by attention to the demon-possessed teacher. The anger that flooded me brought clarity and strength; I felt my Nephilim blood quicken. Pressing my hand against the horrified woman's chest, I reached inside.

"Got you!" I extracted the demon. "Lilith, I presume," I said to the squirming hideous creature.

With my free hand I pulled the clay jar from my backpack and placed the demon in the jar, securing the lid.

Exhilaration swept through me. I'd done it.

I turned to help Rogan.

He had managed to subdue Ashmedai once again was extracting him from the boyfriend's chest to place him in the jar as the security guard, having regained his feet, was once again grabbing him from behind.

I ran across the room and slapped my hand against the guard's back.

"Be still!"

I reached into his back and seized the demon. But in the tussle, we knocked the clay jar out of Rogan's hand. It crashed to the floor and shattered.

Ashmedai fled, disappearing through the ceiling.

Ornasis proved to be a slippery little devil and stronger than Lilith. I fought to control him, but he managed to elude my grasp. He too flew through the ceiling.

Exhausted, Rogan slumped atop the boyfriend who had passed out. I knew the feeling.

"We have to get out of here," he said.

At any moment a fiber optic cable was going to protrude from the air conditioning vent.

Running to the door, I threw it open. "Kids, get out of here! Now! Run!"

A stampede ensued. And just as the fiber cable poked into the room, Rogan and I implemented our exit strategy. We stepped into the walls.

———

While Jana's camera crew captured footage of the reunion of parents and children, she completed her interview with the SWAT chief and was coiling the cord of her microphone.

"I'm not telling you a story, mommy," she heard a little girl saying. "They were angels. Angels rescued us."

"We'll talk about this later," her mother said.

Jana approached them. "What makes you think they were angels?" she asked.

The mother shielded the girl. "She doesn't know what she's saying."

"Please," Jana said, "this is important. I promise I won't use her statement on the news."

"It was Rogan," the girl said. "Rogan the angel."

Jana knelt.

"Are you sure?" she said.

"That's what the other angel called him. His name is Rogan."

———

It was well past midnight before we stepped out of the elementary school wall. All was quiet. The SWAT command post was gone, so too were the news crews.

When we reached my car, I handed Rogan the jar containing Lilith. While we had saved the children, we'd failed to capture two of the three demons. It was only a matter of time before more lives would be endangered.

We rode back to his hotel in silence.

After dropping Rogan off, I returned to the laundromat to get my clothes. The lids of the two washing machines were open, the tubs were empty. While there was a lost and found bin on a back table, my clothes weren't in it.

Considering the events of the day, the loss of my wardrobe was a small price to pay.

"I saw flickering faces," I muttered with satisfaction. "I captured a demon."

I drove home.

CHAPTER
29

A MILD OCEAN BREEZE TEASED THE LINEN CURTAINS OF Rogan's screenless window. He was on the fifty-second push-up of his morning routine when he heard someone knocking on the door. He ignored it.

His first week in the room he answered the door whenever someone knocked, but soon grew weary of it. He had better things to do than to deal with a jealous wife looking for her husband, a jealous husband looking for his wife, a sailor who had previously hooked up with a girl in this room, or a disoriented drunk.

"Rogan? It's me, Jana."

He rolled over and looked at his watch. *5:30 a.m.* After the previous day's battle at the elementary school, he'd slept in and was just starting his routine.

Grabbing a towel, he opened the door.

Jana glanced at the sweat-soaked shirt clinging to his chest.

"Sorry for my appearance," he said. "Morning calisthenics."

He wanted to apologize for the room . . . not just the room, the whole building. Standing in a classless hallway was the classiest woman he'd ever known, stunning in a periwinkle blue ankle length dress with sleeve ties.

"I wish you'd called first," he said. "I would have met you somewhere."

"I know you're an early riser. Are you going to invite me in?"

He stepped aside.

She strolled in and looked around, impressed by the bed with its taut blanket and hospital corners. At the desk she ran a fingertip across the title of his copy of the Tanakh.

"Interesting Mexican pottery collection," she said, noticing the line of jars set against the wall. She bent over to pick one up.

"Um . . . I'd appreciate it, if you didn't," he said, stepping between her and the jars.

Her eyebrows raised. "Is there a story behind the pottery?"

"Is that what you've come for? A story?"

"Actually," she said brightly, "I thought we could go out to breakfast. Sort of pick up where we left off at the mall. I can wait for you downstairs while you take a . . ."

Her voice trailed off when she realized there were no facilities in the room.

"A communal bathroom down the hall," Rogan explained. "How about if I catch up with you at the restaurant?"

The thought of her waiting in the lobby of a seedy hotel was unacceptable.

"There's quaint breakfast nook a block away," she said. "We can meet there."

She gave him directions.

While he showered and shaved, Rogan pondered Jana's early morning appearance. She was up to something. An unannounced visit was obviously her attempt to put him off balance. Was this about yesterday? What did she know?

It was possible Grant had said something to Sue. If so, it wasn't unlikely that Sue would have confided in Jana.

It was also possible that she'd seen SWAT footage of the schoolroom. Had the fiber optic camera caught a glimpse of him and Grant?

But then it might be something as simple as a further explanation as to why he'd followed her to the elementary school, or why he'd ducked out of the newsroom after viewing the airport footage.

Whatever her motives, it was a distraction. His failure to capture Ashmedai and Ornasis infuriated him. Twice he'd had Ashmedai in his grasp. Add to that he was no closer to finding their prince, Nosroch. And it was only a matter of time before the Archangel Michael discovered his location and demanded the return of Solomon's ring. Game over. Without the ring, all of his efforts to this point were for naught.

As Rogan left the hotel for the restaurant, his military training argued that Jana was an unnecessary entanglement. He should just walk away and focus on the mission.

"You clean up nicely," Jana said as he pulled out a chair and sat opposite her.

Rogan was wearing a shirt and pants she'd picked out for him at the mall.

He'd found her sitting at a table for two tucked away in a corner of the cozy restaurant. It wasn't the kind of place he would have frequented on his own—with embroidered white tablecloths, watercolor paintings of country scenes on the walls, and curtains edged with lace—but it was a perfect setting for Jana, who looked positively beatific.

A matronly waitress with an ample waistline appeared and Rogan ordered coffee.

"I apologize for interrupting your workout," Jana said. "Do you exercise every morning?"

Rogan described his routine—the calisthenics and the run by the bay.

His coffee arrived.

"I know so little about you," Jana said after the waitress left. "What do you do after you exercise? How do you fill your days?"

"I manage to keep busy." He picked up a menu. "Have you eaten here before? What's good?"

When she didn't respond to his question, he looked up. Jana was staring at him.

"Why are you still here?" she asked.

"I haven't eaten yet."

"Why are you still here in San Diego?" she clarified.

"Are you growing tired of me?"

"You're not consulting with the Navy," she said. "You don't ask about things that interest tourists. And I've been around military men enough to know that a man of your rank would have certain obligations."

"I think I'll order the biscuits and gravy," Rogan said, setting down the menu.

"Why were you at the elementary school?"

"I told you. I wanted to see you in action."

"You've done that. That's how we met, remember?" Jana said. "I was reporting on the SEAL training, you were watching. Would you care to amend your answer?"

The waitress came to take their order. Rogan indicated his choice. Jana said she was fine with tea. When they were alone, Jana continued staring at him as though he was a puzzle to solve.

"Does this have anything to do with Grant being Nephilim?" she said.

"Nephilim?" Rogan scoffed. "Jana, there haven't been Nephilim since ancient times. What has Grant been telling you?"

She sat back and folded her arms, giving him a don't-mess-with-me glare.

"The three airline flights," she said. "You started to tell me something at the mall and we were interrupted."

Rogan sat back and folded his arms, mirroring her posture. Things had changed since the mall. Focus on the mission.

"Yesterday," Jana ventured. "The threat to the children simply vanished. One minute they were being held hostage in a room with dead bodies on the floor; the next, the threat was gone and they ran out of the classroom. SWAT could offer no reasonable explanation."

"I shouldn't have to remind you of that which you know so well," he replied. "The military is rarely forthcoming with facts, especially with the press."

Jana smiled, relaxed, stirred her tea, and took a sip.

"You'll like this," she said brightly, her demeanor changing. "One little girl I talked to who was in the room said they were rescued by angels."

"Sounds like a little girl with a big imagination."

"She said she even knew the angel's name."

Rogan grew uneasy.

"Do you know what she told me? She told me the angel's name was Rogan."

Checkmate.

Rogan fingered the ring. Jana had put all the pieces together. She knew about Grant, which came as no surprise. She knew that hostile demons were in the area. And she'd placed him in the schoolroom.

He hesitated, then leaned forward and removed the ring, showing her the corresponding tattoo beneath it.

"I am a member of an elite team of Sayeret Matkal, a blood descendant of Solomon," he said, keeping his voice low. "We specialize in the supernatural. Our commander is the Archangel Michael."

Jana unfolded her arms.

"This ring," he held it out to show her, "was once given to Solomon by the archangel. It gave him, and now me, the power of Nephilim, power over demons."

Jana showed interest. Nothing he said appeared to surprise her.

"You're here on a mission?" she asked.

"You were right about the airline flights," Rogan said. "There were three demons onboard, Ashmedai, Ornasis, and Lilith. I captured them during a mission in Israel when they kidnapped a busload of children, but only after they killed two of my men. I thought I'd disposed of them. Somehow, they escaped."

"You saw them on the airport footage arriving in San Diego. What are they doing here?"

"Coming after me."

"So yesterday, at the elementary school . . ."

"They knew putting children in danger, just as they had in Israel, would draw me out."

"But you were in San Diego long before they arrived. What brought you here?"

Rogan smiled. Nothing escaped this woman's notice. "A vow to avenge the deaths of my men. I tracked the demons' prince, their handler, to San Diego. I have yet to find him."

"And yesterday, you captured them again?"

"We managed to capture Lilith. She's in one of the pottery jars you saw in my apartment. Ashmedai and Ornasis got away."

"We? You said, we."

It was no slip of the tongue. There were no secrets any longer.

"Grant and I."

"Grant knows about you and the ring? For how long?"

"Since the dinner when you introduced us."

CHAPTER
30

Opening the dresser in my bedroom, fresh from the laundromat for the second time in as many days, I placed the clean underwear in the drawer and closed it. I hung up two shirts and a pair of pants in the closet. Besides what I was wearing, they were the only clothes I had left. I had only myself to blame. Had I not waited so long to do the laundry, my loss would have been a lot less.

I was walking down the hallway for a trip to the mall to replace the lost articles of clothing when the front door flew open.

"Grant Alexander Austin!"

Jana stormed in. She was angrier than I'd ever seen her. She hadn't used my middle name since our epic quarrel in high school when we broke up.

"After all we've been through," she shouted, "why didn't you tell me about Rogan?"

She stood in front of me, hands on hips. I was a deer in headlights, afraid to move in the face of certain disaster.

Rogan trailed in behind her. "Sorry, Grant," he said. "She figured it out on her own."

I offered her the same line I'd given Sue. "It wasn't my information to—"

"And the two of you," she cried, cutting me off, "at the restaurant when I tried to get Grant to reveal he was Nephilim. I feel like a fool. Well, I hope you had a good laugh."

"Jana, it wasn't like that," I said.

"Speak for yourself," Rogan said. "I thought it was funny."

Jana wasn't amused.

"Sword fighting at the naval base," she said, turning on me. "Jumping through membranes. And demon hunting, Grant? Demon hunting? Does Sue know? Of course she doesn't; she would have told me."

"Know what?" Sue said coming through the open door.

I moaned. This couldn't get any worse.

"Grant and Rogan have been hunting *demons*," Jana's voice rose a pitch higher. "Rogan has a whole line of jars in his hotel room filled with demons they've captured."

Sue gasped. "Grant, is that true? How could you do something so dangerous without first talking it over with me?" She was more hurt than angry.

"Rogan I can understand," she said. "He's . . ."

She looked at him.

". . . well, he's built for it, and trained. While you're—"

"Go ahead and say it," I said. "Here, let me help you—weak, scrawny, uncoordinated, clumsy."

"I was going to say a writer," Sue snapped.

"I think Grant's description of himself is more to the point." Rogan was enjoying this, but he was the only one finding this humorous.

"So that's what you wouldn't tell me?" Sue asked.

"It wasn't my information to tell!"

That was my excuse and I was sticking to it.

Jana chimed in. "Rogan has a magic ring that gives him Nephilim powers," she told Sue.

"It's not magic," Rogan objected. "It's endowed with angelic powers. It was given to Solomon by—"

"Once again I appear to have come at a bad time," observed a new voice. Nosroch.

Just when I thought it couldn't get any worse.

My heart leaped into my throat as my gaze bounced between Noz and Rogan.

"Yes . . . yes," I stammered, approaching Noz. "Bad time. Really bad time. A lot of personal stuff going on here. It would bore you. You need to leave."

"You're the angel that followed us after the Spectacle," Jana said, recognizing him.

"His name is Nosroch," Sue informed her.

Jana blinked. "You know him?"

"Nosroch!" Rogan cried, drawing his sword.

The appearance of the sword intrigued Noz, but didn't seem to concern him. His gaze moved down the length of the blade to Rogan's hand and the ring.

"So you're the one," he said.

While Jana and Sue couldn't see the sword, Rogan's stance, and the vengeful fire in his eyes, told them all they needed to know.

Rogan glared at me. "Nosroch in your apartment? It all makes sense now," he thundered. "Knocking the jar from my hand, letting Ornasis slip from your grip. That was no accident. It was intentional."

"How can you say that?" I protested.

"Grant, why didn't you tell me you knew this man?" Noz asked.

"Because he knew I'd kill you," Rogan said before I could answer.

"Put your sword away," Noz said. "I will not fight you."

"Grant Austin, I would speak with you," Abdiel said, appearing.

"Lord, have mercy," I moaned.

Abdiel's gaze took in the room in an instant. His sword appeared, an imposing silver blade.

"Capt. Dorn, what are you doing here?" he said. "Michael is eager to speak with you."

Rogan wasn't listening; his white-hot focus on Nosroch was unwavering.

"And Grant," Abdiel said. "Once again I find you consorting with rebel angels. Do you not see his black sword? I thought you would have learned your lesson with Belial."

"Step aside, angel," Rogan said to Abdiel. "This one's mine."

With a war cry that would curdle the nerves of a host of battle-hardened warriors, he attacked.

Before I knew it, my sword was out. Stepping between Rogan and Noz, our weapons clashed with an explosion of light.

"Grant, stand down!" Rogan shouted.

"You would defend Nosroch?" Abdiel said.

Rogan swung again, and again I blocked his blow.

"Noz," I said, my arms tingling from the force of Rogan's attack, "I think it's best if you leave."

"As you wish, Grant," he said, and disappeared.

With two drawn swords still in the room, I kept my guard up. Then, there was only one. Abdiel's sword vanished.

He looked at me. Didn't say anything. He didn't have to. The disappointment on his face communicated his feelings all too well.

He disappeared.

That left me and Rogan.

His chest was heaving. His eyes were filled with loathing and betrayal. The tip of his sword was circling a short distance from my face.

"Is this what you want, Rogan? Do you really want to fight me? Abdiel just left. Michael can't be far behind."

"The pretense has been stripped away, Austin," Rogan spat.

"Drop your sword, Rogan," I pleaded. "Let me explain."

"Explain what? Your true allegiance is clearly evident. A word of warning. Don't get between me and Nosroch again. I will not hesitate to go through you to get to him."

Without lowering his guard, he backed out of the apartment, leaving me alone with Jana and Sue.

"Grant," Jana said, "What's going on here? Not telling me about Rogan was one thing, but you've been associating with a rebel angel since the Spectacle? And, Sue," she turned abruptly to her friend, "you knew about Nosroch?"

Her eyes filled with angry tears.

"Jana," Sue pleaded.

Jana waved her off. "I can't deal with this now."

She closed the door behind her.

It was just Sue and me.

Wrapping her arms around my waist, she laid her head against my chest.

"Are you all right?" she said.

I pressed my cheek against her hair. My heart was pounding, my hands sweating. It was going to take a while to calm down, to sort through the collapsed house of cards that was my life. But this was a good start.

"And here I thought I was going to brighten your day with some good news."

"Holding you is all the good news I need."

"How sweet," she said, releasing me and giving me a peck on the lips.

She started toward the door.

"You're leaving? What about the good news?"

"Later," she said. "I'd better catch up with Jana and try to explain."

The door closed and then it was just me.

This whole fiasco had started and ended in minutes, leaving me alone with my to-do list for the day, a list with only two items on it. One had already been checked off as completed: Go to laundry. That left: Go shopping for clothes. Not on the list was: Disappoint a close friend, make an enemy of Sayeret Matkal, and get caught in the middle between two eternal enemies.

There are days when you look back on events and think that never in your wildest dreams could you have imagined what just happened. This was one of those days.

———

Later that evening, now that I was free to tell Sue how I lost my clothes without having to dance around the truth, she took me shopping. It helped having her along. It also gave me the opportunity to tell her about my training with Rogan and the events at the elementary school while she was distracted my size, color, and fashion. It wasn't that she disapproved of my Nephilim activities—especially when it came to rescuing children—what she disapproved of was that I'd kept it a secret from her.

Apparently women prefer worrying themselves sick while a loved one is battling evil, over hearing about it afterwards and being deprived of worrying themselves sick.

Shopping also gave Sue an opportunity to fill me in on what happened after she left my apartment.

"Jana wasn't home when I got there," she said. "She'd gone

after Rogan since they'd driven to your apartment in her car. She caught up with him walking down Main Street."

"What . . . he was going to walk all the way downtown?"

Sue shrugged. "Anyway, she convinced him to let her drive him to his hotel, and along the way they talked."

"Don't tell me," I said. "She's taking his side."

The two packaged dress shirts Sue was holding flopped to her side. "Grant Austin, for someone so smart, you can really be dumb at times. She told him that she trusted you and that he should trust you too."

Sue was right. I felt dumb.

"Rogan broke it off with her," Sue said. "He told her her relationship with you was toxic."

"That's what he said? Toxic? How did she take it?"

"She's hurt, angry."

Sue handed me three pairs of pants and directed me to the dressing rooms, where I tried them on and modeled them for her. Had I been alone, I would have bought them without trying them on. She shook her head at all three and we kept shopping.

"Were you able to patch things up with her?" I asked.

"I apologized for not telling her about Nosroch. Then we talked about how dumb men can be."

A common theme. At least I had company.

"Is she talking to me?" I asked.

"In Jana's words: 'Grant will always be Grant.'"

I didn't know what that meant, but it sounded as though I was off the hook.

As we were standing in the checkout line, Sue said, "Oh, on a different note, I was talking to a couple of students about you. They're both double majors, history and literature. They've read your book, *The Divine Warrior*, and want to meet you. I thought

I'd bring them by your apartment tomorrow and you can sign their books."

"That's the good news you wanted to tell me?"

"Isn't it? I thought writers loved being fawned over by adoring readers."

"I don't know," I said. "Now isn't a good time."

I wasn't feeling very writerly.

"It'll be good for you," Sue persisted. "It'll take your mind off things for a while."

"I guess it'll be all right."

"Great. Expect us tomorrow around one o'clock."

CHAPTER
31

THE NEXT MORNING I AWOKE FEELING DRAINED BY THE CATA-
clysmic emotions of the showdown in my living room. As I showered—gratefully without company—I consoled myself with the
thought that I no longer had to live a life of secrets. But my sim-
pler lifestyle came at a cost.

Try as I might, I couldn't get Abdiel's look of disappointment
out of my mind. Then again, if I had it to do it all over, I still
wouldn't have told him about Noz. Abdiel's reaction to seeing the
rebel angel in my living room was exactly what I'd feared it would
be. He'd had the same reaction the time he'd walked in on me
and Belial. And while he'd been proved right about Belial, he was
wrong about Noz . . . maybe.

The jury was still out. Every time new evidence came to light
casting suspicion on Noz, upon further examination it had proved
unfounded. He was likeable enough, but that could be an act. I'd
been fooled before. He was persistent; which was admirable if he
was good, despicable if he was bad. I guess for me it came down to
the good ol' American way—innocent until proven guilty. Good
for a national legal system, but would it hold up in the court

of heavenly intrigue where, according to Abdiel, everything was either holy or not?

Rogan was a different matter. Where did he come off accusing me of deliberately sabotaging Ashmedai's capture? He hadn't even given me a chance to explain. For him it was guilt by association. The man was obsessed with revenge, plain and simple. Even so, he was the only other person who knew what it was like to be Nephilim. I was going to miss that.

Which brought be back to Abdiel. Why hadn't he summoned Michael immediately? He could have done it with a word and Rogan would have had no choice but to surrender the ring.

Something wasn't adding up.

When I walked into the living room, Nosroch was waiting for me.

"That was quite a convocation yesterday," he said.

"The only one missing was Semyaza."

Nosroch didn't see the humor in the comment. Either he wasn't big on sarcasm or I'd struck a nerve.

"Why did Capt. Dorn attack me?"

"He thinks you command Ashmedai, Ornasis, and Lilith."

Nosroch nodded, putting together the pieces. "When you challenged me about them, it was Capt. Dorn who was the source of your misinformation. Why have you not corrected him?"

"And say what? That I've been meeting secretly with one of Lucifer's lieutenants and he told me he wasn't their prince?"

"A little heavy on the sarcasm today, Grant. You're frightened."

Finally, somebody got me.

"Grant, I want you to know that I'm aware your association with me has put a strain on your relationships. Hopefully, in time, all will be resolved."

I got the impression he wasn't talking only about *my* relationships.

"You and Abdiel," I said.

"It's been eons since I've seen him. Before the rebellion we were brothers in arms. Me, Abdiel, Michael, Semyaza . . . Lucifer."

I was with him right up to the point when he said Semyaza.

"What do you want, Noz?"

"Before we get to that, I want to tell you how much I appreciate that you defended me. Your actions indicate that you trust me. For that, I am grateful."

I'd acted instinctively. But now that he mentioned it, I realized he had a point. Had I not believed he was being honest with me, I never would stepped between him and Rogan.

"Now to the matter at hand," Noz said.

A movement in the ceiling corner caught my eye. It was a demon in all his slimy glory, hanging there, looking at me. I took a step back. There was only one of them. Had there been more, I would have drawn my sword.

"Grant, there is nothing to fear," Noz said soothingly. "This is my son, Elihu."

"What is he doing here?" I asked without taking my eyes off the demon.

"Given recent events," Noz said, "I was hoping you'd reconsider my proposal. I believe you know you can trust me."

"You want that to possess me," I said, just to be clear.

"A mutually beneficial cohabitation," Noz said. "You will afford Elihu a measure of peace and he will provide you with assurances as to the sincerity of our cause where words alone are inadequate."

"No."

"Grant, you've demonstrated you trust me, now act on that trust. And of all men, you should be sympathetic to Elihu's situation. As he is now, you soon will be. Someday you will appreciate a similar act of kindness."

"Look, I have no doubt Elihu was a nice guy when he walked the earth. Call it what you will—mutually beneficial cohabitation—but it's demonic possession pure and simple and it's not going to happen."

"You realize, of course, I don't need your permission."

Was that a threat? It felt like a threat.

"You told me the decision was mine to make," I said. "If you're the angel I think you are, you'll respect it."

Noz stood there looking at me. This wasn't the outcome he was hoping for. I braced myself for what would happen next.

Nosroch made a gesture toward the demon. It vanished through the ceiling. He looked at me and said, "Grant, reconciliation is founded on bravery and sacrifice."

He vanished.

Sue and her students arrived promptly at one o'clock.

The two young men were clean-cut. They both wore dress shirts and Dockers. They were carrying copies of my book. Sue provided the introductions.

"Grant, this is Stephen and Tib."

Stephen was the taller of the two with pronounced dimples. Tib was wiry with a shock of unruly black hair he kept brushing out of his eyes. They were both grinning in a way I hadn't seen in a long time, like they were meeting someone famous. Little did they know.

I shook their hands and invited them in.

"Tib," I said. "There has to be a story behind that name."

"Short for Tiberius," he said sheepishly. "Both my parents were history majors."

They sat on the sofa, one on each side of Sue, both of them hyperconscious about the arrangement, the way young men get whenever in close proximity to an attractive woman. Sue was oblivious to it. I was content to let them have the moment, remembering what it felt to be that young. I grabbed a dining room chair and sat in front of them. I signed their books.

"You have questions," I said.

They asked the usual: What was it like being a writer? Did I write every day? Where did I get my ideas? Did I always want to be a writer? How long did it take before I got my first publishing contract?

While I had been dreading this meeting, I found myself caught up in their enthusiasm. It was refreshing to talk about something other than demons and angels and spiritual warfare.

Sue sat between them smiling; proud of them, proud of me.

"What was it like working with the President of the United States?" Stephen asked.

I asked them if they'd read my book, *Lionheart: The R. Lloyd Douglas Story.* They hadn't, though they'd heard about it.

"Grant was awarded the Pulitzer Prize for that book," Sue said.

"Which has since been taken away," I added in all honesty, "when the truth behind his presidency came out."

"Still, the Pulitzer Prize jurors wouldn't have given it to you had it not been a quality piece of writing," Sue said.

"There is still some value to the book from a historical standpoint," I pointed out. "It's an interesting study of how presidents attempt to shape their legacy. If you'd like, I think I have a couple of copies I can give to you."

Sue beamed as the boys smiled at the offer and I excused myself to get the books that were buried in back of my bedroom closet. Something troubled me as walked down the hallway, something about Stephen's smile. It wasn't right. Maybe it was my imagination, but I thought I saw a glimpse of mockery in it that was unsettling.

Sliding the mirror panel closet door to one side, I got down on my hands and knees to move aside boxes of old income tax returns and research books, still troubled by Stephen's reaction. I told myself it was nothing, probably just a flash of testosterone that is prevalent on college campuses among male academics.

As I pulled up cardboard flaps and extracted two books from the box in the back corner, I concluded that my old insecurities were showing, and that I was being foolish to feel intimidated by an underclassman. Even if I had detected a hint of mockery in his smile, it had only been a brief flickering—

Alarmed, I sat back on my heels.

Only once had I seen the tell-tale sign of demon possession, and that was at the elementary school in the heat of battle. To think that because I'd done it once I could do it all the time flew in the face of experience. Seeing swords . . . walking through walls . . . seeing cloaked angels . . . all these abilities that I could now do with ease had sputtering starts. Had I really just invited a demon-possessed man into my—

Sue!

She was sitting next to him right now! And if he was possessed and that was a mocking smirk I saw, the demon knew who I was.

I scrambled to my feet. A new thought struck me.

Or . . . the man sitting next to Sue was simply an insufferable underclassman and I was getting all worked up over nothing.

How could I know for sure? If I went back out there and saw nothing, would it mean there was no demon, or that I couldn't see the demon?

Regardless, I had to assume there was a demon in my living room, which meant capturing him before he could hurt Sue. But even if I could see him, then grab hold of him, what would I put him in? Just my luck I was fresh out of Mexican pottery jars. I searched the closet and bedroom for some sort of container.

Finding nothing, I searched the adjoining bathroom and came up with a plastic prescription bottle with child-proof lid and a Band-Aid tin. Too small. There were Tupperware containers in the kitchen, would they work?

"Grant?" Sue called. "Did you get lost?"

"The books were deeper in the closet than I thought," I shouted back. "I'll be right out."

I paced in a nervous circle trying to figure out what to do. I needed help. I needed to call Rogan. There were two problems with that plan. First, my cell phone was on the dining room table. I suppose I could get it, make some excuse about needing to make an important phone call and then retreating to the bedroom to make the call. But even if I succeeded in doing that, there was the second problem. Rogan thought I was the enemy.

I stopped pacing. Time for a reality check—

I was on my own and Sue needed me. One other thing: I was Nephilim. What was it the professor told me? *Hupernikomen. We are more than conquerors.*

I tucked both books under my arm and headed down the hallway.

"Took you long enough," Sue said as I entered the room. "Tell the truth. Did you climb out the window and go to a bookstore to buy them?"

I forced a smile. "Not possible," I said, keeping my tone light. "They're out of print."

Second reality check—

Sue was unharmed. As for my ability to see demon possession—the good news was that my Nephilim abilities had kicked in; the bad news was, there were two of them. Both boys were possessed. The really bad news—I recognized them. Ashmedai and Ornasis.

I handed the books to them, first to Stephen/Ashmedai, then

to Tib/Ornasis. At this point my plan was to play along, to give no indication I could see them, let alone recognize them, and if possible get Sue safely away from them.

Stephen opened the cover to the title page. "It's already signed," he said. "Thank you, Mr. Austin, you're the best."

I wanted to smash his face.

"Are you just going to stand there, Grant?" Sue said.

I sat down in the dining room chair in front of them.

"Tell us about the Pulitzer Prize ceremony," Stephen prompted. "That must have been an amazing experience. Were you nervous?"

So focused was I on thoughts of getting Sue out of there, the question sounded like it came from the back of an auditorium. I was lucky to have heard it at all.

"The ceremony," I repeated, forcing myself not to look at Sue, if I looked at her I was lost.

I glanced aside, the way people do when they're remembering an event.

"The ceremony was . . . surreal. . . ." I said. "All at once amazing, yet nothing like how you imagine it's going to be."

When I looked back, I saw Stephen's face flickering. There was a moment of recognition, enough to create a hiccup in my narration, and the next thing I knew Tib sprang from the sofa and slapped me so hard it knocked me out of my chair.

Sue screamed. "Tib! What are you—"

Before I could do anything to stop him, Tib backhanded her into silence.

Sue slumped against the sofa, a hand to her reddened cheek, confused and frightened.

"They're possessed!" I found myself shouting. "These are the demons Ashmedai and Ornasis."

"The great Grant Austin," Ashmedai mocked, standing over

me. Then, in the voice of Stephen, "Thank you so much for signing my book, Mr. Austin! You're the best!"

He kicked me in the gut and I doubled over.

"Let Sue go," I wheezed. "She has nothing to do with this."

"That's where you're wrong," Ashmedai said. "She has everything to do with this. It was our prince who informed us that the professor's lap dog was your weakness."

"Just let her go and I'll give you what you want."

"You would presume to know what we want?" Ashmedai said.

"You want to turn me into a demon."

"Grant, no!" Sue whimpered.

"All in good time, Nephilim," Ashmedai said.

"You also want Rogan," I said, "and Lilith returned to you."

"You're not as dumb as you look," Ashmedai replied.

They were careful to keep out of reach to prevent any attempt to capture them. While I made no attempt to stand, I did manage to scoot over to Sue's feet, positioning myself between her and them.

"I know where Rogan is keeping Lilith," I said. "Leave Sue here and I'll take you to him."

"In your car? Would you take the freeway?" Ashmedai asked.

"Of course. I could have you there in thirty minutes."

"Much too dangerous, wouldn't you say, Ornasis?" Ashmedai said.

"You'd never get me in one of those death traps," Ornasis replied.

"What do you think, Sue?" Ashmedai said. "Is it true that innocent people are sometimes killed in car crashes? Wives, perhaps? Children? Maybe even *professor's* wives and children?"

They were toying with us.

"Here's an idea," Ashmedai said. "How about if Ornasis takes Sue for a ride?"

It was just the kind of threat you'd expect from a demon. Ornasis could crash the car, killing Sue and Tib, and leap into someone else's body unharmed.

"You want me to call Rogan," I said.

"Now why didn't I think of that?" Ashmedai ragged.

"He won't come. Maybe you didn't get the memo, but we're not exactly on speaking terms."

Apparently being facetious only went one way in this conversation. Ornasis took a threatening step toward Sue. I raised my hand ready to order him to be still and he backed off. He knew he couldn't possess her and at the moment he couldn't get close to her without me ripping his slimy self out of Tib's chest.

"Make the call," Ashmedai said, in a tone that indicated the banter portion of our afternoon session was over.

Both of my phones were on the dining room table; my personal smartphone and the burner phone that I used only with Rogan. I stood and reached for Sue.

"Stay close to me," I said.

"She stays on the sofa," Ornasis growled.

"Fine. Then you bring the phone to me."

"I'm not your lackey."

"Then we are at an impasse. I'm not leaving Sue's side."

Ashmedai glared at me. Then, he made a barely perceptible nod and Ornasis backed away. So close did I keep Sue to me our transit to the table was awkward and halting, like we were in a slow-motion three-legged race.

I picked up the burner phone and punched the only number that was programmed into it. The phone rang on the other end. Once, twice . . . four times. There was no recording, no voicemail.

I tried again with the same result.

"I told you he wasn't speaking to me," I said.

JACK CAVANAUGH

"One way or the other, you get Rogan over here or this little meeting will come to a sudden, bloody end," Ashmedai said.

"Try using your smartphone," Sue suggested.

It took both of us to make the call. Sue read Rogan's phone number from the burner phone while I dialed.

Still no answer.

"With Rogan on the run, he's not going to answer an unrecognizable number," I said.

"Given the fact that he knows you're trying to reach him," Sue replied, "he's got to suspect it's you calling, doesn't he?"

The demons were growing impatient. Rogan wasn't going to answer. I had to come up with an alternative strategy. I could back Sue into the narrow kitchen and take a stand at the only entrance. It wasn't much of a plan, but it was our only option. There were two demons and I had two hands. Our chances of success were about as good as Butch Cassidy and the Sundance Kid charging into an open courtyard, guns blazing. They died in a hail of bullets.

I snatched up the burner phone and dialed again while at the same time signaling Sue with my eyes to start moving toward the kitchen.

"You have a lot of nerve calling me, Austin," Rogan said, answering the phone.

Without giving him an excuse to end the call, I spoke the words I knew would get his attention. "Ashmedai and Ornasis. They're here. In my apartment. I need help."

"You dance with the devil, you pay the consequences," he replied.

"Rogan, listen to me. You need to get over here right now."

"That's low, even for you," he replied. "I don't know what you promised your demon buddies, but you're on your own. You disappoint me, Austin. I would expect a trap to be more imaginative."

"Rogan, I'm serious! Please, hear me out!"

But there was no reason for him to listen.

Sue grabbed the phone from me.

"Rogan, this is Sue," she said, her voice trembling. "It's all my fault. I brought them over here. They possessed two of my students and I didn't . . ." Sobs choked off the rest of the sentence.

I didn't hear what Rogan said to her, but Sue nodded and handed the phone back to me.

"They want Lilith," I told him.

There was a pause, a long, gut-twisting pause.

"It will take time to get the jar and then get to your apartment," Rogan said.

"How long—"

I was speaking to a dead phone. Dropping the device onto the table, I turned to Ashmedai.

"He's coming. But it'll take time."

"How long?"

"At least thirty minutes, probably more."

"More than enough time to make your death a painful one," Ashmedai said, "after which I will deliver your wretched demon self to our prince."

"But first we're going to have a little fun with your lady friend," Ornasis added.

"Don't touch her!" I shouted. "I did what you asked."

"We wouldn't think of touching her," Ornasis said with a wicked grin. "Once I enter you, you will."

I began backing Sue into the kitchen. Ornasis and Ashmedai came toward us like jackals closing in for the kill.

"While it's true we cannot possess Sue—" Ashmedai said. Turning to Ornasis, "Shame, isn't it? Imagine all the naughty little things Lilith could teach her." Back to me, "—you, on the other hand, Grant Austin, have been possessed so often you should post a 'Space Available' sign on your forehead. Once Ornasis has taken over that scrawny body of yours, the things he will make you do to Sue will torment you for eternity."

Behind me Sue was frantically opening drawers, looking for something big and sharp to defend herself. I retreated a few steps.

The two demons in student bodies continued advancing. As they reached the narrow threshold that divided the dining area from the kitchen, they had to close ranks. I could let them come to me, or—

In a rage I lunged at them, my arms extended, my hands aiming for their chests.

I shouted, "Be—"

Anticipating my attack, Ashmedai stepped back, turned, and used my momentum to throw me across the room. I crashed against the wall and fell into a heap on the floor. Using the agility of the young body he possessed, he closed the distance between us before I could recover.

That's when Rogan flew out of the wall, bowling over a surprised Ashmedai. Landing on top of him, Rogan slammed a hand against the boy's chest and shouted, "Be still!"

Startled, Ornasis swung around just as Sue swung at him with a knife. Her swing was wild and missed him.

What happened next was a replay of the struggle in the elementary schoolroom. Rogan had Ashmedai pinned and was reaching into his backpack for the clay jar. Ornasis came at him from behind. I managed to catch my breath and lunge at Ornasis, slapping my hand against his back.

"Be still!" I shouted.

The demon froze.

Reaching into Tib's body I held the wriggling Ornasis as Rogan extracted Ashmedai and shoved him into the jar. This time my grip on the slippery Ornasis was like a vice. Rogan held out the jar and I shoved Ornasis into it, hoping that two demons sharing one jar would be an uncomfortable fit because they were going to be in it for a long time.

Rogan shoved the lid in place.

Demon free, Stephen and Tib lay dazed on the carpet.

Sue emerged from the kitchen, the knife in her hand leading the way.

"It's all right," I told her. "Ashmedai and Ornasis can't hurt you now."

She ran to me, arms outstretched, knife in hand and I had to back away to keep from being inadvertently stabbed. Sheepishly, she tossed the knife onto the dining room table and gave me a ferocious hug that was all at once painful and glorious.

Rogan stood at a distance and watched us stone-faced.

"You were outside the apartment when I called," I said to him. "You could have at least told me."

He stared at me. Didn't reply.

Then it dawned on me. "You were staking out the apartment, weren't you? Do you still think it was a trap?"

The two boys had gathered their wits and were glancing around, frightened.

I offered them a hand. "It's all right now, you're safe," I said. "You have questions. I'll try to explain."

Apparently they didn't have questions and didn't want an explanation. They scrambled out the door before I could say another word.

"Maybe I should go, catch up with them," Sue offered.

"Are you up to it?"

Sue smiled wearily. "No, but I feel responsible for them."

I hugged her. She gathered up her things and headed out the door, leaving the signed copies of my books on the sofa. Just as well. I doubted Stephen and Tib would want a reminder sitting on their shelves of what took place here.

Once Sue was gone I turned to Rogan. "We need to talk," I said.

Not a muscle moved in reply. His steely gaze was absent of emotion.

"So that's you're plan?" I asked. "You're just going to stand there staring at me?"

"NOSROCH!" Rogan shouted at the ceiling. "I've got your boys!"

"That won't work. Believe me, I've tried."

"Nosroch!" he shouted again.

"I'm telling you it doesn't work that way. Angels don't like being summoned."

Rogan wasn't listening. With the clay jar tucked under an arm, he stormed toward the front door and nearly tore it off its hinges as he threw it open. Marching into the center of the grassy court-yard, he placed the jar on the ground, backed away a few steps and shouted at the sky.

"NOSROCH!"

I followed him out and watched as he circled the courtyard, bellowing.

"Nosroch! I've got your boys!"

Doors opened and residents appeared to see what the ruckus was all about.

"Nosroch!"

"Rogan, I'm telling you, he won't—"

Nosroch appeared.

All around the complex, people were pulling out their cell phones and recording the showdown in the courtyard. Some were turning their backs to the event to take selfies.

The clay jar lay between the angel and the Israeli soldier. I was standing on the edge of the courtyard, thinking I should probably do something but not knowing what. Nosroch didn't acknowledge me; his gaze was fixed on Rogan.

"I've got your boys," Rogan said, pointing at the jar, "Ashmedai and Ornasis. Lilith is safely tucked away at another location. If you want them back, you're going to have to go through me to get them."

His sword appeared. It was darker than I'd remembered it.

"I will not fight you, Capt. Dorn," Nosroch said. "You have been deceived. Your grievance is not with me."

"I say it is," Rogan replied. "As for fighting me, it doesn't appear you have a choice."

Rogan charged, leaping over the jar, barreling toward the rebel angel.

Noz observed the attack with patented angel stoicism. When Rogan was a few yards away, he levitated out of range.

Enraged, Rogan leaped, flailing his sword, striking nothing but air. He leaped and swung again, and again. To his credit, there was no give-up in the man. He circled beneath Noz like a fox eyeing a bird, trying to figure out how to grow wings.

"Are you in danger, Grant Austin?" Noz asked.

"Not now," I told him. "Ashmedai and Ornasis used Sue to come after me. Rogan came to our rescue."

Nos looked down at the soldier circling him below. "Commendable," he said. "That's twice you have captured Ashmedai and Ornasis."

"Lilith, too . . . earlier. It was a team effort," I said. My male ego couldn't stand by and let Rogan get all the credit.

Rogan didn't like us talking about him like he wasn't there. Noz's compliments fell on him like burning coals. Rogan took to low grumbles that sounded like growls that escalated to a roar.

"I'm not afraid of you, angel," he shouted. "Let's have this out here and now."

"I will return at a time that is more suitable for conversation," Nosroch said to me.

"That would be best."

Rogan was having none of it. "If you leave," he shouted, "I'll go after your partner! Grant!"

It was an empty threat. At least I hoped it was an empty threat.

"Are you in danger, Grant?" Nosroch asked again.

I looked at the seething Israeli. He thought me a traitor, his enemy. But deep inside he knew me, didn't he? I couldn't imagine him harming me.

"I'll be all right," I said.

Nosroch disappeared.

Rogan clenched his fists, flexed his arms, and with the veins bulging on his neck and forehead and his face turning beat red, he let loose a furious roar.

With no angel to fight, Rogan turned on me. Seething, he came toward me, pausing only long enough to scoop up the clay jar. I retreated to my doorway.

Do you know those movies where, near the climax of the film the muscle-bound hero has reached the breaking point and he walks straight toward the camera in slow motion and everyone in the theater scoots to the edge of their seat in anticipation of a good old-fashioned, Dirty Harry butt kicking?

That's what I saw coming at me.

I closed the apartment door and locked it.

If I'd learned one thing from Rogan, it was the advantage of surprise. He didn't know which room I'd be in, or from which direction to expect me. Of course, being the experienced special forces commando he was, he'd anticipate me attacking from any direction, through doors, through walls. So I hid behind neither.

I hid in the sofa. It was the same principle that was used to hide in walls, only instead of wooden studs and electrical wires, I was lying horizontally in cushion stuffing and wire springs. It was in that unlikely hiding place a plan came to me. My first thought had been to stay out of reach until he calmed down, but Nosroch had proved that strategy ineffective. Successfully staying out of reach did anything but calm Rogan down.

My second thought was to try to talk to him, to convince him that he was wrong in thinking Nosroch was the prince of Ashmedai, Ornasis and Lilith. I mean, it only stood to reason, didn't it? Nosroch showed no concern that the three demons had been captured. But rational arguments don't work in emotional confrontations and Rogan was running on pure 100% emotion.

I needed somehow to immobilize him, but how? Wrestling him to the ground wasn't an option even in my wildest fantasy. If I couldn't immobilize him, maybe I could wear him down until he was too weary to fight. The only problem with that plan was that he was Sayeret Matkal and I was a skinny writer who got winded typing long sentences.

That's when the plan came to me. There was a risk. In order for it to work, I was going to have to do something I'd never succeeded in doing before. But it was my best shot. So I settled inside the sofa and waited.

I half-expected him to storm through the front door like a raging bull; shock and awe, the time-honored battle plan of barbarian hordes and Sayeret Matkal. Instead, I heard nothing, and hearing nothing when you're expecting the mother of all explosive entrances was even more unnerving.

I eased myself lower in the sofa so I could see down the hallway. At I saw nothing but an empty hallway. Then, Rogan appeared at the far end of the hall. He was walking on cat's paws and coming straight toward me. He stopped. Listened. Then stepped suddenly through the wall into the closet, only to emerge a couple of seconds later.

He made his way into the living room and skirted the perimeter. Feeling into the walls? I couldn't see. He passed in front of the sofa. All I could see were his boots and the blades of grass plastered to the sides.

He was nearly in position.

I knew of the membrane's location because it was the one Abdiel had used to dump me back in my apartment when he caught Rogan and me training at the naval base. Had the membrane portal always been there or had Abdiel created it by choosing my apartment as a destination? Do membranes eventually fade out from lack of use? Good questions for which I had no good answers.

Rogan was steps from where I needed him to be. I eased myself out of the sofa, knowing that if I made the slightest sound, I was going to have to opt for Plan B. And there was no Plan B.

Rogan was in place.

I crouched and my shoe scraped the floor.

Rogan swung around.

But he was too late. My shoulder hit him in the midsection, my legs drove like pistons, and my momentum propelled him into the membrane portal.

CHAPTER
32

ROGAN LAY ON HIS BACK IN THE DUST, MOANING, HIS EYES closed. Having been pulled through membrane portals myself, I knew how he felt, like he'd been run through a screen door at sixty miles an hour. This time, for me, it was different. I felt no residual ill effects. But then it was the first time I'd passed through a portal under my own power. I was the yanker, not the yankee. Apparently that made all the difference in the world.

I was feeling particularly proud of myself.

Rogan stirred. His eyes fluttered open. "Where are we?"

"Welcome to Sheol," I said.

With Rogan being a student of the Tanakh, I didn't think he'd need any further explanation. For me, the historical background of the place had not lost its appeal. The spirits of Abraham, Moses, King David, all the departed souls of the Old Testament, had once dwelt here awaiting redemption.

"No," Rogan muttered. "That's not possible."

"The best thing about this place," I quipped, "is that the cruise ships haven't yet discovered it."

Sheol resembled a massive cavern, its limits stretching beyond the available dim light. It had a vaulted ceiling—with no pillars or supports of any kind—that appeared to be made of red rock. With no sun, or moon, or seasons, there was no way to measure the passage of time; that is, if time existed here. The atmosphere was acrid, burning our throats. And a thick red dust coated everything which, when scuffed, revealed a surface with a translucent quality through which sparks of lightning flashed, and with each spark I could feel my energy being drained. Rogan did too. That's why I brought him here. Between the violent passage and the constant drain of energy, I'd hoped it would slow him down long enough for us to talk.

Rogan moaned and rolled over. He had pushed himself up into a sitting position. He tried to brush the dust from his hands. When that didn't work, he attempted to stand. His legs hadn't yet recovered, and he collapsed back to the ground.

"This really isn't Sheol, is it?" he asked.

"As we live and wheeze."

"Why are you standing when I can't?"

"Easy, I'm in better shape."

Rogan gave me a deadpan expression.

"If you haven't realized it yet," I said, "you're a captive audience."

Rogan made another attempt to stand and again failed. However, he was making progress. My arms and legs were beginning to feel like they were filling with sand. There was no time to waste.

"Since you wouldn't listen to me at the apartment," I said, "let's try a different approach. You ask the questions, I'll answer them."

That seemed agreeable to him. He said, "What are you going to do once I become strong enough to stand?"

"All right. Not the topic I was expecting, but since you asked: If necessary, I'll kick your butt."

"Now that's funny," he said.

"Is it? I have experience fighting in Sheol, you don't."

"I'll adapt," he replied.

"There's another reason why I'd kick your butt. Look at your sword."

Rogan glanced down.

"Dingy gray," I said, "not as sharp as it once was. Now look at mine."

I brandished it. Even in the dim light it was shiny silver, its edges sharp.

"Your obsessive vengeance has corroded your weapon, Rogan," I said. "Any other questions?"

I'd scored a point. Rogan stared at his sword.

"How long have you been consorting with Nosroch?" he asked.

I cringed. He wasn't going to like the answer.

"Longer than I've known you," I said.

"You knew where to find him all the time we were training and you said nothing?"

Rogan's rage gave him strength. He got to his feet.

I spoke quickly. I told him how Noz stalked me following a Spectacle. I told him about the splinter group of repentant rebel angels and of Noz's patience in the face of my skepticism. I told him I believed Nosroch's repentance was sincere.

"You're a fool," Rogan said. "You're being deceived. Rebel angels are evil."

"I am no stranger to angelic deception," I countered. "I've been deceived before. Semyaza. Belial. I know evil. You're the one who's being deceived. Nosroch is not your enemy. He is not responsible for the death of your friends. His is not the prince of Ashmedai, Lilith, and Ornasis. Their prince is Semyaza. Abdiel has confirmed it."

"So Abdiel believes Nosroch is no longer evil?"

He had me there.

"And yet, despite the disapproval of an archangel, you continue your association with this rebel," Rogan said.

"I don't think you want to play that card, Rogan. Like you're so eager to see the Archangel Michael again."

"That's different. My cause is righteous."

"Your cause is misguided."

"At least I'm not siding with evil."

"So then why is your sword in such sad shape while mine is shiny silver?"

We were arguing in circles and I was feeling the effects of Sheol, while Rogan, having regained a measure of strength, was feeling for a membrane portal. I did nothing to stop him. What was the use?

He found one. I watched as he explored it with his hands. Stepping back, he lowered his head, jumping into it, collapsing on the ground in a swirl of dust. He tried three more times, each time with the same result.

"Get me out of here!" he shouted.

I considered leaving him here for while to cool off, but concluded it would only enrage him more.

"What are you going to do when we get back?" I asked. "Beat the tar out of me?"

"I'll decide that when we get back."

"Tell you what," I said. "I'll make you a proposition. In case you hadn't noticed, I was able to transport us through a membrane portal. I'll wait while you applaud."

"I figured your rebel buddy taught you."

"No, I did it all myself. What's more, that was the first time I've done it successfully."

"So you're not sure you can do it again?" Rogan said. "For all you know, we're trapped here."

"I hadn't thought that far ahead," I admitted. "But here's the proposition. As a show of good faith, I'll teach you how to access the portal. You go through first. Once you have successfully crossed over, I'll follow. Then, once we are back in my apartment, if you still want to grind me into dust . . . have at it."

He looked at me suspiciously.

"Rogan, I'm trying to prove to you that as far as I'm concerned, it's still you and me . . . like we were at the naval training center, atop the Emerald Towers, hunting for demons on the streets, saving children at the elementary school. I am no threat to you."

"You got that right."

"Yeah, wise guy? How about I leave you in Sheol?"

"I'm making no promises," Rogan said.

"I haven't asked for any. Do we have an understanding?"

"Show me what you've learned."

"All right," I said, mustering up some energy. I hoped I hadn't overextended my stay. "The first thing you already know. When you're pulled through a membrane, it really takes it out of you. However, when you make the trip under your own power, you feel no draining effects at all."

"Got it," Rogan said.

"Now, when it comes to passing through the portal, we've been thinking of it all wrong. We've approached it as a threshold to cross and consequently have been bouncing off it. Momentum, speed, brute force, don't work. So don't think of it as a threshold, but as a cocoon, or possibly a warm blanket."

"That makes no sense."

"Maybe not, but it got us here, didn't it?"

"How did you figure it out?"

"That time atop the Emerald Towers when you said I disappeared briefly? I remembered feeling as though I'd stepped into some gelatinous mass with its edges curling around me. This time when we entered, I pulled the edges around us like I was wrapping us in a blanket."

"Unconventional, but it worked, so who's to question it? How did you know the portal would open here in Sheol?"

"I didn't. That was the greatest risk. I thought it possible we would end up on the naval base since that's how I knew about the portal in my apartment in the first place."

"You chose the destination? How?"

"Just by thinking it. Same way I'd do if I thought, 'I'm going to the store.'"

"That's it?"

"That's it," I said with a shrug.

"All right, let's do it." Rogan was on his feet feeling for a portal as he had before. When he found it, he positioned himself in front of it. This time there was no running, no leaping. He simply stepped into it, wrapped it around himself, and disappeared.

I stood all alone in Sheol, taking a moment to look around. Without anybody in it, it was a sterile, lonely place.

Facing the membrane, I prepared myself to step into it, not knowing what awaited me on the other side, wondering if I'd be greeted with a fist to the face.

CHAPTER
33

THE NEXT MOMENT, I WAS IN MY APARTMENT. THERE WAS NO fist to the face, only Jana and Sue waiting for me. They both jumped at my sudden appearance.

"Grant, you're safe!" Sue said, running to me.

"Where's Rogan?" I asked looking around.

Jana answered. "He went to the bedroom, returned with a clay pot, and left."

Sue was brushing red dust from my shirt. I got the impression it was more about assuring herself I was all right than concern over my appearance.

"Did he say anything?" I asked.

"He told us you shoved him into Sheol," Sue answered.

She and Jana exchanged a glance. There was more. Something they weren't telling me.

"He said to tell you that it wasn't over between you and him," Jana said.

I didn't expect it was. But for now, with Rogan gone, for the first time since my home had been invaded by demons I let my guard down. A wave of relief swept over me, accompanied by post-stress emotions that moistened my eyes. I took Sue in my arms and held her tight.

"Are you all right?" I whispered.

"Still shaken, but I will be," she said, her cheek pressed against my chest.

I filled them in on the events that transpired after Sue left—Rogan's fury, Nosroch's appearance. As I was talking, Jana kept glancing at the door.

"Go after him," I told her. "Maybe you can convince him I'm not the spawn of evil."

She hesitated, not wanting to choose between us and Rogan. I assured her it was all right.

"I want a full explanation when I get back," she said, closing the door behind her.

Sue and I migrated to the sofa. I took the books—the ones Stephen and Tib brought with them, the signed copies I'd gotten from the closet—and tossed them to the floor. We huddled together, me holding Sue in my arms.

We didn't speak. I just held her. She was shaking.

Later that night we sat in Sue's office at the college, concluding it was safer here than at my apartment. Sue sat behind her desk, Jana and I in the visitor's chairs facing her. The neutral location gave me the opportunity to get them up to date and to answer their questions. No more secrets.

Jana listened, legs crossed, one foot tapping the air. It was a mannerism with which I was all too familiar. She did it when she was angry. I couldn't blame her. Ever since Rogan had arrived, she'd been the odd man out. It hurt her especially that Sue had kept things from her.

"Grant, give us a moment," Jana said.

While Jana and Sue leaned over the desk talking in whispers, sorting things out between them, I stood and moved to a neutral corner, taking in Sue's office. How different it looked from when it was the professor's office. It was neat, orderly, everything in place, the desk clean. The professor had been a stacker. Books everywhere, wedged into shelves, in piles on the floor. I remembered the day Sue and I cleaned out the office after his death. It had been a bonding moment for us.

Jana sat back, conversation over. While it appeared they'd reached some sort of resolution, there was still a chill in the room. Jana would get over it, but knowing her, it would take time.

"How was Rogan when you left him?" I asked, taking my seat.

"Angry. Determined. Furious with you for highjacking him to hell."

"Sheol," I corrected her.

"His words," Jana said, not appreciating the correction. "He's even more furious with you for allowing yourself to be in alliance with the son of Satan. Again, his words."

"Lucifer is Satan," I said, "not Noz."

"Not helpful, Grant," Sue said.

"It's an important distinction," I insisted. "Now more than ever. And when you say he's determined, am I safe in my apartment?"

In my mind I could see Rogan hiding in walls, storming out when I least expected it.

"You know him better than I do," Jana snapped.

"I would speak with you, Grant Austin," Abdiel said.

The suddenness of his appearance startled all of us. Trust me when I say it's never something you get used to.

Abdiel stood over us like an angry father.

"The professor would be disappointed in all of you," he said. "Grant, I thought you would have learned your lesson with Belial. Nosroch is not to be trusted."

"He's changed," Sue said.

Her defense of Nosroch surprised me—whether from recent events or out of loyalty to me, I didn't know.

"Rebel angels don't change!" Abdiel thundered, his voice shaking the walls.

"How do you know?" I said, standing. "When was the last time you talked to him?"

"Not since before the rebellion."

"Maybe it's time you got reacquainted."

"I have nothing to say to him."

"Then just listen."

"He has nothing to say I want to hear. A master of deception, he speaks nothing but lies. Grant, I cannot urge you strongly enough: Whatever Nosroch is telling you is a lie; have nothing to do with him. If you should see him again, speak my name and I will bring a legion of angels."

"Abdiel, listen to me—"

"NO, GRANT AUSTIN, YOU LISTEN TO ME!"

The force of his words released a pulse of energy that knocked me back into my chair, toppling it over. I found myself on the ground staring up at a very indignant angel in full glory.

"I know Nosroch. I have witnessed his Spectacles throughout the millennia. It was Nosroch who led the Israelites to worship a golden calf while the great lawgiver Moses was receiving the commandments atop the mountain. It was Nosroch who seduced Jezebel into persecuting the prophets and establishing guilds to support the worship of Baal and Asherah in the land of Israel. It was Nosroch who loosed a legion of paranoia demons on Herod and his household that led to the murder of his wife and three sons and the slaughter of innocents. It was Nosroch who orchestrated the Sanhedrin to bring the Father's son before Pilate and throw James from the pinnacle of the temple and club him to death. It was Nosroch who provoked the Romans to martyr Polycarp, a godly eighty-six-year-old Bishop of Smyrna and disciple of the Apostle John.

"There is not enough time to tell you of the fear and superstition he has sowed among the peasants during the Middle Ages, or of the murderous rage he implanted in Catholic kings to slaughter Protestants, and Protestant kings to slaughter Catholics, or of the numerous incidents when he seduced individuals to commit suicide, be unfaithful to their spouses, abuse their children, commit acts of terrorism, rampage the countryside and towns in killing sprees. This is the Nosroch of whom you speak so fondly."

The big guy knew how to make a point, you had to give him that.

Getting up from the floor, I stood before him on shaky legs. Sue and Jana were shaken too; I could see it in their faces.

"Grant Austin," Abdiel said in a more subdued tone, "in the past you have made decisions I deemed unwise, decisions that put your life in danger. Each time you managed to survive. But this time, you have gone too far. You have invited the devil into your house and are endangering not only yourself, but everyone you love."

His scolding subdued all of us.

"I will take my leave," Abdiel said. Before he did, he gave one final warning. "Grant, you once took a noble stand against Lucifer. Don't join forces with him now."

Then he was gone.

None of us spoke. Words weren't necessary to know that each of us was questioning the wisdom of our actions, especially Sue and me.

CHAPTER
34

THE DAYS FOLLOWING ABDIEL'S TIRADE WERE DARK AND gloomy. That's not a weather report, rather a description of the state of my soul on the eve of an impending Spectacle showdown.

When we left Sue's office, we did so with the understanding that Sue and Jana would keep their distance from me. Veterans of supernatural conflict, like all true warriors, their instincts were to engage in the fight. Jana had performed heroically on the Coronado bridge, and then again during the Laughing Jesus Spectacle. Sue had something to prove. Having bailed on me following the professor's death, she wanted to demonstrate the same loyalty to me she had shown to him.

While I appreciated their support, I argued that until we had a better grasp on what we were facing, it would be best for them to remain out of the line of fire.

That didn't mean there was nothing for them to do. With Jana taking the lead, they would go after Rogan and try to convince him that I was not a threat to him. It was a long shot, but worth a try. I know what I'm talking about when I say I've been on the opposing side of a determined Jana and Sue tag team.

My goal was to avoid an Israeli Defense Forces assault long enough to ferret out Nosroch's true intentions—Abdiel having placed serious doubts in my mind—and pray I could do both before Semyaza came knocking at my door. Proceed with caution was the order of the day.

It would be foolish to think that Rogan would back off now. Since our trip to Sheol, he began stalking me again, surveilling my apartment, hoping I'd lead him to Nosroch.

It didn't help that I'd been watching videos of the Sayeret Matkal on YouTube. The researcher in me thought it would be a good idea. Know your enemy. What I learned scared me even more. Their method of operation was to strike first, strike hard, create chaos, take out the enemy. I was the enemy. I began walking randomly through the walls of my apartment, checking to see if he was there.

In the days that followed Sue kept me up to date on Jana's progress with Rogan. More accurately, the lack of it. He refused to see her. Diplomacy had failed.

My life balanced precariously on a knife's edge, looking over my shoulder, never knowing what awaited me around the next corner. Every minute I wondered who would show up first. Rogan? Semyaza? As it turned out, it was Nosroch.

He appeared in my apartment to brief me on his upcoming Spectacle, the goal of which was to make a plea to the Father on behalf of all the repentant rebel angels. As he spoke I couldn't help but think that the real Spectacle had already begun, back at the restaurant at 4th and Broadway, downtown San Diego, that the woman and her baby had been but a ruse to lure me out. I remembered Nosroch standing across the street. He'd paid no attention to the unfolding events, watching me the whole time. Had all of this been a plan to get me to lower my defenses, to earn my trust? To what end, I didn't know. But I felt I was going to find out soon.

Semyaza had played me in similar fashion twice: once by taking the form of Myles Shepherd, the other time using Belial and the Laughing Jesus Spectacle to get me to relinquish the Father's mark of favor.

"Grant, something's troubling you," Nosroch said. "You're not paying attention. Are you having doubts about the Spectacle?"

Actually the elements of the Spectacle, at least the parts I knew, were brilliant. More than once Semyaza had reminded me that they've been doing Spectacles for millennia. Nosroch's plan indicated as much. He was a master.

"Abdiel came to see me," I said.

"I see." Nosroch folded his arms and looked at me.

"That's quite a resume you have."

He didn't reply.

"How could you do those things? The plotting, the intrigue, the deception, the pain and suffering, the destruction of lives, the deaths?"

"I have always been honest with you about my past, Grant."

"Have you? You failed to mention one little thing. The mind-numbing, horrific details."

"What do you want from me, Grant? I cannot change the past."

"I don't know . . . some sort of plausible explanation for why you did all those things."

Nosroch lowered his head in thought.

"I was fighting for a cause," he said. "At the time, I believed that cause was right. The actions I took were for that cause. We were at war. And as in any war, human or angel, there are terrible, unspeakable atrocities. Destruction. Misery. Death. It was the cause that drove me. But then, one day, the day you spoke in

Sheol, I stopped believing. Oh, how I long for the time before the rebellion, but that can never be. But you, Grant Austin, helped me realize that while I cannot change the past, I don't want it to be my final legacy. I choose to believe that our fate is not determined by our past. We can change it. All I have is now. And now, I choose to be the angel I once was. No longer a rebel, but faithful to the Father. What that means for the future, I do not know. What I know is this: Here I stand. I can do no other."

It was a moving speech. I particularly liked the ending quote from the great Protestant reformer, Martin Luther. I wanted to believe him, and probably would have, if not for one thing. As he spoke, his sword remained as black as the ace of spades.

CHAPTER
35

It was S-day. The day of the Spectacle. The stakes were high, especially for Nosroch. If it worked, he and his splinter group of repentant angels would once for all make their intentions known to the Father. If it didn't work, they would be at the mercy of Lucifer.

That is, if what I knew of the Spectacle was his real plan.

Nosroch's plan was bold, risky, and downright frightening. I was having flashbacks of the heavenly battle over the Coronado bridge. I hoped it wouldn't come to that.

My consolation was that this time I wasn't the lowly Spectacle pawn; this time I was one of the architects. The initial salvo in the Spectacle was mine. For it I'd drawn my inspiration from Semyaza.

Semyaza's luring me to Sheol proved to be an addendum to a greater worldwide Spectacle that featured the Laughing Jesus. In this Spectacle, my part was more of a prelude to Nosroch's plan. It targeted Rogan. By getting him a front row seat to a mass confession of faith by a splinter group of rebel angels, I thought that maybe then he would be convinced he was wrong about me and Nosroch.

"It's time," Nosroch said.

The first domino to fall would be a phone call, initiating a sequence of events that could not be stopped.

"Here we go," I said.

It took four attempts, but finally Rogan answered.

"Rogan? Grant. Don't talk, just listen. This has to end. Meet me atop the Emerald Towers at noon. Nosroch will be there. For whatever it's worth, you have my word that we will not leave the towers until this is resolved between us . . . all of us."

I ended the call and turned off the phone. I turned off my personal cell, too. I wanted no distractions.

"Now we wait," I said.

Nosroch nodded, then vanished.

Waiting is excruciating; tedious clock-watching compounded by the uncertainty of what would happen once the waiting ends. I'd considered driving to the Emerald Towers for no other reason than it would give me something to do. But there were too many potentially problematic variables. Traffic. Finding a parking space downtown. Car troubles, a very real possibility given the fact I couldn't remember the last time I'd had an oil change. In the end I opted for the supernatural expressway, a membrane portal.

Twice I started to go and stopped myself.

Give him time to get there.

By the time I left, my legs were weary from pacing.

Pulling the membrane around me, I stepped onto the roof of the Emerald Towers. A stiff ocean breeze greeted me. Gravel crunched beneath my feet. I was the first to arrive, but I didn't have to wait long. Nosroch joined me.

"You look stressed, Grant," he said.

"Good. I'd hate to have all this anxiety with nothing to show for it."

Nosroch stood infuriatingly serene. He took in the view and I could only imagine what was going through his mind. It occurred to me that while he'd orchestrated countless Spectacles, this one was different. This time there was more at stake than pride over a well-crafted scheme. His destiny hung in the balance.

The selection of the Emerald Towers was a mutual decision. The site of my stand against Lucifer, Nosroch thought it a symbolic location upon which to take his stand. Angels are big on symbolism. For me, it was a familiar battleground.

I glanced in the direction of the bridge and Coronado, letting my gaze wander to the naval base and the angel encampment overhead. In the city below it was a normal business day—drivers waiting impatiently at traffic lights, employees, shoppers, pedestrians, tourists, all of them oblivious to the supernatural world around them. I longed to be one of them. I couldn't remember what a normal business day felt like.

"He should be here by now," I said.

"Patience, Grant," Nosroch said. "He'll—"

A hand thrust out of the gravel and seized my ankle, followed by a leg sweep that knocked my feet from under me and sent me crashing onto my back, knocking the breath from me.

"Stay down!" Rogan ordered.

His sword appeared. He leveled it at Nosroch who levitated out of reach.

"Not this time," Rogan said to the angel.

"Rogan, don't do this," I wheezed.

"Grant!"

The sound of Sue's voice sent a chill down my spine.

She came running from the direction of the stairway. Jana was right behind her.

"What are you doing here?" I cried.

Sue and Jana slowed to a stop a safe distance away, trying to make sense of what they were seeing. They both carried a clay jar.

"Rogan said you were in danger, that you needed us," Sue said.

"I tried calling you, Grant," Jana added, "but your phone's off."

Strike fast. Strike hard. Surprise is everything. Controlled chaos. Rogan had acted in true Sayeret Matkal fashion. What I hadn't foreseen was Jana and Sue. I felt like a chump.

Rogan began making his way toward them without lowering his guard. I had no idea of their role in this. I feared more chaos.

"Here's how it's going to go, Nosroch," Rogan said. "These ladies are going to take your demons to Grant's apartment."

"We will not," Jana said with fire in her eyes. She didn't take kindly to being deceived and she certainly didn't take orders from former boyfriends.

Sue looked to me.

"Do as he says," I told her. Anything to get them off the roof.

Rogan's eyes were fixed on Nosroch. "You and I are going to fight. To the victor—the one who survives—go the spoils."

"Your strategy is flawed," Nosroch said. He looked at the jars. "Ashmedai, Ornasis, and Lilith, I presume. I am not their prince."

Prince or not, my blood pressure was pounding in my ears. The last thing this Spectacle needed was for those three demons to escape, whether intentionally or unintentionally. It made me nervous just seeing Jana and Sue so close to them.

"If it is as you believe," Nosroch said, "what's to keep me from releasing them now and ordering them to attack you?"

"It's an option," Rogan said. "But I'm counting on the fact that you're a warrior and your angel pride won't let you be bullied by a human. You'll fight me."

"It appears you have it all figured out," Nosroch said.

"Leave now," Rogan said to the ladies.

They stood there.

"I said leave!" Rogan shouted.

"We can't!" Jana cried. "We can't move our feet."

It was the same tactic Semyaza had used on me aboard the flight deck of the Midway.

"Noz . . . wouldn't it be best if they were to take the jars far from here?" I said.

"They stay," Nosroch said. "It serves my purpose."

What purpose? Having three murderous demons nearby served no purpose that I was aware of.

Sue stared at the jar in her hand. I could tell she was uncomfortable with the thought she might be holding Ashmedai and Ornasis. There was only one reason I could think of that would get her to do it. She was doing it for me.

"As long as they're in the jar, they can't hurt you," I said, trying to comfort her.

Sue's hands were trembling. She looked to Jana.

Jana assured her with a nod.

Nosroch descended. He spoke to Rogan. "Your presence here is a favor to Grant. Respect his wishes and stand down."

But Rogan had no intention of standing down. With Nosroch within reach, he raised his sword and charged.

He didn't get far. Like the girls, his feet were frozen in place, out of sword reach of Nosroch.

Rogan was beyond furious. "Fight me, you coward!" he shouted.

"I have no intention of fighting you," Nosroch said. "But if you persist in your hostility . . ."

Rogan persisted.

". . . they will."

Rebel angels appeared, surrounding Rogan. There was easily

a thousand of them, their black swords drawn. They encircled Rogan, their bodies forming an arena.

Nosroch released his hold on the Sayeret Matkal soldier.

CHAPTER
36

"ROGAN, YOU DON'T NEED TO DO THIS!" I SHOUTED.

Apparently, he did. Assuming a fighter's stance, he held his sword at the ready, his eyes enraged. He moved in circles, anticipating an attack from any direction. Was he really going to take on all of them single-handedly?

Whether he was brave or foolish—I couldn't tell—he was a product of his heritage. More than once the Israelis had been victorious against incredible odds.

Five rebel angels separated themselves from the others and closed in on him.

Rogan wasted no time. He attacked one of them, their swords clashed, sparks flew. Another angel attacked from behind him. Rogan pivoted, anticipating the move, blocking the blow.

And so it went. Five against one. Rogan alternately defending, then attacking, pivoting in a circle. Each one of the angels was his equal, in strength and skill, and he was never a threat to them. They fought patiently, keeping him off-balance, never pressing their advantage, and it became clear that they had no intention of harming him.

Rogan began to tire.

Advantage angels. I knew what it was like for Rogan, having fought in an arena, and I'd only fought two of them.

Breathing heavily, drenched in sweat, Rogan's blows became sloppy. The five angels saw that he was weakening and pressed their attack.

Realizing he couldn't keep this up indefinitely, Rogan attempted to escape, dropping through the gravel ceiling, leaving the same way he'd come. Two angels went after him and pulled him back into the arena.

With nowhere to go, Rogan fought, barely able to hold up his sword. He dropped to one knee and continued fighting until his strength gave out, collapsing onto his hands and knees, exhausted.

The five surrounding angels did not lower their guard, anticipating a ruse. But Rogan was done, he had no fight left in him.

"End it!" he shouted at them.

But that was not the plan.

The five angels drew back.

Had it been any other rebel angel leader, this was the point when the taunting would begin, the long speech declaring the foolishness of humans to think they could thwart angelic schemes. But Nosroch was no longer like other rebel angels.

He turned to me.

"Grant," he said, "allow me to introduce the angels who, like me, had their eyes opened when you spoke so heroically in Sheol."

I found myself the center of attention of a thousand rebel angels. I'd faced a congregation of rebel angels before, but this time they weren't glaring at me with hatred. On every face I saw admiration, something I never thought I'd see. It was overwhelming.

My part of the Spectacle was over and I was feeling pretty good about myself. I'd delivered Rogan and Nosroch had subdued him without injury.

I approached Rogan, but not too close. I'm not an idiot. I wanted to tell him he would understand everything in time. He didn't give me the chance.

"Get away from me, traitor," he spat.

I glanced at Jana and Sue. They shuffled their feet to show me Noz had released them. Despite the lurking danger in the jars, now that they were here, I knew I could say nothing that would get them to leave.

Noz had everything under control. And I had to admit, having witnessed the host of rebel angels paying homage to me, the admiration in their eyes was exhilarating. I'd never been a jock, never knew what it was like to have cheerleaders standing on the sidelines during a moment of victory. And while I hadn't played a starring role, I was part of the winning team and it felt good.

From here on out, it was all Nosroch. I didn't know the specifics, like how he'd get the Divine Warrior to make an appearance so that the former rebel angels could renew their allegiance to him, but I didn't doubt that Noz could pull it off. I was proud to stand with him, and relieved that for once I hadn't been duped by evil. I had been right about him, and soon everyone would know. I only wished Abdiel could be here to see it.

Nosroch rose above the assembly. With his back to us, he spoke to the great beyond, his voice as clear as a resounding bell.

"I have done everything you have asked of me," he said.

I scanned the skies. This was going to be glorious.

Thousands upon thousands of angels appeared.

As they materialized my heart leaped into my throat.

Without exception, every one of them had a black sword, and to my utter horror, standing in the vanguard was Semyaza.

"As promised," Nosroch said to him, "I have delivered to you all of the traitor angels, the wretched Nephilim half-breed, and the ring of Solomon."

"Well done," Semyaza said. "And my children?"

Nosroch motioned to the clay jars Sue and Jana were holding.

It made sense now. Not only was Semyaza prince over Ashmedai, Ornasis, and Lilith, he was their father, having sired them in the ancient days of the Nephilim.

Semyaza looked as insufferable as ever. Nosroch was delivering to him everything he needed to redeem himself before Lucifer at the site of his original embarrassment. Once again, I'd been deceived. Was I ever going to learn?

"Bring the bearer of the ring and the wretched Nephilim before me."

"Really, Myles?" I said. "After all we'd been through, you can't call me by my name?"

The comment earned me a blow from the nearest rebel angel. I landed in a heap beside Rogan.

Rebel angels flanked Rogan and me, dragging us in front of Nosroch, forcing us to kneel before Semyaza.

"Grant," he mocked, "how good to see you again. And once again you have allowed yourself to be deceived. How typical. I look forward to being your prince. My children will teach you what it means to be demon."

I stared up at him and said nothing. What was the use?

"What? No sarcasm? No witty references to being in the mush pot? And you brought Jana with you. You are ravishing as ever, my dear." He looked at Sue. "And the professor's lapdog. I will take pleasure in knowing that I can still hurt him by what I plan to do with you."

Nosroch took his place beside Semyaza without expression. The grand architect of Spectacles had crafted a masterpiece, this time to save his own skin.

Nosroch spoke to Semyaza. "I have done my part," he said. "Now do what you promised."

Semyaza nodded, proud to demonstrate his authority.

His countenance caught fire in an angelic blaze of glory, radiating with light and power.

Lucifer appeared.

He was just as I'd remembered him. More beautiful than any of the other angels, regal, shining with the light of ten thousand suns.

Rogan glared at me without sympathy, an accusing hatred, telling me what I already knew. This was all my fault. He'd been right all along, and I wouldn't listen. There was good in this world and there was evil. Why was it that everyone could see that and I couldn't? He had warned me. Abdiel had warned me.

Abdiel.

Lifting my head, with every ounce of strength I could muster, I shouted.

"ABDIEL!"

In an instant the vast number of angels in the sky doubled as the host of heaven appeared. Abdiel stood over me. Another angel of equal stature stood over Rogan.

The Archangel Michael.

"I thought you didn't care," I said to Abdiel.

"I am pleased to serve the Father," he replied.

"The ring is mine," Michael said to Lucifer.

For a moment all was silent and it appeared we were at an impasse as both sides of the original rebellion squared off against each other. The atmosphere was rife with tension. Who would make the next move? Michael or Lucifer?

As it turned out, it was Nosroch. This was his show.

Leaving Semyaza's side, he rejoined the one thousand. As their leader, he faced Lucifer. In unison, they raised their swords high. To indicate their change of allegiance, their black swords turned silver as they took their stand.

I will remember forever the look of betrayal on Semyaza's face when he realized what was happening.

CHAPTER
37

HUMILIATED BEFORE LUCIFER ONCE AGAIN, SEMYAZA FLEW into a rage. He drew his sword and attacked Nosroch. Like a spark igniting an explosion, the skies erupted into battle.

Adversaries since before the creation of the cosmos clashed, each side distinguishable by the color of their swords. But for the first time in the history of the world, one thousand of the original rebels fought on the side of the faithful.

Michael and Lucifer rose above the din, generals directing their forces.

Abdiel stepped in front of me. "Stay close," he said.

While I'd seen the big guy brandish his sword before, this was the first time I'd seen him in battle. His strength, his prowess, was beyond impressive. As a mentor, he'd been hard on me and I hadn't appreciated him. Seeing him in action, I felt ashamed for all the times I'd disrespected the warrior that I saw now.

I glanced in the direction of Jana and Sue. They had moved behind a large air conditioning unit, protecting the clay jars with their bodies. I wanted to get them to the membrane portal and get them out of here, but that would mean somehow getting them through the heavy fighting without breaking the jars. I couldn't risk it. For now, they were safe where they were. No one was paying attention to them.

Caught in the middle of two eternal forces, I drew my sword and engaged in battle. To my surprise I was able to hold my own, grateful for my training with Rogan. I landed some good blows, blocked opposing blows, sidestepped others, and when my swordsmanship proved inadequate, used my walking through walls skill so that my opponent's black sword passed through me.

I glanced in the direction of Rogan. Weary before the fight began, he was faltering. His lips moved as if forming the same words over and over, and I realized he was praying. While he was engaged with one rebel angel, I saw another approach him from his blind side. Stepping to Rogan's side, I blocked his blow. Rogan glanced at me, grateful, and he began fighting with renewed vigor.

The battle raged. All around us the clash of swords produced sparks that filled the air with what looked like a million fireflies.

Fighting off one, then another, and still another rebel angel, my arms were beginning to tire, and I became aware that, for all the fighting, there were no wounds, no casualties, no fatalities.

The angel code.

Nosroch had spoken of it. Since the original rebellion angels fought with a gentleman's understanding that ensured both sides protected status. But to what end? How would this engagement reach a conclusion? Would there come a point when both sides would simply call it a day and go their separate ways?

More importantly, did that code extend to humans caught up in angel warfare? If not, were Rogan and I the only two potential casualties? Would Semyaza use this battle as cover for ridding me from his life forever?

I scanned the immediate area, but could not find him in the mass of angels. Abdiel said to stay close. He knew I was vulnerable.

Then, from behind me, someone grabbed my shirt and pulled me back.

I swung around, ready to strike.

It was one of the repentant angels.

"What are you doing?" I shouted.

His grip was strong. I couldn't pull free. All of the repentant angels were retreating in what appeared to be a coordinated maneuver. All except for Nosroch who was engaged with Semyaza. He was surrounded by rebel forces, totally exposed.

"We have to help him!" I shouted.

The grip tightened, dragging me farther away.

"Abdiel!" I shouted.

The big angel swung around and came back for me.

"Not me! Nosroch!"

With no one left to fight, Semyaza's forces circled the two combatants as their leader and Nosroch exchanged blows. Several rebel angels came to Semyaza's aid. They were doing exactly what the angels had done with Rogan, wearing him down into submission.

Semyaza fought like a madman, leveling blow after blow on Nosroch.

Nosroch fought bravely, but he was tiring.

Seeing that Nosroch was no longer a threat, some of the angels moved away. Not Semyaza. He leveled blow after furious blow on his betrayer. Weary, Nosroch dropped to one knee.

"We have to help him!" I shouted, trying without success to yank myself free.

No one was listing. No one else was fighting. All eyes were on Nosroch and Semyaza.

The code.

Once Nosroch's strength failed, the battle would be over.

What then? Nosroch's Spectacle would have failed. Would he and his repentant angels be handed over to Lucifer?

Nosroch turned to block a blow from behind him and Semyaza saw an opening. With a victorious cry, he struck, his sword slicing into his foe. The blow was fatal.

In that instant Nosroch erupted in an explosion of color and blinding light that eclipsed the sun, his death sending a shockwave that swept through every angel, rebel and faithful alike, with force, wounding them, as though by his death a part of them died.

The skies were stilled as the angels on both sides exchanged pained expressions. The fight had gone out of them. And as the glory of what was once Nosroch faded, they lowered their weapons.

Semyaza, realizing what he had done, stood forlornly under the disapproving glare of his peers. One by one they vanished, leaving him to stare imploringly at an angry Lucifer.

Lucifer disappeared and Semyaza, his head lowered in defeat, followed.

The last to leave were the one hundred repentant angels. They gathered at the place where Nosroch died, their heads bowed in tribute.

Abdiel stood beside me. "You fought like a warrior today, Grant Austin," he said. He turned to leave. Turned back. "I regret not taking your advice to converse with Nosroch. Today, he was the Nosroch of old. I will miss him."

He vanished.

On the far side of the roof, I watched as Rogan stood before the Archangel Michael, removed the ring, and handed it to him.

CHAPTER
38

SHEOL HAD CHANGED SINCE MY LAST VISIT. IT WAS STILL CAV-ernous, red and dusty, and I could still feel the drain from being here. The thing that had changed was that it was now populated.

"Abdiel told us you were coming!"

A broad-shouldered, virile young man strode toward me confidently. For a shade—that's what people are called in Sheol—he looked remarkably handsome. He extended his hand in greeting.

"Welcome to Sheol, Grant Austin," he said, "or as we like to call it, home."

It was a few days after Nosroch's Spectacle that Abdiel appeared to me in his messenger role to deliver the Father's answer to my petition on behalf of Nephilim. The Father opened Sheol to all demons who chose to live here. It was a perfect solution given the fact that Sheol had been created for the incorporeal spirits of those who had died prior to salvation through His Son. Here the souls of Nephilim could rest until the day of judgment when the Father would determine their—I should say, our—individual eternal destinies.

"I'm pleased to meet you," I said.

He smiled. "This isn't the first time we've met," he said.

"Oh?"

"I'm Elihu. Nosroch's son."

Meeting the son of Nosroch was all at once a pleasurable and uncomfortable. The last time I saw him, he was green and slimy and hanging from my sealing. And so, as is my custom, I said something totally inappropriate.

"I guess the customary, 'You haven't changed a bit,' doesn't apply in this situation."

His laughter was easy and genuine. "May I show you around?" he said.

I fell into step beside him, thinking that his current form must be what he looked like in ancient days when he was Nephilim.

"It's not much to look at now," Elihu said, "but we're learning to adapt. We've discovered we're able to fashion structures with our minds."

He demonstrated by raising a pillar out of the ground. Semyaza had once done something similar, putting me on a pedestal—not in a good way—to torture me in the presence of his legions.

"Here, we are able to live respectable lives like we once did on earth and, more importantly, free from pain. No more clinging to ceilings. No more repulsive demon bodies. No longer the slaves of evil princes. No longer driven by insatiable desires to possess human bodies in order to find a measure of relief."

Elihu saw me looking into the distance at angels who appeared to be standing guard.

"Volunteers," he explained. "Each one of them requested their post to honor my father. They're not here to keep us from escaping—after millennia of torture why would we do that?—but to protect us from Lucifer's legions."

"Are there requirements to get in?" I asked. "For example, would Ashmedai, Lilith, and Ornasis be welcomed?"

"Everyone here must first take an oath of loyalty to the Father and then go through a probationary period. Evil doesn't stay hidden for long. Of course, we have our differences. We all have our human sides."

"What about demons who are under the control of their rebel angel princes?"

"As you would expect, the princes will try to keep the demons under their command from joining us, but from what I've heard, an underground railroad is forming, not unlike the one in American history during the days of slavery."

Elihu motioned to me.

"This way," he said.

The lightning beneath my feet was having its usual draining effect, and I was thinking I was going to have cut my visit short. Elihu, who was not flesh and blood, on the other hand, seemed to feed off it.

"The Spectacle," I said. "You being Nosroch's son, maybe you can clear up some questions I have."

"Let me map it out for you," Elihu said. "Then, if you have any further questions—"

He had my attention.

"My father's goal was to get the angels, both rebel and faithful, in one place so that the penitent angels could demonstrate their intentions clearly and unmistakably to all."

"No small feat," I said.

"Of course, my father wanted you there to vindicate your trust in him. But more than that, he wanted you by his side when they pledged their loyalty. He saw it as a powerful statement of unity. In fact, it was the promise of your presence that convinced the one thousand to assemble. You were their inspiration."

Noz had once told me he wanted us to stand together. I never thought it would happen. It humbled me to think I was anyone's inspiration.

"As you know, it was your task to get Rogan there, knowing that Solomon's ring would bring the Archangel Michael. Turning traitor with the promise of delivering the one thousand, the ring, and the notorious Grant Austin, was an offer my father knew Semyaza couldn't pass up. Since he was desperate to vindicate himself for his past failures, my father was certain he could get Semyaza to summon Lucifer. And, of course, your final task was to summon Abdiel and the faithful angels."

"That's where I have a question," I said. "I didn't know that was my task. Why didn't Noz just tell me?"

"In a pure Spectacle, participants don't play roles," Elihu said. "Situations are set up in which they react according to their true natures. My father knew that if you were pressed hard enough, you'd summon Abdiel."

"Your father could have at least told me it was part of the plan," I said.

"The unknown element," Elihu continued, "was whether Abdiel would respond. My father was counting on a hero's heart from the days of old and Abdiel's love for you. As an archangel and warrior, once Abdiel saw the full force of Lucifer, he would respond in kind."

"Abdiel said something to me when he first appeared," I said. "His usual line: 'I am pleased to serve the Father.' Was that an indication that the Father knew what was happening all along?"

Elihu grinned. "The Father is omniscient, Grant," he said. "Of course he knew what was happening."

"Then why are you smiling?"

"It's only conjecture on my part, but maybe it was Abdiel's way of saying that the Father approved of what my father was about to do."

I liked his interpretation.

"And you knew all along about your father's plan to sacrifice himself?" I asked.

"He called it the Uriah Maneuver. It references the time when King David ordered his soldiers to place Uriah—Bathsheba's husband—on the front lines and then withdraw from him, knowing he would be killed."

"Don't tell me. Noz orchestrated that event, too?"

Elihu laughed. "No, that was all King David. But the maneuver was exactly what my father needed. He could think of no stronger statement than a sacrifice to prove the sincere intent of the repentant angels. Unwilling to endure a third humiliation, once Semyaza discovered he'd been Spectacled, his reaction was predictable."

"Reconciliation is founded on bravery and sacrifice. That's what your father told me. I didn't know it at the time, but he was speaking of himself."

"He was a warrior," Elihu said.

"Heaven's host will be talking about him for millennia," I replied. "What do you think will happen to the one thousand repentant angels?"

"As with all the faithful, they will serve and trust the Father to execute perfect justice in the day of judgment."

Elihu had led me to a large area resembling a public square where hundreds of shades had assembled, the entire population of Sheol.

"I hope you don't mind," Elihu said. "They wanted to meet Grant Austin, the one responsible for giving them a place where they could live free from pain and oppression."

"I didn't do it," I protested. "It was the Father's grace."

"But you proposed it to Abdiel, who presented it to the Father." He motioned to those who were standing before me.

"Grant, meet your future neighbors."

———

We sat in a booth beside a window overlooking the downtown intersection of 4th and Broadway. Sue sat beside me; Jana and Rogan sat opposite us. It was a farewell dinner for Rogan.

After placing our orders, I described to them my experience in Sheol and meeting Nosroch's son, Elihu. When I'd first told Sue about Abdiel's announcement that my petition to the Father had been granted, she squealed with delight and hugged the stuffing out of me. When she heard that Sheol would be my future home, her enthusiasm waned—completely understandable given my earlier descriptions of the place. My visit with Elihu eased both our minds.

Conversation at the table turned to the events atop the Emerald Towers.

"How much were you able to see?" Rogan asked the girls.

"We saw everything," Sue said.

"What did you think of the fiery dragon?" I asked.

"There was no dragon, Grant," Sue said.

She was used to my antics and loved me anyway.

"Don't ever let her get away, Grant," Rogan said.

"Did we actually see Lucifer and the Archangel Michael?" Jana said. "What I wouldn't give to get the two of them in a studio and interview them."

"What about your old heartthrob, Myles Shepherd?" Sue remarked. "He said you were ravishing as ever. Is there something going on between the two of you you're not telling us?"

Jana choked.

"According to Abdiel," I said, "there's not much chance any of us will ever see Semyaza again. Abdiel said he'll never recover from breaking the code."

"What a relief," Jana exclaimed

"There are plenty more demons in the sea," I said.

"We knew Semyaza was evil," Sue said, "but who could have guessed he'd fly into such a rage?"

"Noz did," I said. "You see, a pure Spectacle has no roles; it's set up for participants to react according to their true natures."

Jana nodded thoughtfully. "That's a remarkable insight, Grant,"

"Five bucks says he plagiarized it," Rogan scoffed.

"It's called research," I protested. "Elihu was merely my source."

"Are you going back to your unit?" Sue turned to Rogan.

Rogan nodded. "It was really quite remarkable. The Archangel Michael himself spoke to my commander and then addressed the entire unit on my behalf. Most of them had never seen an angel before. He explained to them the special nature of those under his command and the situation at the winery. He told them I'd acted in the highest tradition of Sayeret Matkal."

"And the ring," said Sue curiously. "Will you miss it?"

Rogan rubbed the tattoo where the ring had been. "I'm not going to lie to you. I'll always wonder what's around me that I can't see. I'll miss the strength and the Nephilim abilities. It's going to take me a while to adjust. I'll probably be bouncing off walls for a while. And, of course, I'll miss sticking my hand into Grant's chest."

Sue hugged my arm. "Hands off, mister. He's all mine."

Rogan looked at Jana. "And I'll miss being here."

She blushed.

I couldn't help but note the irony. Rogan had what I longed for—being human and nothing but human. But did I really? Given the chance, would I walk away from being Nephilim?

Gazing out the window, I looked across the street to where

I first saw Noz. I felt his loss as keenly as I felt the loss of the professor.

Our order arrived. An impressive bowl of The Devil's Own Decadent Mac and Cheese was set before me. I endured the usual jibes about calories and how I never gained weight and dug in. This was as human as it gets.

Jack Cavanaugh has published over thirty books to date. His multivolume American Family Portrait series spans the history of our nation from the arrival of the Puritans to the present. He has also written novels about South Africa, the English versions of the Bible, German Christians who resisted Hitler, and the Great Awakening (with Bill Bright). His books have been translated into six languages. He is also a two-time winner of the Christy Award for best fiction.

Jack has been writing full-time for more than twenty-five years. He was a pastor of three Southern Baptist churches in San Diego County and draws upon his theological background for the spiritual elements of his books. Jack and his wife have three grown children, and live in Southern California.

Visit him online:
Website: *http://jackcavanaugh.com/*
Facebook: *novelistjack*
Twitter: *@novelistjack*
Goodreads: *novelistjack*

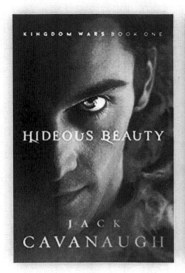